DATE DUE

STRANGER IN PARADISE

STRANGER IN PARADISE

JACKIE GRIFFEY

FIVE STAR
A part of Gale, Cengage Learning

GALE
CENGAGE Learning™

Detroit • New York • San Francisco • New Haven, Conn • Waterville, Maine • London

GALE
CENGAGE Learning

Copyright © 2009 by The Griffey Family Irrevocable Trust.
Five Star Publishing, a part of Gale, Cengage Learning.

ALL RIGHTS RESERVED
This novel is a work of fiction. Names, characters, places and incidents are either the product of the author's imagination, or, if real, used fictitiously.
No part of this work covered by the copyright herein may be reproduced, transmitted, stored, or used in any form or by any means graphic, electronic, or mechanical, including but not limited to photocopying, recording, scanning, digitizing, taping, Web distribution, information networks, or information storage and retrieval systems, except as permitted under Section 107 or 108 of the 1976 United States Copyright Act, without the prior written permission of the publisher.
The publisher bears no responsibility for the quality of information provided through author or third-party Web sites and does not have any control over, nor assume any responsibility for, information contained in these sites. Providing these sites should not be construed as an endorsement or approval by the publisher of these organizations or of the positions they may take on various issues.
Set in 11 pt. Plantin.
Printed on permanent paper.

LIBRARY OF CONGRESS CATALOGING-IN-PUBLICATION DATA

Griffey, Jackie.
  Stranger in paradise / by Jackie Griffey.
    p. cm.
  ISBN-13: 978-1-59414-753-1 (hardcover : alk. paper)
  ISBN-10: 1-59414-753-1 (hardcover : alk. paper)
  1. Young women—Fiction. 2. Male immigrants—Fiction. I. Title.
  PS3607.R544S77 2009
  813'.6—dc22   2008049392

First Edition. First Printing: March 2009.
Published in 2009 in conjunction with Tekno Books.

Printed in the United States of America
1 2 3 4 5 6 7 13 12 11 10 09

Stranger in Paradise

Chapter One

"She wanted what?" Laura tilted her head, puzzled by Mack's statement.

She studied him as he looked down, his attention on her Aunt Sophie's will in front of him. M. C. McKinley. He looked exactly like what he was, an attorney at law, but also her aunt's attorney since he took over his father's law office and a trusted family friend.

He spoke without looking up. "Sophie wanted, above all else, for you to be happy, Laura. She talked to me when she arranged all this. She felt you've had to spend too much time just working in the bookstore and with her—"

Indignant, Laura started to protest.

"She meant lately, since her illness. Too much time working. Not enough time enjoying yourself."

Her Aunt Sophie's death still too recent and painful to allow her to express her feelings, Laura sat fighting tears as both of them looked at the papers on his desk.

Then Mack looked up and smiled at her, his smile taking years and responsibility off his face. His affection for her and her aunt showed as he spoke. "She arranged a holiday for you."

"A holiday?" Laura wondered if she'd heard right. "You mean, a trip of some kind? But, Mack—"

"No buts accepted." He tapped the paper on top of the file on his desk. "Says so right here. And yes, a trip. She was set on it."

Laura sighed. "I know she was set on something. But I thought she was—that her mind was wandering."

Laura caught a tear in the corner of her eye with her fingertips. "Sometimes, Aunt Sophie was a little unclear. Whatever it was she wanted, I promised to respect her wishes, as she called it, just to make her happy. I had no idea what she was talking about."

"Well this is what her wishes are. And her mind was not wandering. Not about this. As I said, the will is just as you would expect it to be, except for this one thing. She wants this trip taken care of. She not only got your promise, whether you understood it or not, but she made me promise, too. She wanted to know that I'd 'see to it,' as she called it." He paused, remembering Sophie and how determined she was. Laura sat silent and he added, "So, if you don't approve, don't expect any help from me."

"Well," Laura found her voice and scolded him in mock indignation. "Fine friend you are." She raised an eyebrow to keep from laughing at his chiseled-in-stone attitude about the trip. When he smiled like that he looked like an eight-year-old behind that big desk. The way he looked when she had first met him after coming to live with her Aunt Sophie. Back then, his father did Aunt Sophie's legal work.

Looking back in those few seconds lifted her heart and she asked curiously, "Just where is it she wanted me to go?"

"That's not in her instructions. What she did was appoint Rose and Daisy to see that you go and get the works at the beauty salon, buy whatever clothes you will need for the trip, and get in touch with a travel agent. Someone professional who can arrange the trip for you."

"A travel agent? That is a serious trip, all right. And she didn't say where she wanted me to go?" Laura stopped, looking determined again. She shook her head. "Mack, this isn't practical, not like her. Maybe her mind was wandering. No," she shook her head again. "This isn't—"

"Never mind what it isn't." Mack was all business, grown up and in charge. "It is what Sophie wanted. And I promised her the same as you did, that I'd take care of it." He gave her a stern look. "I'm not going back on my promise."

"But Mack—"

"Where was I?" He was pointedly ignoring her protests. "Oh, yes, go to the beauty salon and get the works, whatever that is." He looked as puzzled by it as she felt. "And go shopping for clothes. And you and Daisy and Rose are to go to a travel agent. Her exact words were 'someone who knows his business,' to select a vacation spot."

His eyes were drawn like magnets to the papers before him as he stressed her Aunt Sophie's wishes. Some of them he had read word for word. "You're to spend from two weeks to thirty days there. *There* being wherever you want to go."

Laura made note of the legalese. Mack's instructions were positive about this. He wouldn't listen to any excuse she offered.

He studied the instructions before him, lost in thought a few seconds. "I think she wanted you to go somewhere that's foreign and romantic, the way she looked when she talked about it." He gave the papers a pat, looking up again. "But on where to go, the choice is yours."

Laura sat still, dejected, slumped in her chair. Her beloved aunt was gone. There were so many things to do at the house and at the bookstore, and now she had to worry about this pointless trip. Mack almost weakened, she looked so helpless.

He spoke again, more softly. "You can come home in two weeks if you want to. Or you can stay for four, the full thirty days." His eyes begged her to understand. "Laura, I think she wanted you to enjoy yourself so much you'd want to stay the whole time."

She sat listening patiently until he had finished outlining the rest of the things he had taken care of for her, including some details about the trip. That was part of Sophie's wishes for her, too, to discuss all of it and arrange things so all she had to do was choose a place and go. Mack would never understand how hard that one seemingly simple thing was for her.

She gave up the fight. "So, you mean I've got to do all this before getting down to business and back to work. Your mind's made up."

"Sophie's mind was made up." He gently made the correction.

"Just pack up and go somewhere for two weeks. And you're going to insist on that?"

Mack's boyish grin was back. "Excellent summing up! Would you like a job in my office?"

They laughed together and Mack gazed at her, feeling a little encouragement for the first time. He couldn't even remember when he hadn't been in love with her, not that she had ever noticed.

"If you don't want a job, how about dinner?"

He admired her ash blond hair and classic features, innocent of makeup.

Laura remembered his kindness the day of Sophie's funeral. It was dark and rainy that day, as if nature mourned with her. Nothing else had seemed quite real to her that day, only Mack's supporting hand beneath her elbow. Even with Rose and Daisy standing nearby, his support was the only thing that seemed steady and comforting to her.

Laura felt she should go to dinner with him. He'd been so good and dependable. And she knew he was right about her need to get out more. She peered out the window, seeing him from the corner of her eye. She decided he was nice looking, in a conservative sort of way. They both sat a few seconds, gazing at other things, each busy with their own thoughts.

She noticed the sunshine on the shrubs outside the window. Mack stole a glance at her as he replaced the papers, waiting for her answer about dinner. The thought that she needed him warmed his heart. Maybe with Rose and Daisy both helping at the bookstore now, he and Laura could spend more time together.

Laura finally sighed and got up, making up her mind. "Thank you, Mack. I'd like to get out, to go to dinner. The house is so empty without Sophie."

"Good. I'll see you at seven, then."

Chapter Two

At home, the house was so cold Laura caught herself listening for echoes in the lonesome quiet. The silence seemed to wrap around her until she straightened her shoulders like a brave soldier and marched upstairs.

Turning on the radio in her room helped a little. Looking through her closet, she found the dress she had worn to the funeral. It looked just like what it was: a funeral dress. She hung it back and brought out the other new black dress she had bought, holding it up to look at it.

The second black one would do fine, though no one seemed to mourn anymore. Maybe she had got as set in her ways as Aunt Sophie seemed to think. Set in Aunt Sophie's ways. Sophie had been a generation ahead of herself, she thought sadly.

The dress she chose was a versatile two-piece dress that looked more like it was for going out than mourning. And since she felt better with something to look forward to, she picked out a necklace and earrings to go with it.

She showered as if she could wash off sadness, missing Sophie and knowing how Sophie would scold her for moping around as she had been ever since the funeral.

Her heart felt lighter; she was glad Mack had asked her to dinner. Laura pulled herself together, determined to be strong and have a good time, and not ruin Mack's evening while she was at it.

Applying a touch of lip gloss, Laura smiled at her image in

the mirror when she heard Mack's car in the drive. She had forgotten what a lift it gives you to get dressed and go out. Goodness, had it been that long?

When she opened the door she could see the admiration in Mack's eyes. *I must still look all right for a nearly twenty-four-year-old "old maid,"* she mocked herself as she smiled at him.

"You look nice." Mack confirmed his admiration. "Sophie told me you'll be all right, that you're a survivor," he teased her. "She always had confidence in you."

"Thanks, I know she did. After all, she taught me all that perseverance and so forth. And I'm going to get back to some volunteering and other activities, maybe one of the literary groups. Or even go back to school, now that I've finished junior college here in Greenfield." She gave him a sideways smile. "And get out more, as you advised me to."

Mack listened patiently, approving her determination and good intentions. He took her to a small but nice Greek restaurant, one of the two good restaurants in Greenfield.

"I did some legal work for the family who owns this place," he told her on the way. "So I feel like I'm among friends. And when I have clients I want to impress, I bring them here." He assumed a comically hopeful smirk as they went in. "Are you impressed?"

"Very impressed," she pronounced solemnly and then smiled. "Also hungry! Something smells good . . ."

Seated in the attractive restaurant, Laura enjoyed Mack telling her about the Greek dishes on the menu, and having someone familiar and dear to Sophie to talk to.

The Greek cuisine was as good as the scents that had greeted them when they came in, and the service was fast and friendly. Filled with delicious food and enjoying her evening out, Laura listened as Mack talked about Sophie's business as well as the good food the place was famous for. It was a friendly, family business and they had earned their reputation.

As they waited for dessert, Mack told her, "Sophie's will is mostly a matter of signing papers. Transferring the store, and the other things, and legal instruments in her name to yours."

Laura nodded as the waiter came to serve their dessert and pour more coffee.

"Oh, this looks delicious." Laura's eyes danced as she looked at Mack. "What did you say it is?"

"It's baklava. It's my favorite, too. I can think of nothing better to go with coffee." At that moment something caught his eye and he raised his cup to a young woman across the dining room. A beautiful, dark-eyed young woman smiled back at him before turning away to help the waiter serve another table, and Mack literally attacked the baklava.

Laura laughed at Mack. He seemed content as a puppy with a bone as he happily bit into the pastry, dropping crumbs on his tie. His eyes met hers and he laughed with her, never missing a morsel of the sweet, crusty baklava.

"Getting back to the will, since you're making sport of my table manners." Mack grinned good-naturedly.

"Oh, yes." Laura sobered a bit. "It's like Sophie to plan a holiday for me. I told you she never said what it was she wanted me to do when she talked about it. I guess that's why I thought her mind was wandering. She only hinted about some wishes she had. It was so vague, Mack, I was surprised when you told me about the trip. But you're dead serious about insisting I go, aren't you?"

"Yes. I'm going to hold you to it. It was her wish. But the trip is the only surprise. I'll bring some more of the papers by for you to sign in the morning. It's all routine. We'll get it all done eventually . . ."

The next morning Laura called Mack at his office and arranged to meet him there.

"I'm getting dressed now to go to the bookstore, at least for a while. I'll come by there first and sign whatever that was, if it's all right with you?"

"Fine," Mack's pleasure could be heard in his voice. "I'll be expecting you. Come on in when you get here. My receptionist won't be in until later, something about her child's school."

"That's the problem with having to hire human beings." Laura laughed lightly. "They all have lives of their own. I'll be there soon."

Her smile faded as she replaced the phone. *They all have lives of their own except me,* she thought. Maybe her Aunt Sophie was right to plan this trip for her.

Mack's office door was open, waiting for Laura when she got there. He motioned her to a chair and explained each document as he gave them to her to sign.

"I didn't know there was so much documentation involved." She grimaced as he handed her another. "The people who have an awful lot of money and accounts and property probably have writer's cramp most of the time."

Mack chuckled. "I don't think I'd mind, as long as everything I signed meant some asset for me." He waited patiently and replaced everything neatly in a folder.

"Is that all of it?"

"All except the final disbursement after you get back from your trip."

"Nag, nag, nag." Laura wrinkled her nose at him.

"That's everything except for the money set aside for the trip, is what I mean. And the things she left to Rose and Daisy. She had already given me power of attorney for those. Have you given any thought to the vacation trip?"

"Yes, might as well get it over with. I'm meeting Rose and

Daisy at a travel agency tomorrow to decide where to go. I think we should do that first, so I'll know what sort of clothes to buy, if I need to buy any. I'm not going to buy very much. And I'm sure two weeks will be plenty of time, wherever I decide to go. I need to get back here and take care of business at the bookstore."

"You're already wishing you didn't have to go," he accused her. "That's exactly what Sophie was afraid of, why she made you promise."

"And you. I didn't really know she was serious or what she wanted. But you promised, too," she reminded him.

"Yes, I did." No sign of weakening in his attitude or tone of voice. "Let me know when you've decided where you're going."

Laura glanced at her watch as she rose, "I will. Soon as I get it all figured out. Thanks, Mack."

Rose and Daisy were waiting for Laura the next day when she arrived at the travel agency. Both of her elderly, honorary aunts were more excited about the trip than she was. Laura was amused at their animated faces as they went in. Both of them stretched their necks trying to see all the posters displayed around the office.

"Business must be slow." Rose spoke softly, giving a slight nod at the one agent who was talking on a phone.

"Good," Daisy quickly agreed. "The agent will have more time to spend showing you good places to go, Laura. Oh, she's beckoning to us!"

It was soon obvious the travel agent knew her business, and also about everybody else's business as well. Greenfield being small, she knew of Laura's loss. She was sympathetic as she told the three of them about various vacations spots and the particular attractions afforded by each one.

The literature and bright pictures didn't interest Laura. All the things, festivals, sights, and tourist attractions there were to do and see in the popular places made Laura tired just listening about them. She wondered how long she could hang on to her phony smile and mask her feelings.

The stack of discarded brochures on the side of the large desk had grown to a colorful stack. The agent's list of fun destinations was dwindling, and Laura hadn't shown any enthusiasm about any of them.

Darting a sympathetic glance at Daisy and Rose as Laura's eyes wandered around the office, the friendly agent tried another approach. Rummaging in a desk drawer, she smiled at Laura as she brought out another brochure. Its colors were beautiful, too. It showed a palm-studded island set in the sea like a jewel. She laid it in the center of the desk in front of Laura, but where all three of them could see it.

"This is Isla Verde. It's a lovely little island just off Puerto Rico." Her look was speculative. "You reach it by a pretty little shuttle boat, and the plane lands in San Juan. The small village and the beaches there are like a private little Eden." She looked at Laura's face. Pale, no makeup, no interest in anything she'd shown her yet.

The agent hesitated, finally letting her sympathy show. "If you would like to go somewhere just to get away and lie in the sun a while, Isla Verde would be the ideal place."

Laura slowly picked up the brochure. "Lie in the sun and rest? That sounds good to me."

When Rose and Daisy nodded, she said, "I'll pick out a couple of good books to take with me and just loaf. I'll lie in the sun and rest and read. What do you think about that?" She tilted her head, looking at Rose and Daisy.

"Wonderful," Rose decided.

"Yes, it sounds good to me too," Daisy approved. "Do you good to just get away for a while, to have some time to yourself."

She was beginning to wonder if they would find anything at all Laura would think was right for her trip.

"All right. It's settled then." Laura nodded for emphasis. "Isla Verde it is." She smiled, looking happier—or at least relieved—as she handed the brochure back to the agent.

Getting reservations and paperwork taken care of generated an atmosphere of excitement, since they wanted to wrap everything up and get on with the rest of Sophie's instructions.

Rose and Daisy hung on her every word as the agent worked, and they still had time to examine every exotic location represented in the colorful posters surrounding them. Laura's main amusement was watching Rose and Daisy.

They left the agency in high spirits. "I knew there would be somewhere that would be just right," Rose exclaimed.

"Oh, and that's not all. I've made an appointment for tomorrow at Chez Pierre's to have my hair styled and get a facial. Do you suppose that could be called 'the works,' or should I do something else?"

"Why don't you have your colors done too?" Daisy put in quickly.

"My what?"

"All they do is look at your coloring, your face and hair. You're getting a facial anyway. And they can tell you, from an expert's point of view, what colors are the best ones for you."

Laura didn't comment and Daisy went on, "A friend of mine had it done and the colors really do make a lot of difference. You'd be surprised," she insisted.

"What about a pedicure?" Rose suggested, "I've always thought that would just be the ultimate luxury."

Laura looked doubtful. "I don't know about that. I'll decide on that when I see how much it is. I'll be wading on the beach, after all. But I will get the color thing done. Let's go to our house and have some coffee before we go back to the store."

The house didn't feel so lonely with Rose and Daisy there talking about the coming trip. They spread out the brochures on the table.

"It doesn't say much about anything entertaining in this brochure we brought with us," Daisy commented, sounding disappointed.

Laura poured coffee. "That's fine with me. That's why I chose it. I don't want to get involved in a lot of things that don't interest me. I'm going to do exactly what I said, rest and enjoy the sun. And don't let me forget when we go to shop day after tomorrow, I want to go by the store and get a book or two. Or three, maybe."

"Or three?" Rose was horrified. "Laura, you've got to look up once in a while and enjoy all that expensive scenery!"

Laura laughed. Both of them looked so serious. Rose's glasses slid down her nose.

"We're only going to have one day to shop for clothes," Daisy reminded Laura. "You're getting the works tomorrow, and that will only leave Saturday to shop. The plane tickets you are supposed to pick up at the airport are for Sunday."

Both of them turned concerned looks on Laura. "Maybe it's too much to do. Did you really want to go that soon?"

Laura nodded. "Positive. The sooner I go, the sooner I'll get back. And I don't intend to buy too many clothes anyway. Mostly things I can use when I get back, too. I'm sure I'll have to get something to dress for dinner and the rest will be casual. To rest in, like the travel agent said."

Chapter Three

Returning to the bookstore, they opened for business and Laura went back to the office to call Mack.

He answered immediately. "Isla Verde?" His voice was puzzled as he repeated the name of the destination she gave him. "I've never heard of it."

There was an audible grin in Laura's voice. "I doubt anyone else has either. That's part of its appeal."

"Where is it?"

"It's a tiny little island off Puerto Rico. I'd never heard of it either, Mack. It's one of those little places where there's only a small village and beautiful beaches. A place to just lie in the sun and rest."

Mack listened, still trying to place Isla Verde.

"I'm going to get 'the works' at Chez Pierre tomorrow, shop Saturday for a couple of things, and leave Sunday."

"Sunday! So soon?"

Laura laughed. Daisy and Rose were shocked too. "But that's another selling point for the place. I guess there's no waiting for a quiet place like Isla Verde. Anyway . . ." her voice got serious again. "I want to get it over with and get back to the store."

"Well," Mack said slowly. "It sounds like a good place to rest." Laura pictured him lightening up when she heard his little laugh. "And they probably don't speak English, so no one will bother you while you're lying out there on the beach with your books. You can get a good rest before jumping back into the rat race."

"Sure." Laura laughed at that with him. "The bookstore is quite a challenge! Maybe you should have said 'mouse race.' "

Mack laughed again, glad she sounded happier. "Call me tomorrow after you get the works and we'll go out for dinner and a movie. No sense in wasting all that expertise and gorgeousness, not when I like you just fine the way you are."

Something in the way Mack said that bothered her. "Okay, I'll call you tomorrow—even if I turn out looking like an alien?"

"I'll chance it! Glad you found a place to go."

Glad you found a place to go? I must be getting paranoid. Laura sat looking at the phone a minute, thinking it would be fun to paint her face green and see how he took that when he showed up at her door.

Pierre himself met Laura when she entered the beauty salon a few minutes early for her appointment.

"Ah, good timing." He beamed at her. "Come, we see what we can do to gild the so beautiful lily."

Taking the compliment with a grain of salt didn't keep Laura from enjoying it as she sat where he directed.

He touched her hair, glancing in the mirror behind her.

"I don't want much cut off," she explained cautiously. "But if you might just, shape it a bit . . ." her voice trailed off as he continued his scrutiny of her hair and face. He didn't seem to be listening.

Pierre was concentrating. He was obviously making an assessment of everything good and bad about her. He looked so serious; she wondered if there was anything at all he thought was good. Her eyes followed him anxiously.

"Beautiful," he put her worries to rest. "We only bring it out a little. We put in a few sun streaks to bring out the shade, you agree?"

Laura nodded, and ran on blind faith from there on. Pierre worked mostly silently with her turned away from the mirror where she couldn't see.

When she thought he was finished, he still did not turn her chair around. Instead, he brought out a basket of scarves. He draped them one after another about her neck, and several operators sent interested glances their way. Two of them who were between appointments came openly to watch. Nobody spoke, some smiled approval from time to time.

Once Pierre frowned. Laura thought whatever that color was he frowned at, she'd never, ever, be caught dead in it. She wished she could see what it was.

Finally, Pierre spoke. "You are lovely, and no mere lack of color can change that. But for you, the best colors are these. I understand from Ms. Rose, you are going to shop for some things tomorrow?"

Laura nodded cautiously. "I will give you a brochure with a palette of colors most becoming to you." He had his hand on the chair. "And now, voila!"

Pierre turned the chair around to face the triple mirror, and Laura gasped.

She looked up at Pierre. "You've worked a miracle, Pierre. I've never looked this good in my life!" Laura giggled like a schoolgirl.

Several operators came to admire Pierre's work.

"I feel like the Mona Lisa—small-town edition, of course," she told him, setting off a wave of laughter around them.

When she got to work, Rose saw her first as Laura entered the bookstore.

"Oh, Laura, you're beautiful!"

"Yes, you are. You always were, but your hair is just right. And I didn't know what a difference a bit of makeup could make." Daisy nodded like a bobble-head, agreeing with Rose.

"Too bad there's no one in here. I'd like to have had a store full of people to show off to!" Laura laughed, delighted, still feeling sophomoric. "And I bought some of the makeup Pierre used to take with me. What do you think; would Sophie think I'd got my money's worth?"

"Definitely. Yes!"

"She would, no doubt about that!"

"Now all we have to do is shop tomorrow. But it would be nice to—I mean, if you had somewhere to—" Rose tried to get her foot out of her mouth.

"You can stop worrying about that. I'm going by Mack's office and if he's as impressed with Pierre's work as we are, he said he would take me out to dinner and a movie."

Arriving at Mack's office, Laura looked down at the teenaged temp at the front desk. "I'd like to see Mr. McKinley, please."

Mack had heard her voice and opened the door. He stopped and simply stood, staring at her.

"Well?" Laura tilted her head. "What's the verdict?"

Mack grinned. "Come on in here before I finish making a fool of myself."

"You approve then?" Laura asked when the door closed behind them. "I wasn't sure if it was approval or shock."

Mack reverted to his skeptical self. "Now, I know Pierre didn't let you out without having you look in a mirror. What do you think?"

"Does this mean I get taken out for dinner and a movie before I have to go home and wash off all this glamour?"

Laura picked up Rose and Daisy the next day, the color chart safely stashed in her purse.

"I'm putting up the 'Back at Four O'clock' sign. Is that all right? We can always come back sooner if we finish." Rose asked.

"Sounds right to me. I'm not going to buy very much."

"Let me see that color chart again." Daisy held out her hand.

With six eyes on colors and her own two on the prices, Laura bought slacks; a one-piece bathing suit; several tops and blouses; a couple of sun dresses; three dinner dresses; and they still made it back to the store by three-thirty.

"What time does your plane leave tomorrow?"

"I'd have to check to make sure, Daisy, but I think it's ten-thirty."

"Would you like us to come and take you to the airport?" Rose asked.

"No. I hate saying goodbye in public places. I'll just get a cab, then a redcap to help me with all this luggage. I intend to wear every one of these things, and get Sophie's money's worth."

That night about eight o'clock, Mack called and asked if he could take her to the airport.

"That would be nice of you, but you may want to back out when you see my luggage."

"That's right. Today was shopping day, wasn't it? I've been working on a merger with a complicated stock transfer and haven't had a chance to think about anything else."

"Rose and Daisy offered to take me to the airport, but I don't really think Rose should be driving with her eyes the way they are."

"You're probably right. Since the plane is not leaving at the crack of dawn and you have to be there early for security reasons, why don't we have breakfast and then go to the airport? Pick you up about eight-thirty?"

"Fine. Best offer I've had. See you then."

Laura could tell by Mack's voice how pleased he was. At a

simple occasion like breakfast? It set off an alarm in the back of her mind, and she reminded herself that she shouldn't be too encouraging. She looked down at the phone, vaguely uneasy. She liked Mack, but . . .

Mack and Laura celebrated Laura's holiday departure with a leisurely brunch at Greenfield's largest hotel, which took pride in its cuisine and champagne brunches.

"Gracious, is this how the elite live? I feel spoiled rotten." Laura narrowed her eyes, "Do you have ulterior motives, Mack McKinley?" She grinned impishly.

Mack stood straight and assumed a Dudley Do Right stance.

"Ma'am, my intentions are honorable." He insisted as seriously as he had about the trip, then helped himself to Eggs Benedict.

Laura poured juice, avoiding Mack's eyes. *Honorable, huh? That's what I'm afraid of,* she thought miserably.

"By the way," Mack told her as they sat down. "I've had a couple of inquiries about your Aunt Sophie's house . . . your house now. One, in particular, asked me to let him know before you sold it to anyone else. Do you think you might want to sell? Get a smaller place?"

"No." Laura was positive. "I'm going to stay right there and beat the antiques dealers off Aunt Sophie's lovely old things."

"I'm sure that's exactly what she'd do. Making decisions becomes you, and the works still looks terrific."

"Thanks. Pierre sure knows his business. I might go back to him when my hair needs trimming again, but not for the works. That was Sophie's idea." Her lovely features softened, thinking of her aunt.

"I know. It was a splurge Sophie insisted on along with the other conditions. Besides, you weren't exactly haunting houses before he 'gilded the lily,' as he calls it." Mack made a funny face, imitating Pierre.

Laura laughed. He had the gestures exactly right.

"Maybe you'll decide to get married and want to sell the house later on," Mack said, not looking up at her.

"No." She said it firmly enough to leave no doubt. "I'll get back into some activities when I get home, but I'm not planning on any serious dating or marriage."

She felt better after having made that clear, and the subject did not come up again.

At the airport, Mack stopped in the loading zone and got out her luggage before he left. He pointed out the designated gate as two porters headed for her luggage. Laura felt like telling Mack she was well out of kindergarten and could read the signs herself.

"Have a good time." He kissed her cheek. "And come home safely to us."

The simple goodbye brought the warmth of affection to her heart. It was what Sophie would say. She returned his affectionate hug and turned away, eyes on the line of people ahead going through security.

Laura had chosen one of her new ensembles to wear and knew she looked her best. It was a relief, too, that she'd set Mack straight about her 'intentions,' as he called them. She now felt free of guilt and excited about her trip. She didn't look back, but watched her feet and the jostling crowd until she was safely through all the checking and was seated in the plane. She took a deep breath when the plane lifted off.

She gazed unbelieving out the window at the clouds below. She was on her way to a tiny tropical pinpoint of an island she'd never heard of a month ago!

Something kept reminding her she would have to take a larger plane, that she still had a chance to change her mind about taking such a long trip. Mentally, she laughed at her small-town cowardice. She didn't like to be so far from home. And she liked to have her feet firmly on the ground, too, thank you!

But I'm going, Aunt Sophie! I'm going!

Chapter Four

Finally arriving at the busy airport in San Juan, Puerto Rico, Laura—small town new traveler—looked around, fighting panic again.

Why didn't I ask how I would know the island's representative? Oh, there he is!

A sign on a stick held by a young boy said ISLA VERDE in big block letters. The boy was in casual cotton clothes and looked to be about eighteen. Wondering if he spoke English, Laura waved to get his attention.

He nodded, smiling broadly. He came to her quickly, accompanied her to get her luggage, guiding her, the smile never slipping. As the agent said, she had to take a shuttle boat to Isla Verde. She followed the boy out and they rode a tram to where they would board it, their luggage accompanying them. The few fellow passengers taking the tram looked more like they belonged there than she did. Two of them spoke softly in what she guessed was Spanish.

Their transportation shuttle to the island was a barge-type boat fitted with colorful awnings, a roped-off luggage area, and a small bar that sold iced punch. A big sign on the front awning spelled out Isla Verde in letters as wide as the canvas.

The sense of adventure finally caught up with her. She was as excited as a child, enjoying the ride to the island. The shuttle boat docked and the passengers were taken to the hotel in golf carts. The luggage followed in multi-sectioned trams. She wished

Sophie could be there to see and enjoy everything with her.

The hotel itself was large and beautiful, like a white jewel set above the sand beaches on one side, and wide, well manicured lawns on the other side. The sea surrounded the island like the frame of a seascape in an art museum.

The travel agent's brochure didn't do it justice, Laura thought, wishing her aunt could see the place and know she'd chosen well.

A flood of memories and love almost brought her to tears as she tore her gaze away from the brilliant colors of the sea and sand. Sophie liked bright colors.

Inside the hotel, she headed toward the reservation desk. She walked slowly, looking at everything, and noting the clerks at the desk spoke English much better than she could have managed had she studied Spanish.

Having registered, she turned away from the desk and followed an arrow towards the elevators. As she walked, she glanced at one of the ornate writing desks and saw a man standing there. She caught her breath and stopped, her knees suddenly feeling weak as she watched him. He was strikingly handsome. The classic example of tall, dark, and handsome. She didn't realize her mouth was open till her lips felt dry. The man was preoccupied. He seemed to be deep in thought about something.

Though he wasn't far away, the handsome one didn't see her. He was looking out across the lawn to the sea. He was dressed in a white suit that brought out his tan. Taller than she, with a just-right build, he looked like he was posing for a magazine ad. His hair was just long enough for a dark curl in back to catch on his collar as he gazed out the double glass doors at the tranquil, aqua water.

Laura stood entranced. He was the best-looking man she'd ever seen, even in the movies. She wondered briefly if he might be some sort of celebrity. Maybe a model? Or in some kind of show business? No, she dismissed that idea. He seemed to be alone. There would probably be all sorts of staff and people around him, she reasoned, if he were a celebrity.

He'd have dozens of people with him, catering to his every whim, and photographers around him too. And probably reporters, if he were someone important. An official of some kind, from San Juan?

Laura's heart skipped a beat as he moved a bit and began to turn away from the scene before him.

Prodded into action, Laura hurried to an open elevator. She lugged her big designer purse with all the flapping awkwardness of a bird who'd just spotted a cat about to spring. She made it, and silently, just before the elevator doors closed. She hadn't been caught staring. She took a relieved breath, still wondering who the man was and more important, if he could be staying here.

When she entered her room, she saw her luggage was already there.

There had been time to deliver it and more, while she'd been admiring the handsome scenery. Oh, well. Not as embarrassing as it could have been. But the handsome face came back, unbidden, as if etched on her memory.

She sighed wistfully. There was certainly no one who looked like that in Greenfield. He must surely be someone important, she reasoned; someone who would never notice anyone like her—much less stop and stare, as she had.

Laura Carroll, small-town bumpkin. Make that happy, vacationing, small-town bumpkin, she reminded herself with a smile.

Laura looked around at the room, which was more of a suite, it was so large. The French doors were inviting. She drifted to them and discovered, to her joy, a small balcony that looked down on the beach and the sea.

She hadn't expected an ocean view to enjoy. The gentle breeze touched her face, ruffled her hair. No, she hadn't expected this magnificence, hadn't even asked any questions about the hotel, come to think of it. The room's size, the furnishings, and with the ocean view, too, made her think it must be very expensive. She hadn't thought to ask Mack anything about the place or how much it cost. She shrugged. Mack probably wouldn't have told her anyway. He had been so determined to set up this trip just as Sophie wanted.

Well, I'm here, thanks to Aunt Sophie and Mack. Even Miss Dull from the bookstore can appreciate something like this. And I'm going to really enjoy my two weeks here.

Tentatively touching the glass door, she went out on the balcony to look down at the scene below. There was a small table and two chairs. She smiled to herself. *It's pretty as a movie set. Maybe that was the leading man I saw on the way in.*

She laughed at herself, feeling a little giddy. The view was pretty enough to sell anyone on a trip to Isla Verde. Then she realized with a start she was searching the area below for some sign of that certain white suit with a dark curl above the collar.

Laura couldn't help wonder about the handsome stranger. He could easily be Prince Charming in any fairy tale or Hollywood epic. A movie star or a model, or who knew what? She knew very little about the place she had come to visit. But the handsome man had been alone. She didn't understand that. Her mind wouldn't let the mystery go. Adding to the mystery: he didn't have that self-important air most famous or powerful people have.

She shook her head. *I've got to stop reading so many detective novels and romances at the store. Still, I can't help but wonder who he is, what he's doing here. He just doesn't look like the other tourists.*

The men Laura had seen in the line to register at the hotel came to mind, and she compared them to her dark Prince Charming. Most of them were much older, heavier, and could have had *married* or *taken* tattooed on their foreheads for all the interest they generated in her.

She put the mysterious stranger out of her mind by changing to go for a walk on the beach.

Mr. Good Looking certainly hadn't been dressed for wading along the beach. Laura didn't know whether she was more afraid of seeing him again or of not seeing him again.

Now was the time to start enjoying her new wardrobe. She looked at the new colors, which were supposed to do wonders for her. She turned around to admire her new blouse in the mirror. As she slipped on sandals, she told herself firmly that the brochure didn't advertise beach boys to flirt with the guests. This brought an immediate denial from somewhere inside, that the handsome stranger should be classified with beach boys.

Heavens! One look and I can't bear to think ill of him. I've got to get back down to earth. Fast! Some sand in my sandals should do it. She put them on and left.

Outside, a gentle breeze ruffled her hair as she took off her sandals to walk in the foaming edge of the water. There wasn't anyone in sight where she was walking. No one but her to enjoy all this beauty. After walking a while, she sat on a piece of driftwood and let the gentle waves lap over her feet.

During the next two days she enjoyed the beach, eating lunch in the hotel dining room, breakfast or brunch in the coffee shop, and exploring the hotel's shops. The day after that, she got braver and went to some of the closest shops in the village. She fell into a sort of restful routine. The hottest part of the afternoons she spent reading the books she'd brought with her.

By the fourth day, in spite of the beauty surrounding her, the shopping, and the books to read, Laura had to admit to herself she was bored.

She walked along the beach, her sandals in her hand, thinking regretfully of the handsome man in the white suit. He must have just been passing through, or maybe just leaving. She sighed.

Reentering the lobby, a sign caught her attention.

There was a picture of a man in a colorful costume and something in big letters under it about the dinner hour. It was in three languages, and she didn't bother to read it. It did remind her she hadn't had the pleasure of dining stylishly late in the dining room and enjoying the music here.

Much as she hated to eat alone, Laura decided to dress for dinner and dine in style that night. She told herself there would probably be other guests dining alone, so she wouldn't be too conspicuous. And after all, she had shopped for this occasion. It was something to do. How could she face Daisy and Rose if she hadn't even been brave enough to have dinner in the dining room?

Her thoughts returned to the bookstore. She wondered what Daisy and Rose were doing. They were probably picturing her having fun in the sand and the water. They'd been more excited about the trip than she had. She missed them. She wanted to go home. *One more week*, she sighed to herself.

That night she selected one of her new dresses, and after applying makeup as Pierre had showed her, decided she looked pretty good.

Not that it matters any. She frowned back at the mirror's image.

The late dinner was worth dressing for. The food was world-class gourmet fare, accompanied by music from the hotel's excellent band. The musicians added brightness to the décor with their uniforms. They wore black pants, but their shirts more than made up for that drab shade with their rainbow of colors and ruffles.

Turning to look as they started playing, her attention was caught by the movement of a man who was shaking maracas.

She gasped, eyes wide, staring in surprise. There was the handsome one she'd seen on the way in. Or was it? She narrowed her eyes.

It's . . . no, it can't be. But it is. He works here. He plays in the band at night; that's why I haven't seen him.

A comfortable distance away, Laura studied her handsome Prince Charming as the band played. *He's probably a little older than I am, but not much. He must live in the village; he's not any youngster.* She remembered the expensive looking white suit he'd been wearing when she first saw him and then remembered it had been Sunday, after all.

So now she knew. He was not any kind of immortal, or a celebrity. He was working. He was a normal human being, not a movie star.

Laura's eyes moved over the rest of the musicians. All of them seemed to be accomplished and professional. *They're probably very good and play here all the time. Maybe the good looking one is married!* Her heart sank. *As if that's any of my business. And even if he isn't, I wouldn't want him to be nice to me or pay me any attention just because I'm a guest here. What am I thinking? I haven't even met him!*

The flush of warm blood was so hot, Laura could feel it rising up her neck. Yet her eyes held to this tall, dark, and handsome image, and she gazed at him, fascinated.

Her dream man's hands moved to the beat of the music, the rhythm seeming to be natural and a part of him. He smiled at the leader once, his teeth showing in a smile that made him even handsomer. Laura watched, admiring him as she sipped her coffee. She had no idea what they were playing. Aware only of him and the rhythm. Then, with a start, she realized the music had stopped and the handsome face across the room turned toward her.

Her cup arrested in mid air, their eyes met. She could not turn away. She sat, lips slightly parted, until the man turned away to resume his seat.

The spell was broken, leaving only shock at her reaction to the dark eyes that had captured hers. Holding her breath a moment, Laura steadied her hand to set down her coffee cup.

It had been only a few seconds, but she had felt as if they were alone in time and space, that no one or nothing else was present or mattered.

She got up, and moving as if in a dream, signed for her dinner and managed to get her legs to work. Not daring to look back at the band, she left the dining room.

The next two days Laura avoided the dining room. She liked eating in the coffee shop anyway. It was smaller, less formal, more Greenfield-friendly, she guessed, missing home.

That night, having already dined earlier, she went to the entrance of the dining room and stood near a large potted plant. Admitting to her skeptical self she was hiding, she pretended to look at the plants and the menu that was posted there. She waited patiently.

She peered through the greenery when the band began to play. She frowned when another man got up to play the maracas. He was an older man with graying hair.

Maybe if I kissed him he would turn into the handsome one again. She was as enchanted as someone in the fairy tales Sophie used to read her, ridiculous or not.

It was obvious the handsome musician must just play at the hotel part-time. Laura pictured herself slinking along behind the potted plants for nothing for the last couple of days. And Prince Charming wasn't even there.

Guess it's just as well I didn't buy any glass slippers . . .

The next morning, the first thing she noticed going to breakfast was a large sign that had been set up in the lobby opposite the elevators. It was even larger than the one she'd seen earlier.

She quickly stuffed the little cards Mack and Daisy and Rose had written into her purse to look at later. Feeling guilty she had not sent them cards, she stopped to read the poster.

There was a picture of the shuttle boat she had come to the island on from San Juan. She stepped closer for a better look and read the lettering.

Chapter Five

Obviously, the poster facing the elevators was in the best place to get attention. It was about a carnival in San Juan. The costumes in the pictures of the carnival crowd were bright and elaborate. It looked like a Latin Mardi-Gras, or the pictures she had seen of the Krewes in New Orleans. It looked exciting, too, as if everyone in the pictures were having fun. She could almost hear the hotel's music as she looked at the picture.

Laura smiled to herself. Daisy and Rose would be impressed with all that—the color and music and costumes and excitement.

Concentrating on the English words under the Spanish ones, Laura read that the shuttle boat would be making trips every afternoon for those who wanted to go to the festival in San Juan.

Picturing Greenfield, it seemed old-fashioned black and white beside all that color and excitement displayed on the poster. She could almost feel the rhythm of the Latin music as she caught the excitement, knowing she would never get to see anything like that again.

Quickly Laura turned and went to the desk in the lobby, looking around impatiently for a clerk. A man of fifty or fifty-five came out of an office door behind the desk and smiled at her. He didn't stop, but pointed to a young man who had followed him out.

The young man came to her and smiled expectantly.

"That sign over there." Laura pointed. "The shuttle boat that goes to San Juan? I'd like to go tomorrow. Do I make my reservation here?"

"No need reservation." The boy smiled with teeth almost as perfect as the mysterious maracas player's, giving her heart a lurch.

This must be where all the toothpaste ads get their models, she thought sarcastically, not wanting to be reminded of that handsome face or her embarrassment.

"Boat leave first trip, five o'clock. You be at dock where you land when you come, get on boat."

"How much is the fare? In American money," she added quickly.

The young clerk looked nervous. Young and anxious to please, his nervousness elicited sympathy from Laura's soft heart. She realized he might not know any more about American money than she did about Puerto Rican money, and she had a sudden inspiration.

"Could I just charge it—the shuttle boat—to my room? Like I do my meals?"

Relieved, the clerk nodded enthusiastically. The older clerk smiled approval as she nodded that she would do that.

"Thank you." She left, heart dancing, resolving to get to the dock early to board.

A festival! She resolved to remember everything she saw and to take home some of the brochures about it to show Rose and Daisy. She was finally getting excited about being here, as Aunt Sophie had hoped she would be.

When it got closer to time to leave, she chose the new yellow sundress they had shopped for to wear to the festival. Next, she looked over the cosmetics she had bought from Pierre and carefully applied makeup to her face.

Finally ready to go, she shook her head slightly, tossing her hair, peering critically into the mirror.

She was pleased with the way Pierre had shaped her hair. She brushed it, shook her head, and it fell neatly into place without a lot of bother. And she was going to a festival! That excitement brought joy and added sparkle to the new makeup.

The image in the mirror was happy and flushed with excitement. She pictured the brightly decorated little shuttle boat as she hurried out.

At the landing there were already people boarding and waiting to board the boat. A long line quickly formed behind her as she waited, but the shuttle was deceptively roomy and held more people than it appeared to. There were still seats along the low rail and wall for those who wished to sit down.

Stepping onto the boat, she gave the uniformed man her name and room number and made her way to stand by the rail and look out.

She smiled to herself as the breeze ruffled her hair. She tossed it back and glanced along the rail, looking at the people on board until her eyes were arrested by a familiar face. She gasped, and her heart skipped a beat.

There he was, her mysterious musician. The handsome-as-a-movie-star maracas player himself! She realized her mouth was open and smiled to cover up her surprise.

I don't know why I didn't see him as soon as I got on. He's wearing his uniform, if you can call anything that bright a uniform. And he sees me!

Her heart began to beat a wild tango in her breast as he looked straight at her. And he was, quite obviously, liking what he saw.

As he moved slightly, Laura realized with a start he was looking around to see if she was alone. He was alone, too, or seemed to be. She didn't see anyone near him. And now he was getting up. He was coming toward her!

She watched him making his way carefully and politely toward her in the crowd.

Determined not to show her nervousness, Laura tried to breathe slowly and not look so interested as he came closer. He didn't bother to hide his own interest, she noticed. This was as fascinating as everything else about him. She took a couple of slow, deep breaths, tried to still the rapid beat of her heart. A vein in the side of her neck thumped so, she wondered if it showed. She stood still, anticipating what to say to him.

At last, he stood before her. He was tall, dark, and breathtakingly handsome, swaying slightly with the motion of the boat. They were underway, on their way to San Juan.

Fascinated, Laura gazed up at him, her hand reaching for the rail as the boat rocked a little harder in the wake of a pleasure boat passing by. She wet her dry lips a little and smiled up at him.

When he spoke, his voice was strong, masculine, but pleasant. It went perfectly with his handsome face, she thought.

Then her brows drew together. She hadn't understood a thing he said to her!

Laura's hand tightened on the rail. "I . . . I'm sorry, I don't speak the language here." She hesitated. "No Spanish." She managed to get out reluctantly.

"No English," was his quick reply, looking just a tiny bit displeased.

Laura's disappointment showed in an anxious expression as she gripped the rail behind her. As weak as her knees, her timid smile had faded. Fearing he would simply turn away, she tried to think of something to say, to no avail.

But he didn't turn away. Instead, he placed his hand on his chest.

"Esteban," he said earnestly, looking into her eyes as if hunting for the smile that had disappeared.

Stranger in Paradise

Laura's face lit, catching the idea. "Laura." She placed her hand over her own heart.

"Laura," he repeated it and smiled. He looked down at her as if Laura was the prettiest name in the world.

She smiled back, pleased, but at a loss about how to continue.

Esteban pointed to himself, then slowly pointed to her, then across the water toward Puerto Rico, and to a poster on the wall about the festival. She watched. Then, last, he pointed back to her and to himself, then to the island of Isla Verde. He raised his brows and stood waiting hopefully, watching her.

He was so careful and slow in all this pointing, Laura had no trouble understanding he was asking her to accompany him to the festival, and that he would see her back to Isla Verde. Her smile came back full force.

Her heart lifted and she nodded, pushing back a lock of hair the wind blew across her forehead.

He smiled at the gesture and moved forward to stand beside her at the rail. Both of them looked toward San Juan.

"Esteban." She liked the sound of his name. "I'm going to talk to you anyway. I know you can tell a lot about what I'm saying. And maybe, if you decide to talk, too, I will pick up some Spanish words." She added hopefully, "I have a friend who took Spanish in school. Maybe I will recognize some words."

He said something in Spanish that sounded pleasant. But the only word she caught was *festival,* or something that sounded like it.

She breathed in the warm air, remembering the posters with pictures of the costumed crowds. "The festival will be something I will remember all my life and something I can tell people at home about." She gestured toward San Juan as she spoke to him.

Esteban made a comment from time to time, but didn't seem

to expect answers. In no time, they were docking, ready to leave the little shuttle. Excited, Laura took in everything around them.

Getting to the city and into the melee of the festival was a simple matter of walking up the hill from the dock at San Juan, holding Esteban's arm. They were soon surrounded by people, some in costume, some not. The noise and music surrounding them was too loud to talk anyway as they looked at the ornate costumes. Some were really spectacular. The scene was all the poster at the hotel had seemed to promise.

"I've never seen so many happy, laughing people and bright costumes. Look at that man on stilts!" Laura pointed, delighted.

Esteban nodded then pointed to a large papier-mâché head coming toward them.

Laura was glad to have Esteban holding her arm close to his side as she looked closer at some of the revelers.

"It would be easy to get separated and lost in a crowd like this," she said sounding a little scared. "And most of them look like that wouldn't worry them one bit!"

Esteban laughed with her as two clowns went dancing by.

When some of the revelers came too close, Laura cringed closer to Esteban, and he put his arm protectively around her shoulder.

Pressing to his side, a safety she was at a loss to explain overwhelmed her. It was almost as if, together, they were enchanted, invincible. She told herself he was simply being a considerate companion—but it felt good.

Feeling safe and enjoying herself, she thought of Daisy and Rose. *I can't wait to see their faces when I tell them I got into the carnival spirit and picked up a date on the boat. They'll think I've lost my mind!* She smiled happily to herself.

After walking a while, they stopped at a café with outside seating and had a light supper with red wine. Esteban ordered, talking briefly with the waiter, who seemed to be the owner as well.

Laura watched, thinking Esteban was probably acquainted with people here, as Isla Verde was so close. And of course, there was the shuttle. She was distracted by the waiter's return. She tasted the food set before her.

"This is good. Good," she pointed to her plate smiling, feeling like the village idiot trying to make him understand. But he seemed to know what she meant.

"*Si. Bueno,*" he agreed.

"*Bueno,*" she repeated, knowing *bueno* meant good. She was happy to have earned Esteban's approving smile with her one word and tried to remember some she'd learned from the friend who took Spanish.

After the stars came out, the lights and music and colors around them seemed even brighter, and Esteban stopped at one of the booths packed with goods to sell. He bought a large, brightly colored shawl, and folding it carefully, carried it over his arm. He made no explanation.

Laura felt a jealous twinge. Though she knew she wouldn't understand even if he tried to explain, she wondered if perhaps he'd bought the shawl for a wife or a girlfriend. She turned away to hide the flush that thought brought to her face.

Suddenly, Esteban stepped in front of her, bracing himself to steady a man who had nearly stumbled into them.

"I didn't see him," Laura said as the man recovered his balance and continued on his way.

Later there seemed to be a dwindling of the crowd. There were also more people who had been drinking, or who had bottles of wine with them. The night had turned cooler and Laura shivered.

Esteban stopped and released her arm. He unfolded the colorful shawl and placed it around her shoulders.

He bought it for me! The shawl was for me! she realized happily. *I guess he could see I'm just one of the foolish tourists who don't know the nights here get much cooler. Me and my new sundress!*

She smiled and said one of the few Spanish words she knew. "*Gracias,* Esteban."

"*De nada,* Laura." He smiled and pointed to another café where people sat drinking coffee and watching the crowd of costumed revelers.

The coffee was strong and hot. Tired, Laura wondered how to suggest they leave. She didn't want Esteban to think she was not enjoying the festival.

As if he had read her mind, Esteban rose and pointed down the hill toward the dock, tilting his head to watch her reaction.

She nodded as she rose and took his arm. They started back toward the shuttle boat.

"I feel so safe with you, Esteban." She nestled closer as a group of singing revelers passed close to them. She smiled up at him. "This has been such a nice evening, right now I feel like a high school girl with a crush on a movie star, and you're the movie star. It's a good thing you can't understand a word I'm saying, or I'd die of embarrassment and Daisy and Rose would disown me!"

Esteban paused to adjust the shawl slightly and smiled with her before he turned away to scan the distance in front of them. She pressed against his arm, enjoying his closeness on the dimly lit walk back down the hill.

A gay crowd of young people overtook them, and Laura laughed at a couple who stopped, arms entwined, and kissed right in front of them, oblivious to anyone else.

The shuttle was filling to return to Isla Verde when they boarded, the breeze rocking the little boat gently as they took their places again by the rail.

The evening was cool and Laura reached up to adjust the

shawl. Esteban caught her left hand and held it. He touched the third finger, a question in his dark eyes.

"No," Laura shook her head. "No, I'm not married, and I'm not engaged or anything," she added as he continued to hold her hand.

Esteban raised his left hand to show her he wore no ring and nodded to let her know he understood. Then he pointed, indicating he was going to the other side of the boat and would be back, pointing last to the deck in front of her.

Laura nodded, knowing that meant he would be back, amused and excited by their charade of about fifty percent body language and the other fifty percent mutual attraction.

While he was gone, a wiry little man in dark pants and a t-shirt touched her arm to get her attention, and handed her a paper tumbler.

"What is this," Laura asked. "It looks like Coke. I guess you don't speak English either." She tried to look pleasant. "Thank you. Gracias." She raised the glass and drank deeply, not realizing how thirsty she was. "Goodness!" Laura turned red, gasping for air, her throat burning. "You people must put chilies in everything!" She took a breath at the fellow's concerned expression, and cautiously tasted it again. She couldn't finish it and looked at the stranger, wondering how to explain, how to refuse his kindness.

The stranger glanced behind her and his face blanched. Esteban was approaching with a stormy expression on his face. The stranger hurried away, pushing his way through the other passengers to the other side of the boat, and Laura tried to explain.

"Oh, dear, I'm afraid I've insulted him, but this drink . . ." She held it out. "I—" Laura shook her head. "It's just too hot—"

Esteban took the paper tumbler and tasted, then threw it into the water. He turned without a word, his head swiveling, searching the faces around him as he went. He disappeared around the side of the shuttle's pilot house. The crowd closed behind him.

It was a few minutes before he reappeared.

Laura waited by the rail, enjoying the cool breeze and the starlit night, the strange drink spreading warmth which was not unpleasant. She heard footsteps and turned to see Esteban coming.

He looked happier. *He must have taken offense that that fellow tried to talk to his date,* she thought—if this chance meeting was officially a date. She would like to think Esteban was jealous. The wistful thought amused her. She felt like laughing but stifled the giggle.

"There was some sort of commotion on the other side of the boat, Esteban. Did you see what happened?" She pointed that way, raising an eyebrow, wondering if there was trouble with the little shuttle boat.

Esteban shrugged, his expression bland as he glanced at a couple passing by.

"Oh, well, I guess it was nothing too important. It hasn't seemed to slow us down." She smiled at him. "Anyway, I'm glad you're back."

Esteban stood beside her and they turned to look toward Isla Verde together. The wind off the water was cold and Esteban pulled the shawl close about her, covering her arms. Then, the wind off the water getting colder, Esteban stood behind her. He wrapped her in the shawl in his arms as they stood looking over the dark water toward Isla Verde.

"I can't remember ever feeling so warm and safe, and happy," Laura murmured, resting her head for a moment against his shoulder. She straightened up.

"I guess I'm too comfortable, I'm getting sleepy." She turned her head, hoping he might kiss her. He smiled and lightly kissed her cheek.

When the shuttle docked, Laura's feeling bordered on panic as she fought her emotions, the attraction she felt for Esteban, as well as the groggy feeling that had come over her.

She wished she could talk to Esteban. She felt like crying at the thought that she might not ever see him again if he didn't come back to play in the band until after she left. How awful that seemed. Sad and sleepy, she shook her head, trying to wake up. She couldn't fall asleep now; they were pulling up to the pier.

Laura and Esteban stood still, letting the others get off, and Laura thought Esteban must be a good and loyal hotel employee, letting the others disembark, seeing that they got safely started toward the hotel. But he was too good looking to be a mere shepherd. She felt as much like giggling as she had a moment ago when she felt like crying. Then Esteban, arm around her shoulders, helped her go ashore. Safely off the shuttle, Laura stood on the firm ground, feeling disoriented, as if she were still on the rocking boat, and looked up at Esteban.

This might be goodbye for us, she thought. *Kiss me, Esteban.*

Her heart wanted to shout it, but her lips were better disciplined, and she simply stood gazing at him and hoping.

Looking a little uneasy now, Esteban kissed her forehead, then, amused at her disappointed expression, smiled and kissed the end of her nose before he took her arm and started toward the hotel.

Oh, he's going with me, her heart sang.

They stopped once for Esteban to adjust the shawl. The night was really cold on her bare arms. At the hotel entrance, he held the door and walked to the elevator with her. She paused again, thinking Esteban would leave her there.

He probably lives nearby, she thought, fighting the sleepy feeling.

Esteban steadied her as they stepped on the elevator. She

Chapter Six

Laura looked out the elevator doors, a little confused. Somehow, down the hall, the door to her suite looked different . . .

She tried to shake off the groggy feeling. Then, to her horror, she stumbled when she stepped off the elevator.

"I'm so sleepy," she moaned. "And, I don't know what's real anymore. I don't know why I'm so sleepy, Esteban. I don't think I'd have made it from the dock to the hotel without you."

He did put his arm around her then, and held her arm as he walked with her to her door.

At the door, Laura opened her purse, but had to concentrate on focusing her eyes to see. Esteban reached into her open purse and got the key.

He put the key in the door and quickly twisted the doorknob with the same hand. With his other arm he held on to Laura, who was in danger of slipping from his grasp and falling to the floor.

Finally inside, Esteban gently sat her in a chair and turned on the lamp beside the bed before going back to close the door.

"The lamplight looks so cozy," Laura murmured. She was at peace with the world, except for this raging desire she felt for Esteban. She watched him as he turned down the bed, vaguely wondering why she didn't want to get up as he came toward her.

Esteban said something softly in Spanish to her and then held out his hand.

Laura was bewildered, trying to figure out what he wanted, but she still had no desire at all to move. She just sat gazing happily up at him, as if memorizing his face.

He gently pulled her to her feet and put his arms around her, holding her against him, and guided her to the bed.

"Oh, so this is why you came all the way home with me. And I thought you were being such a gentleman!" Things were becoming a bit unreal now, as if she might be dreaming or caught up in one of the romance-suspense novel plots she liked to read. Dreaming a plot with the handsome musician seemed very amusing to her. Her giggle was cut short by a hiccough. Too late, she briefly put her hand over her mouth. The thought come from somewhere in the back of her mind that he, if he really was here, if she really was here, must have the wrong idea about her.

"You must think I'm a party girl," she worried aloud. "Well . . ." She looked around them. "Maybe I am, and didn't know it until now." She gazed earnestly up at him. "Right now, there is nothing in this world I want more than you, Esteban!"

There. She had said it. Or maybe she just thought she had? The words didn't seem to have any effect on him. Good thing, her still-intact inbred caution tried to tell her. She peered at him. He was really as handsome as she thought, but he hadn't said anything. Not that she could understand it if he had . . .

It was hard to tell if Esteban was listening or not, she decided. She giggled again as his hands found the back of her bra and unfastened it. She remembered some of the love scenes in the books she'd read at Aunt Sophie's bookstore. But there was dialogue in those. She took a deep breath. The loosened bra hung. She felt better; she could breathe easier.

"I think my body is glad to be free," she said in wonder at how strangely full her breasts felt. The material of his shirt tickled her as she brushed against it.

Her fingers found the hidden grippers in the costume shirt he wore and loosed them all. It was only fair, some kind of childish logic reasoned. This thought was accompanied by a silly laugh she didn't recognize as her own.

As he stood holding her up, she pressed her breasts against his bare chest—his warm, tanned, desirable flesh. She moved against him, his warmth, enjoying the feel of him. Somewhere inside, her good sense watched in horror but she didn't care—none of this was real . . .

"Esteban! I want you to make love to me!"

He kept his arm around her, awkwardly, silently, holding her up. He did not kiss her or touch her except to hold her up.

She felt groggy again, holding Esteban. Almost out cold, eyes closing against her will, her head leaned against his chest.

She was on the verge of falling asleep when he caught her in his arms. This time he lowered her onto the bed and pulled the coverlet up over her. He carefully tucked the coverlet around her neck, smiling at her peaceful face, lips slightly parted.

Drifting in and out of sleep, she was aware Esteban had lain down on top of the coverlet on the other side of the bed.

Knowing he was there soothed her and she slept, dreaming of the carnival and of Esteban holding her, kissing her in the chaos of the carnival crowd.

Some time in the night she realized he had laid his arm over her, the heavy comforter between their bodies. She drifted back to sleep, feeling comforted that he was still there.

She awoke about ten o'clock the next morning. She sat upright, looking wild-eyed at herself and the bed. The dented pillow next to her brought the night before back with a rush.

Pulling the twisted sheet up over her half-dressed body as she sat in bed, Laura looked around at herself, at her bra on the chair and the lamp that was still on.

She still felt a little strange, but she was aware of what was real and what wasn't as she rubbed her sleep-swollen eyes. Laura couldn't believe she'd spent the night with a strange man she'd brought home from the carnival! A complete stranger, no matter how good looking he was. All Laura could remember, that wasn't in the least bit hazy, was how much she had wanted him.

I'm awake, but I still want him. The thought jolted her. She felt her cheeks burn with embarrassment. She looked around the suite; his clothes weren't there. The shirt she had unfastened last night was nowhere in sight. She didn't even know when he had got up and left.

He must think I'm . . . what do they call it? A One-Night Stand. A silly American tourist here for a fling—

Oddly, it wasn't so much what she had done, but that Esteban was gone that concerned her.

Laura sat on the bed, hugging her knees and feeling sorry for herself. This was certainly not her idea of a happy ending.

But I did finally have a good time as Aunt Sophie wanted me to. I met the handsomest man I've ever seen and he seemed to like me, too, even if we couldn't talk to each other. I don't know who he is, I may never see him again, but I'll remember this and the night at the carnival, always . . . She put her head down on her arms.

A sound, close by, made her jerk her head up. It was the bathroom door opening. She gasped, her eyes on the door.

When it opened, Esteban stood there with one of the hotel's towels wrapped loosely around his waist. He was smiling at her just as he had last night. He was real. He was as handsome as she remembered. And he was smiling at her. She tilted her head, stifling a laugh at herself for being so glad to see him.

"So." It came out on a little laugh. "You didn't go off and leave me. I was afraid you had."

He said something she couldn't understand in Spanish as he came toward her. She hugged the coverlet and held her breath. No book of etiquette she'd ever read covered a situation like this. And she was definitely not a One-Night Stand.

But he was only retrieving his clothes. They'd been kicked under the bed. Probably by that woman, the One-Night Stand, that Laura didn't want to remember.

"Esteban." She didn't know what to say, and he would not understand her anyway. Her best bet was to do the charade they'd decided to use.

Instead of speaking, he picked up his clothes. As he did, he bent over and lightly kissed her lips, then playfully kissed her ear, smiling affectionately. It was somehow like saying "I still like you even if you are a little nuts and not very bright." The way Aunt Sophie used to treat her and make everything all right when she was a little girl and had messed up or got her dress dirty before going to church. It was a good feeling, and she smiled, stretching.

"I've never heard of anyone kissing ears, Esteban." She giggled. "But I like it. Or I guess I like it because you did it. And I guess—I hope—you're telling me we can forget about my making such a fool of myself last night?"

Esteban paid no attention. He just took his clothes and went back into the bathroom.

Laura sighed, feeling rested as she looked around the room. Bright sunshine was streaming in through the French doors to the little balcony. *It's sure a good thing we can't understand each other. I think that's one of his good points, not that there's any shortage of those.* She blushed, glancing toward the bathroom door.

She still felt somewhat giddy and excited, wondering if he would take her to lunch or make other plans. If he planned to stay with her, that is, since he did work for the hotel. And he had, after all, stayed with her. She was puzzling about how to signify "breakfast" when he came back.

Esteban walked out of the bathroom with his clothes on. Neither of them tried to speak. He gave her an amused look and pointed to the shower. She made a little face as if she was disappointed, and he laughed. She saw him reach for the hotel phone as she went into the bathroom.

She heard him saying something in Spanish as she turned on the water. She hoped he was ordering them some breakfast.

Laura took her time in the shower, washing her hair and letting the warm water caress her.

She wondered if Esteban would stay around until she had to leave for home. She didn't know what hours he had to work, except he sometimes played with the band. She didn't want to think about leaving, now that she had found someone to share all this sand and sunshine with her.

Squeezing the water out of her hair she turned off the water, reaching for a towel. *I'm living in a fool's dream, thinking anything could come of this, even if he's been a gentleman so far. But it's my vacation and I can spend it with Esteban if I want to.* She grew sad, remembering the romances she had read at the bookstore. *I guess I'll know when it's over, or maybe it will be just a matter of not being able to stay here any longer. Whatever. I refuse to think about it.*

As Laura left the bathroom wearing a big terry robe furnished by the hotel, someone knocked at the door. Esteban quickly disappeared into the bathroom as she opened the door.

A smiling waiter wearing the hotel's uniform with the logo on it was standing there. He gave her a little bow and wheeled in the room service cart, glancing quickly and nervously around. He reminded Laura of a quick little squirrel with a hoard of nutmeats to deliver.

She noticed Esteban's absence, remembering how fast he had disappeared. Suspiciously fast? She wondered briefly if there was some sort of hotel rule against such things as bringing home your date.

Feeling mischievously naughty, she pressed her hand hard

against her mouth to keep from laughing like an idiot and wondered how they would word such a rule. Just how would they manage to get "do not date the guests" into a job description? And what did they expect, hiring people as gorgeous as Esteban? The nosy waiter was in no hurry to leave and kept glancing around like a sorority housemother.

Esteban stayed out of sight in the bathroom.

Finally, Laura pointedly held the door open as the waiter straightened napkins, poured orange juice, and rearranged the covered dishes, wishing he would just go. Having used up all his excuses to stay and look around, the curious waiter at last finished and made her another little bow before leaving the room.

As soon as the door closed, Esteban came out of the bathroom.

"That waiter was nervous or something. Curious, too, the way he looked around," she told Esteban. "Maybe it was because there was breakfast for two here?"

Esteban didn't answer; he was looking critically into all the covered dishes.

"What are you going to do if the breakfast fails your inspection?" Laura teased. "Fire him? Or maybe just make him eat the mistakes?"

Esteban's face was serious. Then, seeing her expression, he grinned as he held her chair for her.

"This just goes to prove something my aunt Sophie always said about conversation, 'It's the tone of voice that's important.' And this looks good."

They started eating and Laura paused. *"Bueno,"* she said.

"Sí. Bueno." Esteban helped himself to more scrambled eggs. There were coffee, rolls with honey, eggs, and a large covered platter of sausage and bacon. He said something in Spanish, lifting the carafe to fill her juice glass.

Laura smiled and held out her glass. "There's nothing like being happy and on vacation to perk up your appetite, is there?" She smiled, sipping her juice.

When she touched her still wet hair and pointed to the bathroom to indicate she was going to dry her hair, Esteban nodded and went toward the door.

Trying not to panic, Laura went to stand in front of him, helplessly twisting her hands. "I wish we could talk to each other."

Esteban paused only a second. He pointed to himself, to the door, then down at the floor between them. His eyes on hers were serious, wondering if she understood.

Laura said seriously, pointing to him. "You're going out," she pointed to the door. "But you'll be back," she pointed to the floor. "I understand, I think." She nodded, pointing to him and to the floor in front of her and smiled. She nodded again.

Looking relieved, Esteban kissed her cheek and left.

Going to the closet and opening her suitcase, Laura chose a pair of slacks, sandals, and a bright silk blouse with flowers on it. Esteban surely had gone home to change clothes. He couldn't wear that rainbow of ruffles all day. She'd never dreamed her Prince Charming would be wearing ruffles! She wondered where he lived, if he didn't live in the hotel, and if he had far to go to change clothes.

It was not long before Esteban returned. He wore slacks and a sports shirt, and leather sandals. Added to them was an approving expression in his eyes as she came to stand before him.

"You look nice, Esteban." Her eyes held admiration. "Heck! You're handsome." She laughed out loud. "Might as well give credit where credit is due. My Aunt Sophie always told me that."

They left the room hand in hand. She had no idea where they were going and it didn't matter as long as she was with Esteban. Maybe she would find out more about him.

"I'd like to see more of the island," Laura said as they walked along. She looked toward the village as they headed that way. "I haven't had anyone to show me around, and there are no village maps at the hotel. I wouldn't want to wander onto anyone's private property or anything."

She remembered the incident on the shuttle. "Judging by how angry the people here can seem to get on short notice, I wouldn't want any of them angry at me."

Esteban did more guiding than talking as they explored the village. They looked into shops, outdoor stands, and admired the fruit vendors' goods, before he led the way to other streets which branched off the main one of the village. He pointed out residences and gardens. Some of the older looking buildings had signs in front of them. One lovely old mansion had been the home of the governor before the island and the smaller ones around it became part of Puerto Rico.

Laura was getting tired. "I can see there's a lot more territory than I thought there was to explore," she sighed.

Esteban led her to a bench where they could sit and admire an ornate fountain, then pointed down to the intersection of the next street. Laura nodded.

Looking after him she hoped he had gone for something to eat, since that good breakfast was gone. She leaned back and closed her eyes, the sun warm on her face.

Esteban came back, carrying a course-looking sack and set it down between them on the bench. She watched as he drew out of it two large things that looked like burritos and two cold bottles of some kind of cola. He tipped the sack to show her there were honey rolls, too.

"Wonderful! And I see some green onions." She frowned slightly, warning him as she pointed to the onions. "I hope you aren't going to hold my fondness for onions against me," she lifted a napkin to catch the overflow of sauce.

Esteban ate, seeming to savor the onions as much as she did. They rested, enjoying the fountain as they finished their drinks. People strolled by, mothers pushed carriages, and children played in the little park.

When he got up to return a ball to a little boy, Esteban smiled down at her and said something in Spanish, gesturing at the children.

"If you're asking me if I like children, I certainly do." She paused and grimaced, as if making a serious decision. "I think we should have a boy like you," she pointed to a little boy, a little girl, then to herself. "And a girl for me. And of course, live happily ever after."

He made a cradle with his arms and rocked it, laughing.

She nodded, her eyes returning to the children as Esteban gathered up the sack and napkins to throw away.

He beckoned and she took his hand, wondering if he had some particular destination in mind since they didn't stop to look into shops and stalls as they had before.

As they crossed a street, he pointed to a shop with a green stripped awning. She couldn't make out what the sign said, but he said something in Spanish, and she hurried along with him.

"Oh," she exclaimed when they got closer. "It's a costume shop!"

The mannequins were wearing all sorts of things. She stopped to examine an Indian sari as Esteban held the door for her.

A prominently displayed sign advertised costumes for rent, and Esteban gestured with an arm outstretched to tell her she had a wide choice.

She approached a rack of women's costumes, wondering what might appeal to his taste.

Holding up a ballet costume, she held out one of the three quarter sleeves, "This would be warm when the evening gets cool," she touched the other sleeve with her hand.

Esteban tilted his head as he examined it but did not look too pleased. She lowered it and hung it back on the rack as Esteban held up another one for her to look at.

"But, it's the same costume! Oh, no, it's not. This one has the long skirt instead of the shorter tutu. Good, I'll get this one. What about you, Esteban?" She looked to him and around them, pointing. There were costumes for men as well.

He shook his head.

"But, don't you want to wear a costume?"

He smiled and moved his hands as if playing the maracas.

"Oh, you're going to wear your band uniform. Well, it's brighter than most of the costumes in here," she admitted. She moved toward a counter with an old model cash register on it and got out her credit card.

Esteban reached out, pushing her hand back into her purse. "Palacio Isla Verde," he said to the woman behind the counter.

"Oh, I didn't know I could do that here. Are you sure, Esteban?"

The woman got out a short form for her to write her name, room number, and some other information. When she finished, Esteban took it from her and signed his name underneath hers.

"Esteban Aguilar," she read. *Now I know what his name is.* She made a note of how it was spelled and how it was pronounced as the woman read the names and looked at them for confirmation.

"I will have to see our manager," the clerk said. "If you will please wait but a moment," she spoke English carefully.

Through a door past the counter an older, grayer man looked at the signatures when the clerk approached him.

The older man, who was probably the owner of the shop, turned to look out at them. With an affectionate smile he raised his arm in greeting to Esteban. Then, looking with open curiosity at Laura, he smiled at them again and threw a kiss to her as he turned away to speak to another clerk demanding his attention.

Chapter Seven

Laura realized she was standing there with her mouth open. "He threw me a kiss," she said in surprise.

Esteban only smiled and shrugged. He kissed her hand as he took the shopping bag from her.

"I never know what to expect in Isla Verde," she murmured as she followed Esteban.

They stopped at a small outdoor café for ice cream and coffee before starting back to the hotel.

"This ice cream is so rich! I'll have to watch my diet after this. There must be enough calories in this for a whole meal!"

He shook his head when the proprietor held up a coffee pot.

"You know," Laura told him thoughtfully as they walked back. "There is no language barrier when people can understand each other. It's all a matter of listening and caring about each other's feelings, isn't it?"

Esteban said something briefly, taking her hand as they entered the hotel together.

She glanced at the sign advertising the carnival, reading the English words there. "Only two more nights, Esteban." She held up two fingers, "What will we do after that? Do you think it will be a problem?"

Esteban motioned toward the elevators and gave her a look so full of mischief, there was no mistaking his meaning, and pointed upstairs.

Laura blushed, thinking *I understand that, only too well! There's no question of our getting bored as long as we have each other, but how long will that be? Until you get tired of my kisses and company or I have to leave . . .*

Inside the room, Laura threw her purse into a chair and took out the costume to hang it in the closet. Esteban had removed his shoes, and she did not hear him come to her. She turned and he was there, reaching hungrily for her.

She felt she was floating in space, every inch of her tingling at his touch, "Esteban!" She returned his kiss, but pulled him toward the balcony to look down on the beach.

"Sometimes I wish I could talk to you in Spanish, to know how you really feel about me, but I'm a coward. I don't want to know if this is all chemistry and I'm only an unimportant tourist."

Esteban didn't seem to be listening; his eyes followed a child and his mother walking on the beach and he smiled when the child stooped to look at a shell or something. He pointed, raised her hand and kissed it.

"A little blond boy. I wonder if our little boy and girl would have my coloring or yours, not that it matters, since they only exist in my wishful thinking." She watched the little boy carefully hand the woman his shell to keep for him.

"You will probably meet someone else after I've gone back to Greenfield. You'll marry and not even remember your 'fling with a tourist.' But I'll never forget you, Esteban, or this beautiful, magical island, either. Even if we part and I marry someone else later in life, I'll never forget you. I've fallen in love with Isla Verde and you."

He turned and held out his arms. She went into them, her heart fluttering at his touch. He kissed her long and tenderly, as if he treasured her above all else. Her better judgment warned her again to stop reading so many romances at the bookstore. She ignored it.

"You do care for me, Esteban," Laura murmured, her face close to his. "When we're together, and when you kiss me like that, I feel like you do, that surely you like being with me as much as I like having you here with me."

Esteban no longer seemed to worry about understanding mere words. He kissed her on the forehead and beckoned to her, excited again about something.

"What is it?" She looked at the clock. "Oh, it's time to get dressed! I'm coming!"

She followed him into the bathroom to see that there were plenty of towels as he adjusted the water. When the temperature suited him, he pulled her in with him, laughing at her surprise.

They stood in the stream of warm water, clothes and all, laughing, holding each other until Laura wrung the water from her hair, and making a face at him, left the shower. He shut the door again and she laughed as his drenched clothes flew over the door, one item at a time.

When he finished she went into the bathroom. She was drying her hair when he came to the door. She stopped, turning to look at him when he started gesturing.

Esteban pointed to his own chest.

"You." She said aloud.

He pointed to the door.

"Are going." She nodded, pointing to the room door she could see from there.

He pointed to the floor in front of her.

"But you will be back." She smiled, nodding her understanding, and Esteban left.

She assumed he was going to get his band uniform, since that was what he was going to wear to the festival. It comforted her somehow to know he must live somewhere close. She wondered if he would take her to see where he lived. She was reminded she knew very little about him and his life except that he played in the hotel band and he was a considerate companion. These unanswered questions about where he lived always made her wonder if he had befriended other guests who didn't have escorts and didn't know the language. She remembered the shop where they had got their costumes and smiled to herself. *At least I know his name now. Esteban Aguilar.*

As always, when not in Esteban's company, her mind was filled with questions about all the things she didn't know about him. The things about his everyday life that must be important to him. Against her better judgment, hope was building up that he would somehow find a way to talk to her.

But I promised myself I wouldn't think about that until I have to leave. She thought of Daisy and Rose, her "family" back in Greenfield, and she felt better.

She glanced at the mirror to check her makeup and then stepped out on the balcony to admire the view. She knew Aunt Sophie would approve of Isla Verde, but what about Esteban? Would she approve of him?

If I had known what was in store for me here, I wonder if I would have had the nerve to come. I feel as if all this is happening to someone else!

The door opened and Esteban was back, ending such foolish questions.

She smiled and went to him, standing in the hall as he closed the door. He held her hand as they went out.

"I don't think I would be going back to the festival if I didn't have you to go with me," Laura confided as they boarded the shuttle boat. "Even if I'd been brave enough to come by myself once, I would never have had the courage to come back. I wonder why the travel agent didn't say anything about the festival?" she wondered. His answer, if that's what it was, included a word she knew.

"*Hermosa. Hermosa?*"

He pointed at her with his other hand, *"Hermosa,"* his eyes admired her as he repeated the word.

"*Hermosa*, beautiful," a pleased flush rose to Laura's cheeks. "Thank you, Esteban. *Gracias.*" She smiled, pleased about the few words she knew.

Standing against the rail, she turned hopefully to him and spoke carefully, "Do you . . ." She pointed to him, then touched his lips with her fingers. "Do you know any English words?" His expression remained blank, an eyebrow raised. "English?"

Esteban studied her a moment, then brightened a bit. "No smoking," he said seriously, and they both laughed.

They looked out across the water and as she watched his profile, she saw several white hairs just above his ears. She touched them and he turned.

Putting his hand where she had touched the white hairs, he said a phrase including another word she knew.

"*Años*. That's years," Laura clasped her hands, "I can remember some of the Spanish vocabulary my friends told me in school when we studied together. If you're trying to tell me how old you are, or ask how old I am, I'm twenty-three."

Laura held up her fingers to show him ten, ten, three.

She put her hand on her heart. "Twenty-three."

Esteban nodded and held up his fingers. Ten, ten, seven.

"Twenty-seven." Laura exclaimed triumphantly. "That's," she said, gazing at the face which had become so dear to her, and made a circle with her fingers. "Just right. *Bueno.*"

Esteban laughed at the "just right," and put his arm around her as the little boat rocked beneath them. They were at the dock.

It was the last night of the festival, and Esteban took her to a large hotel in Puerto Rico for a late dinner before returning to Isla Verde.

Esteban signed for the gourmet meal and spoke with the

waiter, who seemed to know him.

Laura thought this must be a place he came to splurge once in a while, like Mack went to the Greek restaurant at home. She must be getting the Very Important Person treatment since he brought her here. It was a good choice with good food and it was certainly a beautiful setting, with tiny lights in the high ceiling that looked like a starry sky above. The lighting, cut flowers, and music were as much a feast for the eyes as the food was for their customers. Laura felt special on Esteban's arm as they rose to leave.

The waiter said something in Spanish to him as they left, smiling broadly at Laura. Esteban glanced at Laura as she smiled a little uncertainly.

"*Amigo*," Esteban explained.

"Oh, another one I know. *Amigo.* Friend."

"*Si, amigo.*"

Back in their room on Isla Verde, Laura lay beside Esteban as he slept. He always slept on top of the coverlet. She liked to watch him, admiring him as he slept. Her heart resolved firmly to stay here as long as she could, even if he was only escorting her around because she was a guest of the hotel. But the festival was over, and so were the two weeks Laura had planned on staying.

I'll have to make arrangements Sunday to stay the other two weeks. Aunt Sophie wanted me to stay the full thirty days, so that will give me another two weeks before I have to go home to Greenfield. To leave here. To leave Esteban.

Tears welled up in her eyes. The disparity in her life in Greenfield and life here in Isla Verde was as different as the contrast between a dull black and white film and a Technicolor movie. The only romances Laura had come in contact with were the fiction ones inside the books in Aunt Sophie's bookstore.

Well, this was not fiction. Isla Verde was not the Land of Oz. She smiled to herself, remembering the Oz characters. *And I've got a heart, and a brain, and courage.* She felt sad briefly as her eyes closed. *If only, if only . . .*

She drifted off to sleep against Esteban's back.

Chapter Eight

The next morning, Laura stretched, feeling a little bored. Esteban had left quietly, without waking her.

She wondered if Esteban had something to do on Saturday. Maybe another one of his part-time *turista* jobs? She ordered coffee and sat on the balcony to wait for him.

When she opened the door for him, he was wearing a robe over a bathing suit. He had on thong sandals and handed her a pair, patting his clothes with his other hand. It was then she noticed the basket he had set down beside him.

"Oh," she breathed. "We're going to have a picnic on the beach." She wrinkled her nose, teasing him. "One thing I can do very well in Spanish is eat. I won't be a minute!"

He sat down to wait, the picnic basket beside him.

"This is the first time I've worn my new bathing suit," she called from the bathroom as she slipped on the thong sandals.

She came out and stood posing. "There. Will I do?" She turned around for his approval.

"*Hermosa*." He made a circle with his fingers, the "just right" sign she had showed him.

Outside, they walked up the beach. It looked like it stretched for miles, appearing unexplored, but broken at places by vendors of some sort. Drinks, floats, or other things visitors might want were available. Esteban stopped and got a large beach umbrella for them and set it up on the far side of a large rock.

Laura quickly caught the towel he was spreading when the

wind caught it.

He anchored the towels, set the umbrella at just the right angle and stood surveying their little kingdom before reaching for her hand.

They ran together in the sand and kicked off their thongs to dash into the ocean, splashing like children. Esteban's hands caressed her as they got out where the water was almost deep enough to swim, his flesh exciting as they touched in the salt water.

He was about as good a swimmer as she was, she decided, which was not all that impressive. They did not go out very far, and the waves played rough tag with them as they headed back for the beach.

She stood, panicked for a second, seeing a huge wave about to hit Esteban, not having time to warn him, when an even bigger one crashed down on her. They laughed as they clung together, stumbling closer to the beach. Back at the umbrella, she stopped, looking down at the sand around her. Her signet ring was gone. She touched her finger where the ring had been.

Esteban looked too. Then, reaching out to keep her from moving, he reached down and picked up the ring beside her foot and handed it to her.

"Thank you, Esteban. My Aunt Sophie gave it to me." She kissed him on the cheek. "What is it, Esteban?"

He took her hand with the ring on the little finger and touched the finger next to it. His face was serious, his eyes asking questions.

"I'm not married, if that's what you're thinking." She shook her head vigorously, willing him to understand. "Remember, I showed you I had no wedding ring when we met on the shuttle, and you—you had no ring either."

His face grew so serious; her heart plummeted into her stomach. *Please, she prayed, you aren't trying to tell me you're mar-*

ried, are you? She wondered if the pain showed in her face.

Slowly, she took his left hand and pointed to the ring finger.

"No!" It came out flat and clear in English he must have remembered, maybe from the "no smoking" phrase he had learned. His face was wreathed in smiles. He stood silent a minute and Laura waited, scarcely daring to breathe. He pointed to Laura.

"Me," she breathed barely aloud.

Again he pointed to her and then he shook his head and held up one finger.

A tiny hope crept into her that he meant Laura was the only one he was seeing, or dating, or whatever they called it here.

Again he laid his hand on his heart and held up one finger.

She held up one finger too and nodded, pointing to him.

His arm went around her waist, pulling her close. His other hand cupped her breast beneath the bathing suit and he kissed her long and tenderly.

If I die right now, she thought, her head on his shoulder, *I'm already in Heaven, I feel like I'm going to swoon from pure happiness!*

He gestured toward the basket he'd brought, then sat down and started taking things out.

"This looks like enough food and cola to last a week," she said, laughing at how much he had brought.

Lying on their towels later, she propped herself on her elbow and told him, "I guess it's time to tell you my life story. It's just as well you don't understand, it's so boring."

She told him about her mother and father being killed in a car accident and her Aunt Sophie coming to take her home with her. She told him about Greenfield and the bookshop and that Aunt Sophie was the only family she had except for Daisy and Rose.

Esteban lay gazing up at the sky and watched the gulls. When her voice became sad when she talked about Aunt Sophie's last wishes, he raised up and traced her lips with his fingers, kissing her gently, to make the sadness go away.

They stayed to watch the sunset and its spectacular display of colors and finished the rest of the fruit in the lunch basket before starting back. Esteban left the umbrella at the stand where he got it. The vendor had simply closed his own umbrella and left it there when he was ready to go.

Esteban left her at her door with a kiss and a familiar gesture at the carpet in front of her. She nodded and kissed him back. When he was gone, she stood leaning against the closed door, remembering their happiness, the sunset, her heart strangely at peace, sure this time. She knew, really knew, he would be back.

She tossed her robe away and headed for the shower.

I've got to call Rose. I've got to let her know I'll be staying the whole thirty days. I'd better find out how much money is left in the amount provided for the trip too, the way I've been charging things to my room.

She stepped into the shower and swept her hair up.

Ouch! Her fingertips explored her neck when she got out and looked into the mirror. *Some of that sunset came home with me.*

She used the drier carefully, wary of her sunburn. *I know I've been putting off calling home. I don't know what to say. Maybe only that I'm enjoying my stay here, and how pretty the island is . . .*

A little later, her mouth a determined line, Laura reached for the phone. She waited impatiently while the hotel placed her call for her.

I suppose it's another service they advertise for their guests, but I hate to wait for someone else to complete my call for me. I wonder how Rose, or Daisy if she answers, will take my wanting to stay another two weeks? I know it will be a surprise.

She jumped at the ring of the phone. "Yes? Rose? I'm calling to tell you everything is fine in Paradise. In fact, it's a lot better than the travel agent said."

"Wait." Rose spoke to someone else. Then, "I'm putting you on the speaker so we can both talk to you."

"It's about time we got some use out of that speaker. Good idea." Laura laughed.

"You sound like you're having a good time," Daisy broke in. "What's this about the place being better than the travel agent said?"

The sound of their voices warmed her heart as Laura pictured them. "It is. It's really so beautiful here, there's no way anyone could describe it."

"You mean it even beats those pictures we saw?"

"Oh, by miles! And it's not very far from Puerto Rico. When the plane lands in San Juan, the little shuttle the agent told us about is a fun trip in itself. Then, Isla Verde . . . there's no way anyone could describe it and do it justice. And there was a festival in San Juan the agent didn't know about. And I'm enjoying myself so much, I'm going to stay another two weeks."

"That's wonderful!"

"Yes, it's exactly what Sophie was hoping."

"There's something else I need to ask about. I've been charging things to my room rather than trying to deal with the difference in the money. I rented a costume for the festival, for instance, and some meals. I thought I'd better ask. Will there be enough trip money for me to stay two more weeks?"

"Oh, don't worry your head about that." Rose chuckled. "Just in case you did decide to stay, after I paid the bills for everything here, I put the rest of the trip money into your checking account. So all you will have to do is write a check."

"Right," Daisy said. "There's a little over four thousand dollars we put in, plus of course, whatever amount Mack put in it before that, from other things."

"Good, then I won't have to worry about it." She stopped,

Stranger in Paradise

hearing Esteban come in.

"Laura?" Esteban's voice preceded him from the door she had left open for him.

"Laura?" Rose's voice questioned.

"Yes, Rose, I'm here," she beckoned to Esteban.

"I just wanted to tell you the exact amount of the deposit we made is four thousand, eight hundred and ninety dollars and forty-seven cents."

Laura carefully wrote down the amount and chuckled, "I sure can tell you've been an accountant by trade. I'm always rounding things off."

"You always know where you stand with accurate records," Rose defended herself.

"You're absolutely right, Rose. I've missed you both. How are things going at the store?"

"The store's doing fine. Business is good, but we miss you. And Laura, Mack either stops by or calls about every two days, wanting to know if we've heard from you."

"Yes, he thinks it's odd we haven't had a card and wonders if everything is all right there."

"He's a worrier, I guess." Laura frowned. "I should have sent a card, but to tell the truth, nothing I've seen at the travel agency or postcards has come close to what this place is really like. I've been walking on the beach and enjoying the sun, and exploring the village around the hotel."

"We told Mack not to worry, that bad news travels fast, so you must be having a good time."

"What have you found to do there besides enjoy the beach and the sun? Did you read the two books you took with you?"

"I did, but it's a good thing I finished them before the carnival started or I wouldn't have had time. And since it's in San Juan, to get to it, you take the little shuttle boat they send for you when you fly into Puerto Rico. It's really been fun and different, and . . ." She gazed up at Esteban, her heart in her eyes as he smiled back at her. "Like nothing I've ever experienced before."

"That's good news. I guess Sophie was right, it was just what you needed. She wanted you to stay the full thirty days is why she set aside so much money to prepare for it."

"That's right, so you have a good time and don't worry about costs or things here, and do be careful and take care of yourself."

Daisy stopped, then asked thoughtfully, "You said the festival is in Puerto Rico. Did you go with a group from the hotel? I would be careful about going to a place that big alone, and at a festival time, too."

Laura smiled, feeling loved by her two adopted aunts. "I wasn't alone, Daisy. I met this nice fellow who works here at the hotel. He's a musician. He doesn't speak any English, but he is a big, strong man, and I feel safe with him." She glanced up at Esteban, who was still listening. "And of course, since he works here, he comes back with me, too."

"But," Rose said, puzzled. "If he doesn't speak English and you don't speak Spanish, how do you communicate? But then, I guess you don't have to worry about that much, just coming and going," she answered herself.

"What does he look like, Laura," Daisy asked curiously.

Laura laughed, sounding as happy as she felt. "Daisy, he's the handsomest man I ever saw." Her smile and admiration were so obvious, Esteban's grin was just as broad as he gazed back. "The model agencies at home would fight over him for toothpaste ads alone. He has perfect teeth, and the nicest smile. And as I said, when I go somewhere with him either here on the island or the festival in San Juan, I feel safe, so there is nothing to worry about."

"Is he really that good looking?" Rose was incredulous.

"Maybe he keeps you safe from everyone else," Daisy insisted on worrying, "But what about him? But then, he knows you know who he is and where he works. That's always a good thing."

"Now, Daisy, you're worrying about nothing. He is as nice as he is nice looking. And he's certainly not going to do anything to me that I don't want done. End of worry, period."

Esteban stood behind her now, massaging her shoulders. He pulled back her robe, examining the sunburn, and gently kissed her neck. It gave Laura a little chill of delight, and he kissed the spot again.

"Well, anyway, we're glad you're having a good time. And we'll be looking for you in two weeks. Take care."

"And call us when you get ready to come back and let us know when your plane will get in."

"I'll do that, Daisy. And thank you, Rose. Thank both of you. Goodbye."

Laura put down the phone and stood up. Esteban put his arms around her, holding her close, as if he had missed her the brief time he had been gone.

"Esteban," she told him, knowing the tone of her voice would be reassuring even if he couldn't understand the words, "Right now, here near you, every inch of me loves you. You're wonderful." She laughed at his raised eyebrows.

Chapter Nine

Esteban watched Laura, who looked properly satisfied as she laid out the clothes she wanted to wear. She talked as she worked.

"I'll wear slacks and a top. Casual like you, Esteban. Then we can go wherever you want to."

They spent the day in town, and ate lunch at one of the little restaurants. Coming back, they took off their shoes and walked along the beach in the edge of the water in the moonlight until the breeze began to get cool. They came to the hotel on the beach side and stopped in the patio.

Laura stood on one foot to slip on her shoe, but Esteban shook his head.

"What?" She followed, carrying her shoes, as he led the way to a door she hadn't noticed beyond the patio. There was a service elevator not far from the door.

"This sure beats sand in your shoes," she commented as they entered the service elevator. She smiled at Esteban, "They must serve people on the patio from that door. I keep forgetting I'm with someone who knows the place," she slipped her arm through his.

When they arrived at her room, Esteban opened the door for her then pointed to the floor, indicating he would be back.

She managed to hide her disappointment, and went about straightening the room while he was gone.

She smiled to herself as she picked up the robe she had tossed on the floor in the bathroom. She was gazing down at the moonlight on the sand when he returned.

"Esteban, every time you leave, I worry that you may not come back. There are so many things I don't know about you."

He held up a large white tube of something and made a motion as if opening his shirt.

"We're really getting good at this," she laughed lightly, unbuttoning the top button on her blouse.

He came to her and held up her hair in back.

"Wait, I'll fix it." She went to the bathroom and secured the hair with several pins.

Esteban gently rubbed the soothing cream on her lower neck and shoulders, then, with a large bath towel in his hand, he went to the French doors and beckoned to her. He draped the towel around her shoulders and indicated a chair before going back in to use the phone.

Room service was fast and efficient. In no time they were settled with their coffee and the honeyed rolls the kitchen seemed to fix twenty-four hours a day, to watch passing water craft and moonlight on the water.

"This certainly is the way to enjoy a sunburn," Laura licked honey off her fingers.

She sighed, happy, refusing to think how fast her time on Isla Verde was running out.

The next morning Esteban wanted to go downstairs for breakfast. He pointed at the door and down, his eyebrows raised.

"All right," Laura nodded. "And I've got something I have to do first."

As they passed through the lobby, she touched Esteban's arm and pointed to the desk.

"I'm going to tell them I'm going to stay two more weeks." She held up two fingers when he looked at her. She beckoned and tilted her head toward the desk. "I know you don't understand, but just come with me. This is necessary."

She turned and took a step toward the desk. Esteban hesitated briefly, then accompanied her across the lobby.

Laura looked around; there was no one behind the chest high desk. When she stopped, a young man came through a door behind the counter and smiled at her.

"*Si?*"

"Oh, dear, do you speak some English?"

"*Si. Un poco,* some English," he answered slowly, as if having to think about each word.

"I'm in room four-oh-seven," she told him, speaking slowly. She held up four fingers, made a circle for oh, then held up seven fingers, and pointed upstairs. "And I wanted to tell you I'm not going to check out tomorrow as planned." She shook her head slightly. "I'm going to stay two more weeks. I don't plan on leaving before then, and will probably continue having things I buy in town charged to my room."

Laura smiled, having got it all said, thinking he must understand since he hadn't said anything. "That's room four-oh-seven. I just wanted to let you know." She started to turn away.

The young clerk looked up from the register he had been studying. "I am sorry."

"Sorry?" Laura stopped, surprised.

"The room—not available." The clerk pronounced the words with an assumed impersonal formality as if he had memorized the phrase.

"Not available? What do you mean?"

"The room. Needed Monday," the clerk explained.

Laura stood rooted to the floor, not knowing what to say until she heard a noise like someone choking. Her head swiveled as she felt Esteban beside her.

Esteban had moved quickly; he reached across the counter and took the frightened clerk in an iron grasp, wrinkling his uniform. Esteban's face wore the thunder-and-lightening look it had when he pursued the oily looking little man on the shuttle boat. The clerk's glasses dangled from one ear. Laura held her breath, afraid Esteban would get in trouble for his temper.

"Please," an older voice spoke. The older man Laura had seen once or twice in the lobby came out of the office and gave the young clerk a withering look before facing Esteban.

"I will take care of this, Julio."

Esteban let go of the clerk, who adjusted his glasses and left as fast as possible, going back through the office door.

"And how may I serve you, *Senora?*"

"As I said to the other clerk, I am in room four-oh-seven, and I will be staying on two more weeks. I wanted to let you know."

"Four-oh-seven." The man glanced at Esteban who said nothing, his face still stony.

He doesn't need to say anything, Laura thought, feeling a primitive pride.

"This is, as you say in your country, no problem, *Senora.* We will be happy for you to stay with us for as long as you care to stay."

He shifted his attention to Esteban. "This clerk, he is one of two new men we have just hired, he has not been here very long. I am sorry if he has inconvenienced you."

Esteban inclined his head like a king graciously allowing a condemned peasant to live, and took Laura's arm to leave.

"Well!" Laura exclaimed as they entered the coffee shop, "I'm glad I stopped to tell them I'm staying. I might have wound up without a room."

She sent Esteban a teasing look, "Would you have invited me to stay at your place, wherever that place is?"

He only pressed her arm, stopping to pick up a menu on their way in. They sat at a table facing a large curved window overlooking a garden filled with palms and tropical flowers. He held her chair for her.

"Breakfast looks delicious," she observed when the food was served. *"Bueno. Muy bueno."* She pointed.

"Bueno," Esteban agreed, his stormy expression gone.

They left the hotel to explore the village and turned up a street several blocks away from the costume shop. Esteban stopped at a place which rented bicycles and all manner of wheeled vehicles.

There were men's and women's bikes, tandems; Laura had never seen so many different wheels, motorized and to peddle.

"There's a side-by-side both people can peddle. Let's try it, I've never been on one of those," Laura's eyes asked questions.

Esteban nodded. He made the arrangements and pushed the two-seater out the drive to get into it. She laughed gaily as they pedaled off down the narrow street. "Aunt Sophie has treated me to another happy childhood," she told him. Esteban looked like he was having as much fun as she was.

Pedaling down several streets Laura had not seen before, they turned a corner and pedaled by a church. The priest was standing outside watching some children at play. Esteban stopped, got off the bike, and spoke to him in Spanish, then led him back to Laura.

"Padre Sanduval, Laura Carroll. Padre Sanduval, *me amigo*," he smiled.

"I'm glad to know you," Laura smiled, shaking his hand.

"Welcome to our island," the priest said, smiling at her as he spoke.

"Thank you. I'm really enjoying this lovely home of yours, and of Esteban's." Laura's heart rejoiced that he spoke English. Now she could solve a little more of the mystery of Esteban and his family. She shook his hand vigorously.

"Welcome to our island," the priest repeated, still smiling but a little uncertain.

Laura kept smiling to hide her disappointment. He had evidently learned that phrase so he could have something friendly to say to those who visited his church. *There goes my hope he speaks English well enough to be an interpreter for us.*

The following week was filled with exploring, both in the little village and the beaches around the island. They rented a sailboat and went around the far side of the island to visit a smaller uninhabited island not far from the end of it. She could tell how much Esteban was enjoying showing her around his part of the world.

That weekend, Esteban rose early and left, pointing to the floor to tell her he'd be back soon. Laura lay there a little while, drowsy and reluctant to leave the warmth of the coverlet.

She showered, not bothering to turn on the light, and was towel-drying her hair when she heard the door open.

"Laura?"

Esteban stood staring at the empty bed. There were no lights on.

"Was that a note of panic I heard in your voice?" Laura stuck her head out the door and turned on the bathroom light. "Now you know how I feel when you leave, even when you tell me you'll be back."

He smiled and held up something. She went closer to see what it was. He took her sandals and the thong sandals he had bought her out of the closet. From a drawer he took her bathing suit.

She took out his present, holding it up.

"It's a sweat suit. It looks warm. Even the colors are warm: sunshine yellow and white."

He handed her sandals to her and a sundress to put on.

Everything else he put into a large shopping bag with the hotel's logo on it.

Laura looked at everything he had gathered up. "We're going somewhere. Maybe overnight?"

Esteban didn't answer, pointing to the sundress.

"Seems I'm to wear my sundress and sandals and take my bathing outfit and the sweat suit you brought me. I guess I'll find out in due course, but wherever it is, I'm sure to need underwear and a toothbrush."

She went past him and finished putting some other needed things in the shopping bag. She held up a finger. "I won't be a minute," she promised.

She put toilet articles in on top of her clothes, still talking to Esteban, and then laid her purse on top. "I thought we might be going to San Juan, but this is the best place for swimming, so it must not be there. And the sweat suit? It must be cool, somewhere on the water?"

Esteban put his arms around her for a reassuring embrace, and held the door for her before picking up her things.

She smiled at the sack. "Our Isla Verde luggage." She laughed. "That's part of the fun of going somewhere with you, Esteban, I never know where we're going, but packing's no problem."

They went out through the lobby, down toward where the little tourist shuttle docked, then continued on down the beach to a cove where boats of every description moored, from large ones down to the little sailboats like the one Esteban had rented to take them to the small island. Some of them were large yachts; one or two were anchored farther out in the cove, too big for the marina.

As she looked around at the boats and activity in the area, Esteban put the shopping bag down by her feet and went up the wooden walkway of the pier, stopping, she estimated, about a city block away.

He disappeared for a few minutes, and she wondered if he was boarding one of the boats.

She looked around, a little apprehensive at the wait, then turned to see him coming back.

Esteban stooped, picked up the shopping bag and pointed down the wooden walkway, which creaked and moved underfoot.

This must be an expensive hobby, Laura thought, not talking as she tried to watch her footing and admire the boats at the same time.

He stopped and walked up beside a boat that looked to be about forty feet long, and wide enough to take up two berths.

She admired the sleek lines of the expensive-looking boat. She wondered who it belonged to. There weren't any signs saying there were boats to be rented. This looked like a pricey private marina.

Esteban took the shopping bag and other things and set them on the deck before turning to help Laura aboard. He indicated a deck chair and went up the steps to the controls.

"We must be going to go out in this boat," Laura said, as much to herself as to his back. "I finally figured that out all by myself. Aren't you proud of me?" She followed him up the steps and watched as he maneuvered them out into open water.

"The view is beautiful from up here, and this is a beautiful and no doubt expensive boat. I see now why you brought me the sweat suit. But Esteban?"

He turned his head at her worried expression and the obvious question in her voice.

"This boat?" She pointed to the deck and the floor between them. "Whose is it? I know it's not one that can be rented. There was no sign and this is too obviously a private marina." Lines appeared above her eyes.

"*Amigo,*" Esteban said. Then, because of her still-concerned expression, he gestured around them and at the deck and repeated confidently, *"Amigo."*

"Amigo. It belongs to a friend of yours." She nodded. *He must take care of it to get to use it,* she decided.

They went all around Isla Verde and the three smaller islands near it. They circled the one where they had gone on the sailboat and shared a smile, remembering the day. He stopped in the hidden cove—perhaps to swim?

He led the way down to the deck and held the door of the cabin open for her, bending his head as he entered.

Stepping inside, Laura stopped to look around her, liking what she saw. Everything was beautifully coordinated, and everything needed for their comfort had been very compactly and efficiently fitted into the space available. There was even a television set and VCR. She walked over and examined how they had been secured against any movement.

Esteban opened a door, waiting for her to enter. Laura found herself in a small hallway. A room on one side consisted of closets and storage. The other room was larger and held a king-sized bed with a lamp over it.

Part of the closet and storage area across the hall could be used as sleeping quarters too, she noted. There were bunks that could be unfolded from the wall and had bedding under them.

Esteban stood in the room with the large bed. She stood at the door, looking around.

"All of this is really nice and well done." She gestured at the cabin, believing he could understand the compliment. "It looks so comfortable."

She touched the bed and noticed the table beside it was secured to the floor. A radio and cassette player with magnetic bottoms sat on it. "That's a good idea," she mused, still looking around.

Esteban touched the radio to show her it would not move or

fall from the table. Laura smiled and extended her arms as if embracing the room.

He laughed at the gesture and came to claim the embrace for himself. He left her to explore and went to bring down the rest of their things. More Isla Verde luggage.

When he returned, she waved her arm again, indicating the entire boat. "Your *amigo*. *Bueno*. And it was nice of him to let you use the boat."

"*Bueno*," he agreed, dumping her things on the bed.

He took his suit from the Isla Verde luggage sack and went to change.

Then he was back, beckoning to her.

"You're in luck, you know," she told him.

He widened his eyes, waiting for more or a gesture.

"I can't ask you if you've . . . I mean, how many other girls you've brought for a holiday on this boat."

Her eyes slid to the big bed in spite of herself. He stood listening, not commenting in Spanish or by his expression. "I just have to take you at face value and follow my feelings," Laura said. "And what's worse, you seem to know what my feelings are most of the time." She grinned, realizing how true that was.

Esteban slowly leaned closer to kiss her, his warm hands pressing her close to him. Then grinning, he suddenly pushed her, both of them falling backward on the bed.

She laughed with him, not asking any more questions he couldn't understand—and might not answer if he could. They put on their bathing suits and she followed him to the deck.

As they swam he showed her brightly colored fish and coral and other beautiful and strange things until they were tired of diving.

By the time they got back, Laura was wondering if the little galley had supplies in it.

Esteban held the rope ladder as she climbed back aboard the boat. On deck, he ruffled his hair, pointing to the cabin.

"Shower. That was an easy one," she grinned at him. "And I can see how good that sweat suit you thought of is going to feel. The breeze is already turning cooler."

Esteban had brought big, thirsty towels with the hotel's logo on them, and she had wondered about that. *I guess it's all right as long as we take them back.*

When she went to take her shower, Esteban's arm reached around her to open doors on both sides of the sink. She couldn't read the Spanish labels but could tell what everything was.

She held up some lavender scented hand lotion, "Your *amigo. Bueno. Gracias.*" She smiled. "That's my entire Spanish repertory . . . well, almost," she admitted under her breath and reached for the hair dryer.

Esteban was dressed and putting on his shoes when she came into the room to get her sweat suit. His suit was charcoal gray with the hotel's logo on it. He pointed up and left.

She joined him in the tiny galley where he opened all the cabinet doors so she could see what was in them, an uncertain expression accompanying all the openings. Last of all he opened an under-the-counter refrigerator and stood looking at her, his head tilted to one side.

Not understanding the labels, she looked at pictures, shook cans and packages, and was grateful most of the things in the refrigerator didn't need explanations. She hummed as she worked, shaking her head at Esteban who seemed to be checking to see if she needed help.

The dinner of sautéed pork chops, baked potatoes, and French bread was so appreciated, Laura knew he was surprised to learn she could cook.

Dinner was delicious, and she felt she had earned his

embrace. His indications of approval included cleaning up the galley.

Later, under way, Laura sent him a questioning look. She was beginning to wonder about the direction in which they were heading.

"We're going at a pretty good clip—somewhere—as if you don't know the way back to Isla Verde?"

Esteban shook his head.

"Not Isla Verde?"

"San Juan."

Chapter Ten

When they were in sight of Puerto Rico, they met the hotel's shuttle boat coming back. The man operating the little tourist boat took off his wide brimmed hat and waved it at them. Esteban beamed at him like long lost family as they both returned his greeting.

Laura smiled and waved, too. The greeting lifting her spirits, it was such a happy one. *Esteban is well liked by his friends and people he works with. Or, maybe that man is family. I know so little about him. But I do know his name now. Esteban Aguilar.* Knowing his name made the smile on her face linger, her affection for him growing because he seemed to be so well liked.

She watched as they approached the marina, admiring Esteban's skill at guiding the boat into the slip. The marina was a lot like the one on Isla Verde.

Holding Esteban's hand as they walked toward shore, she looked around at the marina. There were lots of boats, most of them smaller than the one they'd been on.

That one seemed to be the largest boat the marina accommodated. There were larger ones anchored farther out. "This is where we met. On the shuttle."

She smiled up at Esteban as they paused where the shuttle boat docked when it came to Puerto Rico.

He smiled and pointed. He remembered; her heart knew it. His heart and his eyes spoke to her in the language of love, and she took his hand as he reached out to continue walking.

They looked at some of the outlying shops and stands before coming to a sign in Spanish and English. Esteban stopped and tilted his head toward the sign.

"It's advertising an excursion to see the rain forest?" Laura nodded, "That sounds interesting, if you would like to go." She pointed to her heart and nodded, then pointed to him, tilting her head.

He nodded and pointed to the addresses where tickets were available. They made their way to a large and seemingly ancient hotel lobby to get the tickets. The dark woodwork inside was particularly beautiful, rather ornate and antique looking, and polished to a high gloss.

"A parrot," she exclaimed in delight, pointing at the beautiful bird.

Esteban turned, their tickets in his hand, to see what she was staring at with such a rapt expression. The parrot sat on a perch in a very large cage and stared back at her as she admired his beautiful colors.

Esteban laughed softly, pointing to the tickets. He looked up at the clock above the desk and guided her toward the front doors.

The tour bus sitting in the street was not large, nor was it any make Laura recognized. She squeezed Esteban's hand, looking forward to the tour as they boarded the bus.

"We will be able to see everything," she told him excitedly as they took their seats.

A middle-aged woman in a bright skirt and blouse entered and greeted them as the bus pulled away from the hotel. She told them first in English and then in Spanish some facts about the history of the rain forest, as well as some of the tropical flora and fauna they might see on the tour. The accompanying gestures and the slow pace of the bus after they entered the forest enabled them to follow what she was telling them.

She realized why Esteban had laughed at her amazement at the parrot in the hotel. There were many strange and brightly colored birds, as well as ferns and other plants, as they made their way along the narrow road that appeared to have been cut through the living vegetation. They slowed even more to cross a shallow stream, and Laura's hand tightened on Esteban's as she peered out the window.

A large lizard sat on a rock not more than a couple of feet from the bus.

"It's so still, I nearly missed seeing it," Laura breathed, staring at it.

"Iguana." Esteban patted her hand.

"Iguana," she repeated. "They must not be too aggressive and frightening. I seem to be the only one who's impressed by how big he is—must be about three feet or more."

As they moved away from the iguana, she settled back beside Esteban. "This sweat suit is beginning to feel good." She picked up some of the soft material of the arm between her fingers. *"Bueno."*

Esteban nodded, "Laura *buena*," he said with an amused smile.

"This is beginning to sound like, 'me Tarzan, you Jane,' isn't it?"

"Tarzan—Jane." Esteban laughed with her and put his arm over the back of her seat as he gazed out at the lengthening shadows.

By the time they got back to the hotel, dusk had fallen, showing up the intricate iron carriage lights on the hotel entrance. Esteban pointed to a nearby café, which had tables outside with candles already lit on them. They made their way to the little patio bounded by shrubs and potted plants.

Esteban ordered and Laura caught the word "coffee" as the waiter turned away.

The coffee was strong and hot and accompanied by fruit-filled pastries with powdered sugar or honey on them.

There weren't many people around when they returned to the boat. One of the larger boats was leaving, moving toward the open sea with lots of running lights that made it look wraith-like and romantic in the dusk.

On deck, Esteban sniffed and pointed to a boat several slips away from them where a man was tending a grill.

"Smells good to you—*bueno?* I'd better see what I can find to fix for us to eat." She pointed down and left.

The galley and its contents more familiar to her now, she went to work on dinner. It was a huge success, probably due to hunger, and Esteban put his arms around her as they rose from the table, speaking softly to her in Spanish.

"That's a pretty long speech," she murmured against his chest. "So it must be something good."

She stretched up, gently kissing his cheek and pointed up. She wanted to watch him get underway.

He shook his head and picked up a bottle of wine.

She didn't understand and stood waiting.

He put their glasses on an end table and pointed out the window. There were dark clouds over them now, the boat was rocking gently, and the rain had started.

"No Isla Verde."

She nodded and snuggled up close to him to show it didn't matter. They sat on the comfortable couch watching the rain until they got sleepy. They went to sleep in the cabin's king sized bed, Esteban's body curved around hers, cozy and warm.

The morning sun woke Laura. Esteban opened his eyes as she rose to look outside.

"The rain storm's all gone. *Hermosa,*" she pointed to the tranquil water.

"*Hermosa*—beautiful," his arms went around her, drawing her close to him.

"Love for breakfast?" She murmured, wondering how she had lived this long without him, never even knowing this paradise existed. She pushed away her mental warnings that this was only a temporary paradise, not eternity. She wanted him more than she had the first night he stayed with her. But not as just a temporary fling, and he didn't seem to want that either. Or maybe the feeling was because of something she didn't yet know about him.

Laura told herself she must remember this was Esteban's part of the world, not hers. Maybe there was some reason he didn't want to have a closer relationship. But she didn't want to know about it—not now . . .

Laura pressed against him, most of her dangerously willing to make this paradise complete, if only for her last few days. But Esteban moved back. He seemed to draw away from her, kissing her briefly as she spoke to him, her arms still around him.

"Esteban," she leaned closer and murmured against his neck. "Surely you will find a way, or someone to talk for us soon, to tell me if I'm living in a fool's dream to think you love me as I do you."

He did not hold her closer and she sighed, letting her arms fall away. "I hoped the priest at the church would be the one."

She looked sad as she turned away, and he reached for her again, briefly holding her against him to kiss her forehead. Then he moved away.

"Isla Verde," he said.

She went to the galley to find them something to eat.

On deck, she handed him a toast and ham sandwich and coffee in a mug. He waited until he had the boat underway to do more than sip his coffee and smile his thanks.

They went around the big island again, then the smaller one

Stranger in Paradise

where they swam to shore and ate a picnic lunch and explored around the lesser islands before returning. The two days on the boat were more of a vacation trip than Laura had dreamed of when she and Rose and Daisy had been making vacation plans. Greenfield seemed so far away.

As they walked back from the Isla Verde marina, Laura looked up at the hotel. It sat like a medieval castle surrounded by the incredible colors of palms touched by the last rays of the sun. Deep myriad colors, deep shadows and tropical plants, sand; all of it framed by the vivid blue of the sea where the last rays of the sunset hit it.

"The hotel is so beautiful. The sun is gleaming on it as if it's kissing it goodnight," Laura said in awe. "What is the word?" She wrinkled her brow. "*Casa*, that's it!" She stopped and Esteban turned to her.

"*Casa*," she said carefully. "Your *casa*. It's *hermosa*."

He understood, she thought, or liked the sound of the words. He took her in his arms, not caring whether anyone was on the beach or not, and held her tenderly, then pointed to the hotel.

"*Mi casa, su casa.*"

"I know that, I've heard that phrase. It must be one of the first ones you learn in Spanish class. It's lovely. Like a Spanish aloha, I guess." She walked beside him, her hand in his.

When they got to Laura's room, Esteban put down the shopping bag.

"Our Isla Verde luggage does just fine." She tossed back her wind-blown hair and looked fondly at the shopping bag.

Esteban pointed to himself, to the door, then to himself and the floor in front of her.

"Oh, you're going. But you're coming back. I guess you're going to change. I'm getting a little warm in this suit, too. I'll shower while you're gone."

She kissed his cheek and pointed toward the shower. He nodded and was gone.

Waiting for her hair to dry naturally, she slathered cream on her face and steamed it in with hot water before putting on her makeup. She dressed in one of the colorful shirts she had bought for the trip, applied scent to her ear lobes. Then she added a tiny bit to her bra strap, giving herself a naughty grin in the mirror before choosing earrings to match the shirt. She stood there looking down at her bare feet.

I never know whether to put on heels or sandals or—oh, he's back!

Esteban wore light colored slacks and a sports shirt, his thong sandals on his feet.

"Thong sandals it is."

He watched, nodding his approval as she wriggled her toes into them and picked up her shoulder bag. "Lead on!"

This time they walked down the other side of the island, passing the marina. They rolled up their slacks and waded at the edge of the water. "My thanks to whoever it was who invented thong sandals," she watched the water lapping over her feet.

He nodded agreement, taking her arm to guide her around some broken shells. He pointed to a rock big enough for them both to sit on.

"You think of everything." She chuckled. "Sometimes I wish I could just charge you to my room and take you home with me. What do you think of that, and thank goodness you haven't a clue what I just said!"

She laughed as Esteban tilted his head, seeming to think it over, and then pointed toward the horizon. The sun was almost gone now, and the splash of colors looked as if they had been done with a huge paintbrush.

"Puerto Rico *bueno*." Esteban got up and pulled her close, putting his arms around her. They simply stood a moment in silence before he pointed toward the hotel.

I wonder what he wanted to say. It seemed to me he wanted to tell me something. It must be a problem to him too, not to be able to talk. Not that it's been hurting our relationship. She smiled, aware of her hand in his, as if he owned it. *Don't I wish . . .*

At the hotel Esteban went on past the coffee shop and entered the elevator.

I guess this means we won't be eating in the coffee shop.

In her room, Esteban went to the closet and stood, considering the clothes hanging there. Then his face lit up and he picked up her high-heeled dress shoes and handed them to her.

"Oh, you want to dress for dinner. That was an easy one. There's nothing else that combination of gestures could mean," she looked down at the shoes.

She went to the closet and got out the two dresses she liked best and held them up. "Which? Which one do you like better?" She held one out, then the other one.

Esteban pointed to the black one.

"All right, I like this one too."

He pointed out and back, and Laura nodded. She pointed to the bathroom and her hair.

"My, if we were seen at this charade, people would think perhaps we're too backward to learn proper sign language."

He pointed again to the floor in front of her and left the room, smiling.

I've been out in the sun so much; I'd better steam some more cream into my skin.

Laura looked critically at her image in the mirror when she had finished, wondering if Pierre would approve of the job she had done with her makeup.

I'll put up my hair and wear the real pearl earrings Aunt Sophie gave me. I know she would be glad to know I'm wearing them.

She was looking critically at the results of her preparations when she heard Esteban. She made herself walk slowly out into the room, knowing nothing was as unglamorous as trying to hurry. Then she saw Esteban and stopped in her tracks.

She took a deep breath, she could hardly speak. "Esteban, you, you're . . ." She paused. "I already thought you are the handsomest man I've ever seen, but . . ." She breathed deeply again. "But, in that tux, Esteban, you're magnificent!" She laughed softly, "I'm afraid to let you out of here, someone will steal you from me."

She reached for the hands he held out to her as she spoke, admiring him.

He had been looking at her while time seemed to stand still, gazing at her, his eyes as admiring as she felt when she gazed at him. He looked at her hair and the pearls in her ears, and she knew she looked stunning. His eyes were telling her so.

He slowly raised one of her hands to his lips and kissed it. She held her breath; the moment was magic.

Then he seemed to remember something. He pointed quickly to himself, then out, then down at the floor again.

"Oh, no." Laura sighed, not wanting him to go. Reluctantly she nodded, wondering why he seemed to be in such a hurry.

She stood looking out at the moonlight after he left, then turned on the lamp by the bed and went back to the bathroom mirror to look again at her hair. She didn't hear him come in, but she beamed when his reflection appeared in the mirror behind her.

"Ah, you're back. What is that you have?"

He turned her around to face the mirror again. She saw out of the corner of her eye he had laid a velvet-lined jeweler's box on the counter top. Their eyes met in the mirror as he placed a strand of pearls around her neck and fastened the clasp.

"Esteban, they're beautiful!" Laura was not quite sure what to say.

"*Mi Madre—*"

"*Madre*—Your mother's? Oh! Esteban, no, I couldn't. No," she protested.

He took the hand she raised in protest and held it behind her, holding her close and burying his face in her neck. "Umm." He savored the scent she had put on.

"All right, I will wear your mother's pearls, but I'll worry until they're back in the jeweler's box. And we'd better go." She laughed lightly. "Before we decide eating is not all that important!"

Chapter Eleven

Laura and Esteban slept late the next morning. She woke first and lay propped up on her elbow, gazing down at him.

He was smiling. She hoped he was dreaming about their trip to San Juan. She smiled, too. Esteban had never tried to make this what her Aunt Sophie would call an *improper relationship.* He was Aunt Sophie's ideal of a gentleman, as well as handsome as all get-out.

Her smile faded. *Or he doesn't want the problems that might go with a closer bond between us,* she thought. *No, there are villains as well as heroes in all those romances and mysteries I've read. My Esteban is a hero.* She smiled, tracing his eyebrow with her finger before getting up.

She was showered and already drying her hair when Esteban stuck his head in the door. He smiled and disappeared.

"Laura," she heard in a few minutes.

She looked out. "I see you have enough clothes on to qualify for decently covered." She grinned at him, wishing he could understand.

He raised the arm holding his tux, then pointed down then to the floor in front of her to tell her he would be back.

She nodded and returned to finish drying her hair, his image in his tux keeping her company.

I'll probably have plenty of time. He's surely going home. Wherever that is, she added with a frighteningly empty feeling. *When he's gone, all the things I don't know about him come to the surface.*

She studied her concerned expression in the mirror. *It's as if my own good judgment doesn't have a chance to be heard when Esteban is here with me.* She flushed, watching the red surge up her neck. *I can't hear it over the beating of my heart!*

Looking for something to put on, she found two blouses she hadn't yet had occasion to wear.

I guess we really bought too much when we went shopping, but these are things I can wear at home. She ignored the cold, hollow feeling thinking of going home brought on.

She chose a moss-green silk blouse with a ruffle around the low neck and three quarter length sleeves.

This looks feminine and pretty enough to suit my mood. I never would have thought about bringing a sweat suit, she thought, remembering the one Esteban had brought her. *But then, I wouldn't have thought about a trip on a boat, either.*

When Esteban came back, he had the shopping bag with the hotel's logo on it with him. He put it down and came to admire the green blouse, touching the ruffle lightly, approving with his eyes.

"This is one of my colors. I know none of this is getting through," she giggled.

He touched the green silk. *"Bueno. Hermosa,"* he pronounced.

"I guess recognizing the right colors isn't a language thing after all." She glanced at the shopping bag.

"And here's our Isla Verde luggage, I see. Are we going somewhere? Are my blouse and slacks all right?" She touched the blouse, raising her eyebrows.

He nodded, talking to her in Spanish as he went to the closet. As he talked, he took out her robe and looked around.

"I'll bet you're looking for my bathing suit."

She disappeared into the bathroom and reappeared, carrying it. "It's only a tiny bit damp in places, almost dry. I guess I'd better get some face cream and lotion too." She laid the suit on the bed and went back to the bathroom.

I didn't notice anything of his in that sack, she thought as she took the things she wanted from the shelves. *Maybe we're going on his friend's boat again, where he keeps some of his things.*

On their way to the elevator Esteban rubbed his stomach and pointed toward the coffee shop.

"Gross, but understood, Esteban. I could use some breakfast, too."

They had breakfast in the coffee shop, the shopping bag propped against Esteban's leg.

"This has been the most unplanned, impulsive relationship, Esteban. I've never heard of anything like it, even in a novel. I never know what we're going to do next. But it's always been something exciting and enjoyable, or maybe it's just being with you that's those things." She smiled at him, laying down the menu.

He placed his hand over hers, then picked it up and held it between both of his, his eyes on hers briefly, until the waitress came with their coffee.

She turned to look at the flowers and the sweep of lawn to hide the thought that came unbidden and unwelcome. *Take a good look at paradise, Laura; this can't last forever. I will have to leave, and he will have to go back to work. I can't bear to think about the end of it. I won't.*

He signed for their breakfast. She watched him write Esteban Aguilar in bold strokes across the bottom of the check.

Laura wondered briefly if he had signed for her sweat suit in the gift shop too. If she knew how to ask, she would insist on it being changed to a charge to her room. But there was no time to give it more thought. Esteban was already rising from his seat, reaching for their Isla Verde luggage.

They went out the lobby doors in front and walked toward the town's main street. The shops were open, and friendly people greeted them with smiles and waves as they walked along, Esteban returning all their greetings.

She laughed, wondering silently if the whole island population was his family.

He looked inquiringly, but she only shook her head, smiling at him.

He stopped and Laura looked curiously around. The place was like the bicycle rental shop, except here they had larger motorized scooters, golf cart two-seaters, and several kinds of motorcycles. Esteban chose a motorcycle with a sidecar and pushed it out on the apron in front of the business. Laura brought the shopping bag and placed it and her purse on the floor of the sidecar, stepping in beside them.

Esteban put on his sunglasses and checked to see that she had hers on and was seated safely.

She grimaced at the noise as he started the cycle, but was soon too interested in the scenery to notice the racket.

They were out on the open road now and she wondered where they were going, not that it mattered. She smiled to herself. Then the smile faded. *What matters is that room four-oh-seven is mine until checkout time next Monday morning.*

She banished such thoughts and concentrated on the scenery.

She held to the side as Esteban veered off onto a less-traveled-looking road that paralleled the beach. Shortly after that, Esteban began slowing.

We're here. Laura steadied herself. *Wherever here is.*

There had been an alternating fence of iron and stone on the land side of the road for quite a way, and Esteban pulled the motorcycle into a driveway in front of an iron gate.

This looks like some kind of private drive. Laura shifted uneasily in her seat. She leaned forward, looking up the drive, but could see nothing except that the road curved and started uphill, then was hidden by trees and shrubs.

Esteban saw her trying to see and smiled. He pulled a perforated card from his pocket and put it into a slot in the arm of the gate. The heavy looking gate was double and of an ornate iron pattern. It moved inward to let them pass.

"*Amigo?*" Laura got the word out quickly, before the motor could drown her voice.

Esteban hesitated a moment then nodded. "*Amigo.*"

The drive took them steadily upward until Laura could see a breathtaking view of water through the trees on the side toward the sea. Then a slight bend of the road took them up a long, straight grade to a house sitting just below the crest of the mountain. It was impressive. The house itself was massive and beautiful, with stone, glass, and landscaping that used all the scenery to its full advantage.

The tiled front porch had large, white columns, and went across the entire front of the house. The entry was imposing. The double doors were massive, of beautifully carved wood, and the windows flanking it reached almost to the floor.

"What a beautiful house," Laura said, thinking, mansion would be more like it.

Esteban unlocked the door with a key from a large ring she figured must be his caretaker's keys because there were so many of them.

He stepped aside for her to go in. She went in a few steps and looked around in all directions.

"It's beautiful." Laura clasped her hands, "*Hermosa.* It's an *hermosa casa,* Esteban, but it's empty!"

She waved her arms as she spoke. "Does no one live here? What a waste! Surely, even people who only come for part of a year would furnish it. I certainly would." She started exploring.

He watched as she made a small tour of the foyer and the rooms that opened from it. She caught sight of huge fireplaces through the grand archway.

"Oh, Esteban, these big, beautiful fireplaces are really something."

She walked over to touch the poker beside the fireplace near them. "You couldn't run me out of here with a stick if this place were mine," she said wistfully. "I would love furnishing it and living here."

Esteban went to the shopping bag and got out her bathing suit then went out in the hall and opened a closet hidden under the stair. She stood holding her suit; she hadn't realized the closet was there, the rest of the place was so interesting and full of things to see.

He took something from a hook. It was a pair of bathing trunks, and he disappeared toward the foyer.

Going back to the shopping bag Esteban had left beside the fireplace she decided, *I'll leave my things here beside our Isla Verde luggage.*

He rejoined her and they went out the double doors. He led her to the left side of the porch and pointed down. She looked and could see little glimpses of water, but not much else through the foliage. She took the hand he held out to her.

She admired the house as they went around it, then gasped with pleasure. The whole area behind the house was beautifully landscaped, even part way up to the crest of the mountain behind it. There was a pool and the gurgle of water somewhere nearby.

She didn't have time to explore farther. Esteban guided her to a separate building that served as a garage and was as massive as the back of the house looked. There were two cars in the garage, both with covers over them, along with storage and lawn equipment. Esteban went to a golf cart and poured fuel into it from a can. He wiped his hands on a utility cloth and started the motor, beckoning to her.

Their destination was a large lagoon with a small island in

the middle of it, covered with some variety of flowered vine. The water curved around out of sight and gave the illusion of being larger than it actually was. Two swans appeared, their reflections moving in the quiet water with them.

"*Hermosa,*" Laura said, but she wondered if the natural beauty had been landscaped by some artistic hand as the area back of the house had been.

He pointed out beyond the island where Laura saw a float, an ideal place for a swim.

Instead of going toward the water, Esteban got back into the golf cart and continued showing her the estate.

"The roads, plants, and everything is kept in such beautiful condition, even to the potted plants." Laura shook her head. "I can't understand why the people who own this place don't live in it."

Laura smiled at the tug on her hand, "I guess you've got me trained. At least I know most of the time what you mean. I wish I knew how to tell you I've been imagining living here with you. It would be paradise."

It was late afternoon by the time they tired of swimming in the pool, and Laura wondered if there were supplies in the house as there had been on the boat.

They hurried back to the shopping bag and he handed her robe to her.

She rubbed her arms briskly, glad the sleeves were long, and wandered around the room when Esteban disappeared, admiring the dark luster of the woodwork.

"This must be rosewood. And all this glass and these fireplaces . . . this place is beautiful even without any furniture in it."

"Laura," Esteban called from somewhere. She found him in the foyer, which impressed her anew as she entered.

"I know people who would be happy just to have this

entrance." She followed Esteban into the kitchen.

He stood beside some open cabinets and gestured upwards to show her they had their choice of whatever they wanted to eat.

"All right, I guess any further tour of the house can wait a while. I'm hungry too."

She examined the cans, canisters, boxes, and other things in the well stocked larder. *I wonder where the refrigerator is?*

Esteban saw her turn away from the shelves and opened a wide door.

"Oh, the refrigerator is built in! I'd have to look twice even to recognize it."

He gestured toward the top of the refrigerator.

"That must be the freezer section, but it's so big. This refrigerator must be four feet wide. No wonder it had to be built in. The people who own this place must be planning on entertaining—if they ever buy any furniture." She grinned at Esteban.

She examined the packages in plastic wrap because she could tell what they were and then held up a package of pork chops.

The main course having been approved, she got out things to go with it as she sautéed the pork chops.

After finishing their meal, Esteban spread marmalade on one of the refrigerated biscuits she had baked to go with their meal and got up, beckoning her to follow him.

On the other side of a tiered rock garden and some flowering shrubs was a low bench facing a kidney-shaped pond with a fountain at the far end.

Her eyes followed his pointing finger. There were gold fish and carp and something that looked like branches of coral for them to swim through. He handed her a piece of the biscuit.

Some of the fish were already coming toward them. She smiled, crumbling the bread for the fish. Esteban picked up some twigs and branches and disappeared around the side of the garage.

It was getting cooler, she realized as she dusted the last of the crumbs from her fingers.

Laura hoped Esteban was going to build them a fire in one of those big fireplaces. It would not only be pretty; it would feel good. At least someone was getting some pleasure out of this beautiful place. *This must be one of his jobs, taking care of this man's summer place when he's not at his job in the band at the hotel. The boat must be his, too. It's certainly a job loaded with fringe benefits.*

The fire was going well when she came through the door, sending its glow to all but the most remote corners of the large room, pushing back the dark that had descended so fast outside as she washed their dishes.

She stood in front of the fire and gestured at it, *"Bueno."* She smiled down at Esteban.

He had put velour blankets and some pillows near the fireplace.

He stood up, shaking his head as he reached for her.

"Why not *bueno?* As if I wouldn't agree with you no matter what you said." She snuggled close to him.

He held her against him, one hand holding her head, which lay against his chest, the other arm pressing all of her to him.

"Bueno," he repeated, his meaning clear as he smiled. This time neither of them drew back. Laura nestled in his arms, loving the warmth of him, till he moved away, pulling her with him.

They sat down in front of the fire, Esteban arranging the soft blankets around them, kissing and caressing her as the fire warmed them. The glow of the fire danced, reflected in the polished woodwork. Lying nestled in his arms, Laura watched the fire and the sky through the long windows as the stars come out, until Esteban kissed her cheek and got up.

Pulling his robe around him, he went to get more wood, and Laura went to the kitchen. Esteban was back quickly and laid some extra pieces of wood on the hearth as Laura returned from the kitchen.

"I brought us some more biscuits and marmalade," she said as she set down the plate near their blankets. "Marmalade, *bueno?*"

"Laura, *bueno!*" The huge room was comfortably warm now. Esteban settled again on the blankets and pillows and reached for her.

She moved the biscuits a little and went to him. He held her close, his hands gently exploring her body as he kissed her. He didn't turn away as he always had before, and she didn't pull away either.

Laura held her breath; this time was different. This time, Esteban was not turning away from her. Her heart beat faster as he pulled the blanket back to let them touch, and she clung to him. This was the bell-ringing-found-the-right-one chemistry all the happy-ending romances in the bookstore shelves at home described. Laura was in love with Esteban, her heart beating against his.

He stopped, still holding her against him, his eyes holding hers a second before he buried his face in her neck.

In a sudden panic, she wondered if something was wrong, if he was going to turn away again. But his arms tightened around her as if he'd never let her go.

"*Te amo,*" he murmured in her ear. "*Te amo,* Laura."

She lay quite still, listening, then her arms came up around his neck. Her cheek against his, she murmured, "*Yo te amo,* Esteban." She repeated it carefully, "*Yo te amo.*"

She looked at him and held his gaze, her eyes questioning, afraid to believe what he had said. He had told her he loved her in his language.

"The first phrases my friends learned in Spanish were *'como esta?'* how are you?" she said slowly, her eyes holding his. "And *'yo te amo,'* I love you. Do you? Do love me, Esteban?"

He returned her solemn look and said slowly, so there would be no mistake, *"Yo te amo."* He leaned forward and kissed her forehead. *"Yo te amo."*

Pressed against the warmth of him, his hand cupped her breast. Esteban kissed her long and tenderly. Then, touching her upper arm that felt cool, he pulled the blanket up over them. She felt warm and cozy beside him—and he loved her! He had very carefully told her so. She propped up on her elbow to talk, but instead, he pulled her to him, his eyes meeting hers, confident this time.

He still did not make love to her, but he held her close, pushing away the blanket as if pushing away anything that would come between them ever again. And he told her he loved her, made sure she understood the words.

Safe and warm in the firelight, no longer a stranger in paradise, Laura rested in Esteban's arms.

Chapter Twelve

Their love made the empty mansion an enchanted castle with a circle of warmth and light from the fire. When Esteban brought more wood for the fire, he went back to the kitchen and brought honey rolls he had warmed in the microwave. When she reached for one, he held them away and kissed her before handing her the whole plate of them. Esteban's smile was bright enough to compete with the flames from the fire. He laughed as she bit hungrily into one of the rolls.

"Is this a pledge with honey rolls to take care of me and keep me all the rest of my days?" Laura pressed.

Esteban smiled and saluted her with his roll, seemingly pleased with whatever she'd said.

Laura finished her roll. "I guess now that we are in love—*te amo*—*amo* Laura—" Esteban laughed at her stumbling over the word and smiled as he listened.

"We can live in Greenfield," she said, looking into his eyes.

"*Casa*. Greenfield—*casa?*"

"Greenfield—*casa*," he acknowledged, understanding.

"My *casa* is not anything like this." Laura gestured with one bare arm and shook her head. "But it is a nice *casa*." She smiled. "A *bueno casa*. Big enough—*grande?* No. No *grande*." She shook her head. "But *grande* enough for . . ." She held her arms as if holding a baby and held up two fingers.

Esteban nodded, smiling, still looking pleased.

He pulled her to him and kissed her again, as if agreeing with whatever she said. He got up, pointing toward the kitchen.

Feeling warm and loved, Laura lay wrapped in a blanket as Esteban went to the kitchen and returned with bowls of rich Isla Verde ice cream for them.

"Unless I get so fat on this wonderful ice cream and you don't want me any more, we can live there in Greenfield, or here in Isla Verde." Laura pointed to herself and to him, getting serious again. "Greenfield *casa?*" She tilted her head, "Or Isla Verde *casa?*"

"Isla Verde." He answered positively, no doubt in his meaning this time.

"I don't blame you. This is your home, and it's beautiful here. Isla Verde *hermosa.*" She sighed, wondering how much he was really understanding. But no matter; he was getting the important parts. "Laura—Esteban—Isla Verde. *Bueno.*"

He set down his empty plate and pulled her to him, holding her close. "Laura. Esteban. Isla Verde. *Bueno.*" It was a confirmation.

"Well, I guess that's settled. We can sell the house, my Aunt Sophie's house, and get one here. And since I won't be there, the bookstore can be sold too." She busily counted assets in her head, worrying about their future. "That, in addition to the little bit I already have from Aunt Sophie, will give us a small amount of interest to supplement what you make at the hotel. Or maybe we can just live on it. Prices don't seem to be very high here. We'll do whatever you want to do."

She paused, looking at him. He hadn't said anything else, but he looked happy. He hadn't said much except to confirm that they would have a home and it would be in Isla Verde. *And most wonderful of all, he loves me. That's miracle enough for one night. Esteban will see to the things that have to be done, Spanish, English, all of it, and properly . . .*

"I know you don't understand much of what I'm saying, but

we must think of our future. Now, what was that word for money? I remember a friend whose dad was a doctor and she made a joke out of MD meaning *mucho—Dinero!* That's the word. *Dinero.*"

Esteban leaned on his elbow, watching the frown on her face with undisguised amusement, but listening politely to everything she said.

"*Dinero.* I'm talking about an income for us, what we will live on. You and me and . . ." She rocked her arms like a cradle.

She pointed to herself then him, repeating, "Esteban. Laura. *Dinero.* Oh, how wish now I had taken Spanish!"

She looked so frustrated, Esteban sat up, smoothing her brow with his fingers as he smiled at her, wiping away the worry lines. Then, touching her lips for silence, looking serious, he laid his hand on his heart, then on hers.

"*Dinero.* No Problem," he said. "*Todo es bueno. Dinero* no problem."

"Well, that's two words in addition to 'no smoking,'" Laura laughed. "We're making progress."

Esteban pushed the plates out of the way and held the blanket, reaching for her. Laura slept in his arms, happy and warm. No Problem . . .

Chapter Thirteen

The next morning was too chilly for breakfast on the patio. Laura fixed breakfast in the kitchen. Esteban helped her clear away the things they had used and pointed upstairs.

He held out a hand, an obvious "stop" or "wait" sign. He retrieved their shopping bag, pointed inside, then upstairs again.

"Oh, we'll shower and dress up there," she nodded.

Esteban led the way. He showed her a double bathroom off a large bedroom and stopped again, looking up the hallway.

"I'll check around a little more, out of curiosity." Laura touched his arm as she passed him. "I've already seen enough touring downstairs to turn me green with envy for the rest of my life." She stopped him as he started into the bathroom.

"This is nice, but our *casa* will be nice, too. *Bueno.*" Her eyes danced as she gestured around them.

He grinned, lifting his hand and making a circle of his fingers as she had showed him for *just right*. Laughing lightly to himself, he disappeared into the bathroom.

Showered and properly dressed, Laura stood outside by the sidecar and checked the shopping bag to make sure they hadn't forgotten anything while Esteban checked things outside and made sure everything had been put away.

It's good he's so conscientious; it would be a bad time to lose one of his jobs before we even get started on our lives together. Now, what is that signal supposed to mean?

Esteban moved quickly to the nearby elevator without a word and Laura followed, her lips dry.

Esteban did not speak, and his face was unreadable, until they reached the door of four-oh-seven. She knew something must be terribly wrong, or something bad had happened.

Inside, Esteban emptied the shopping bag on the bed and then turned to her. Laura was trying to warm one cold hand with the other, waiting for him to find a way to tell her what was the matter.

She stepped a little closer, concerned for him. "There's something terribly wrong, something important. Can I do anything to help?"

She pointed to herself and to him, and pointing to the door, said, "I will go with you or do whatever I can to help. Do you understand me?" She pointed to him and to herself again, her eyebrows raised, waiting to see if he knew she was trying to help.

He smiled sadly and shook his head, as if he had understood but she could not help. She wondered at his shaken expression, wondered if anyone could help. What could be so terrible no one could help? She could only watch, feeling frightened and helpless, as he began again their language of love.

He pointed to himself. He pointed to the door. He pointed to the floor in front of her, their signal for "I'll be back" that she knew so well. She feared her heart would break with the helplessness she felt, standing as if rooted to the floor. Gestures or not, this time it was different.

He reached for her quickly, his arms swallowing her in a huge bear hug. He held her hard, desperately, as tightly as he could, as if something were tearing him away from her.

Tenderly he lifted her face and kissed her lips and her eyes, then buried his face in her hair, nuzzling her neck as he had when he had first told her he loved her.

Esteban was gesturing again. He pointed to the bag then to her eyes.

"Oh!" She reached into the bag. "My sun glasses, right."

She set the bag and her purse into the sidecar, put on the glasses and gave Esteban a merry "thumbs up" signal.

Her stomach felt suddenly light as they started down the steep hill, and she shouted, "Wheeeeeeeeeeeee!"

Esteban shook with laughter, the motor drowning out any comment he might have added.

They left the motorcycle at the rental place and walked back towards the hotel.

"Another beautiful day in Isla Verde," Laura announced in her best tour director's voice.

"*Hermosa* Isla Verde," Esteban solemnly agreed.

When they arrived at the hotel and crossed the lobby on the way to the elevators, she saw the older clerk hurry toward them, or maybe he was the manager. He had come out and taken over when she'd had to renew her room. He was obviously Julio's boss. She watched him as he walked quickly toward Esteban.

He can probably interpret for us. Why didn't I think of him before? Or maybe there's some reason Esteban didn't . . . She lost the thought as she saw his face.

The clerk, or manager, or whatever he was caught up to them, his eyes fixed on Esteban. His face looked like he had news of a hurricane or some other catastrophe. He told Esteban something quickly, in Spanish spoken so fast Laura didn't catch a word of it. And she knew, somehow, she was not supposed to. She paled, watching Esteban.

Esteban appeared more worried than the clerk. He clutched the man's arm and asked him three questions in rapid succession. He nodded at the answers, deeply concerned, and the clerk hurried away as fast as he had come to them, evidently to do something Esteban had told him to do.

"*Yo te amo,* Laura!"

With that, he again pointed to the floor—and he was gone.

She stood staring out after him, her cold hands clasped together. He had passed the elevator at a run and disappeared, hurrying down the stairs.

Laura reached out to close the door. She leaned against it for a moment, shaken.

She went to the French doors and looked out, unseeing, her lips dry. She didn't know how long she stood there, frightened, knowing somehow something beyond her power was happening. Somewhere in the back of her mind the sound of a plane registered; she hadn't known there was an airstrip on the island. She ran her tongue over her lips and paced the floor, not realizing she was pacing. All she knew was that Esteban was gone. Gone where? Why? She lay down and finally drifted off, the lamp still on.

How she had managed to sleep—if those troubled dreams could be called sleep—Laura didn't know. The sun coming in through the French doors woke her. She got up and went to them, letting the sun warm her.

She could almost feel Esteban's arms as he held her close to him, the way he had before he left.

She brightened, straightened her shoulders. She told herself he would be all right. Her Esteban would be able to handle whatever it was, and he would come back to her. *He loves me. He took time to hold me and assure me of that. And he said he would be back. He pointed to the floor in front of me twice. He made sure I understood that. He loves me and he'll be back.*

She held on to that and felt better, remembering their love words in front of the fireplace. And he had never been away for very long before, so surely he would be back soon.

Time dragged by slowly. Two days, eons long, went by without any word from him. Laura had walked slowly past the desk on her way to eat in the coffee shop, hoping the clerk would beckon to her to tell her she had a message. There was nothing.

She had asked in vain after the manager, but got no response from him; he would not even see her, and the door of the office was always closed.

He either did not know or would not tell her anything. Perhaps he had been told not to tell whatever it was that called Esteban away. Could it be some kind of hotel business? But how could anything as serious as Esteban had looked affect the band? Or maybe this was something to do with one of his other jobs . . .

After that, Laura began stopping by the desk every morning to ask if there were any messages for her, to no avail.

She looked at everything in the hotel shops, exploring them and the grounds. She didn't want to get too far away in case Esteban came back or called her.

Just to hear his voice—to know he's all right. He wouldn't have to talk. Just to say my name, to hear he's all right. It became a daily prayer.

There were fashion magazines and a few paperback books in English in the gift shop. She selected several, and some rose-scented lotion, and retreated to her room. Her monthly period started too, and she slept most of the afternoons away.

She didn't feel like walking or shopping; the afternoons were too warm to enjoy walking on the beach too. Besides, Esteban might call her.

She could not quite convince herself of that possibility, still feeling lost and abruptly shut out of his life.

The days and nights went slowly by. The mornings were filled with walks on the beach when she felt better, and to the marina—places she had enjoyed with Esteban. Looking at the bright awning of the shuttle boat brought more tears to her eyes

Stranger in Paradise

as she turned to watch the sun setting on the water.

She decided to have a light supper in the coffee shop and get a couple more magazines before she went back to her room.

Making a roundabout tour of the lobby, Laura asked if she had any messages before going on to the coffee shop. She sat with the menu open before her, not seeing it, wishing she had known some way to help Esteban, no matter what the trouble was. She ordered a salad without even reading what else was offered.

Getting off the elevator, she remembered she hadn't left a light on.

Esteban always turned on the lamp beside the bed. She smiled to herself. *He loves me; he'll be back.*

She turned on the bedside lamp and picked up one of the paperbacks. She read the first paragraph twice before realizing what it said, then read until she drifted off to sleep.

When she awoke, the sun was streaming in the doors of the balcony. She still wore her sundress, the coverlet tucked around her feet.

Esteban, Esteban, where are you?

She walked out on the balcony and looked down. *What are you doing, silly? Do you think he might have washed up on the beach,* she scolded herself. *Something is wrong, very badly wrong. Something important. But he will be all right. And he will back. He will.*

She showered and put on her makeup. Her hair she tied back in a scarf. She put on the yellow sweat suit and walked down to the beach. The water at the edge of the wet sand was cold. She walked several minutes before sitting down on a flat rock out of the cold water. The sun hadn't burned off all the fog farther out, and the overcast fit her mood.

She walked aimlessly down the beach, moving but not really taking in much around her. In the distance, she saw the marina where she and Esteban had taken the boat to Puerto Rico.

I wonder if the boat is still there.

She walked up the wooden dock along the slips until she saw the boat. It looked somehow abandoned too, everything neatly put away as Esteban had left it. Feeling even more depressed, she turned and started back to the hotel.

Her heart lifted as she got off the elevator. *Maybe he's back! Maybe he's here, waiting for me!*

There was only a silence that screamed, waiting inside the room. Had it been this quiet before? She couldn't remember.

She went into the bathroom, washed her feet, dressed, and went down to eat, moving as if moving didn't matter anymore.

There were no messages for her at the desk. The young clerk barely had time to shake his head at her, he was so busy checking in tourists. The clerk glanced toward the closed door, but the manager was nowhere in sight. *Maybe he just comes out to handle problem guests,* Laura thought, feeling bitter and lonely.

Breakfast was adequate but uneventful. Laura passed the time looking at the influx of tourists. There was a family with two precious small children; two couples. They looked like honeymooners with eyes only for each other. There was an old couple. Probably an anniversary trip. She tried to picture herself and Esteban on a future anniversary.

At a sudden laugh, she turned her attention to a table where four girls sat. They were probably local. Probably they were part of an office crew somewhere, having coffee before they went to work.

For some reason everyone else seems to look nineteen or twenty when you're twenty-three. She frowned. *Maybe Esteban is out looking for a newer model. No! No, not my Esteban. He loves me. He'll be back.*

Time dragged inexorably by, days turning into nights, then back into days again, and still Esteban did not come. Laura had asked every day, sometimes twice, if there were any messages for her. The young clerk behind the desk always dutifully looked behind him at the row of empty boxes before shaking his head and saying, "No, *Senorita.*"

Laura had finally faced another possibility, unpleasant, but knocking insistently at her consciousness.

Esteban told me he loves me, and he did love me. I know he did, as much as I love him. But he did not ask me to marry him. I wouldn't have known the word, but he could have pointed to his ring finger as he did when he told me he wasn't married. No, he didn't ask me to marry him. I am the one who assumed if he loved me, of course he would want to marry me. But suppose he doesn't? He seems perfectly happy the way he is. Maybe he doesn't want to get married.

Laura drifted away from the desk, her mind in turmoil. The young clerk glanced after her, looking sympathetic, until another tourist claimed his attention.

The truth was, she didn't know very much about Esteban at all. He couldn't talk to her and tell her about his people. He never took her to see where he lived, just showed her around the village where he seemed to know everyone. Laura had only decided, since he played in the band, he must live somewhere in or near the hotel.

She shook her head slightly. *No, I won't think such negative things. He loves me. He'll be back!*

Sunday morning came, sunny and beautiful as always in paradise. Laura gazed out the glass doors before getting up.

It's nearly time for me to leave. My room is only reserved until checkout time Monday, and that's tomorrow.

She reached for the phone to call the desk and see if there had been any messages for her, then thought better of it, drawing back her hand.

She had asked so many times in the last few days, and the

answer was always the same. No messages, no calls. She had to go down to breakfast; she would stop and ask then.

Chapter Fourteen

"We will be landing in Paris in a few minutes." Arturo fastened his seatbelt. His handsome face was solemn as he inclined his head to listen to Esteban, his younger brother.

Glancing around to make sure no one was listening, Esteban spoke softly. "I think you were wise not to ask how they managed to get the information from that dog of an informant."

"I doubt it was physical fear but the thought of his future, if he has one, that was most effective. The important thing is that we know where he is being held and by whom."

"You have all of the transcript?"

"Yes. We will make our plans as soon as we are together and leave immediately for the interior."

"No jewel ever created is worth this."

"I pray God we are in time."

Esteban looked out the window at the clouds below, his imagination painting horrors on their cottony whiteness as he prayed silently. "Arturo, I must send a message to Laura." He smiled. "She won't be able to read it but she will understand *'yo te amo'* and that's enough to reassure her." He stopped, thinking. "Or perhaps I will call her and just say that. To let her hear the love in my voice . . ."

Arturo shook his head, looking grave.

"Why not?"

"Would you put her in danger?"

"Danger? No, what do you mean?"

"Esteban, these people know our every move. They had to, to do this. Someone inside, or their own surveillance—more than likely both—are watching us and everyone who is dear to us. They had infiltrated our work force, at least the few that they could contact. The way we knew where to look is thanks to these who risked their lives getting mixed up with these desperados. They were very sure of themselves when they kidnapped our father. They had to be. We cannot take any chances until he is safe. Then our family will be safe too. You must not put anyone else in danger. Our security is working with the law enforcement as we speak. We must find our father first before anyone can move against this group that will stop at nothing."

Esteban looked stricken.

"You said she loves you, and she knows you love her?"

"Yes. I am sure of that." Esteban took a deep breath. "You are right, I cannot put her in danger. I will explain to her when this is over. When we have found him and brought him out alive. You are right. I should have known." He closed his eyes and pictured Laura as he had left her with their "I'll be back" sign and the taste of her lips warm on his. He prayed.

Laura's cheeks still burned with embarrassment as she unlocked the door of her room, balancing the coffee and roll she had brought with her, and her purse.

She had approached the desk on the way back from the coffee shop, and the young clerk had seen her coming. When she got close enough, before she had a chance to ask, he had shook his head and said the dreaded words. "No calls, no messages, *senorita*."

The words fell on her heart like physical blows.

Their plane was circling for a landing. Esteban's eyes were

Stranger in Paradise

focused on their destination, his face lined with worry.

Beside him, the profile of Arturo's face looked carved from stone. Esteban voiced his fear softly. "Arturo, do you think the informant told us the truth—that he lives?"

"He knows if he did not, he is a dead man," Arturo answered without turning.

"I have read the transcript. If he is where he said, the guide coming from that district and the plan you have will get us there faster and with less publicity than I would have thought possible. But we must lose no time."

"We won't. The worst will be getting to the location he gave us, but we will worry about that when we get there."

"Will Miguel and the others be there when we land?"

"Yes. We will meet there and go our separate ways to get to him."

Esteban closed his eyes. He thought fleetingly of Laura, his fist clenched on the arm rest.

Arturo touched his hand, looking brighter. "Come, tell me of this woman, this golden one."

Alone, knowing nothing of what had called Esteban away from her so abruptly and with no word from him, Laura tossed aside the magazine she had been looking at without seeing it. She faced the unpleasant facts.

What am I doing? I might as well face it. I'm just passing the time away until it's time for me to go, that's what I'm doing. I've very cleverly gotten myself into a situation where that's all I can do. Her cheeks flamed as they had when the young clerk shook his head at her.

I guess Esteban has decided he doesn't want to get married and doesn't know how to tell me. That would be hard, all right, even if he could speak my language.

Tears dimmed her eyes. She was still unable to feel anything but sympathy for Esteban, her love so undeniable it hurt to think of him. *Maybe he thought it would be better this way.* The tears spilled over and ran down her cheeks.

She dashed the tears away and got up. Throwing open the double doors of the closet, she began tossing clothes on the bed.

Laura worked quickly, trying not to think, to face the fact she was leaving, would never again see Isla Verde, or Esteban. She threw the two big suitcases on the bed and hurriedly began filling them.

When she came to her yellow sweat suit, she held it to her cheek, savoring its softness, her heart aching. It smelled of the sea. She folded it carefully.

Finally she had everything packed except what she had worn to breakfast. It would do, with a light sweater, for the trip back.

She had put her jewelry in her purse.

But these . . . She tenderly picked up the black velvet box with the pearls in it.

"*Mi madre's,*" Esteban had said. His mother's pearls.

She fought back more tears. *He loved me. I know he did. I don't know why he couldn't just tell me, or find someone to tell me. I'll have to leave these for him in the hotel safe.* She resolutely closed the box.

Laura picked up the phone and called the desk. "Is there some sort of schedule for the hotel's shuttle boat?"

"No, *Senorita*. It leaves every two hours for the trip to San Juan and back."

"When is the next one?"

There was a pause. "It is gone now. *Dos.* It will be two hours."

"Thank you. Can you please tell me the amount of my bill? I'm in room four-oh-seven. Or better still, just get it ready and I will come down and get it."

"*Si.* It will be ready, *Senorita.*"

Laura looked up the airline's number without going through the hotel's switchboard. Somehow that felt good. Like she was back in charge of her life, what was left of it.

"I have a plane ticket for Monday afternoon, but I would like a flight this afternoon if there's a flight available, and I can get a seat."

She waited as the agent checked for her. *At least I won't be sitting here, hanging onto hope until the last minute.*

"There is a seat available on the flight leaving this afternoon, at the same time."

"Fine. I'll take it. You do mean three o'clock?"

"Three o'clock. But, please to be there before—"

"Oh, I'll be there more than an hour before. Thank you."

Everything was packed and ready, she would take the pearls by the desk and leave them for Esteban after she had lunch and check out at the same time. It would be just in time to catch the shuttle.

She sat down and wrote a brief note on the hotel memo pad beside the phone. She hesitated, knowing someone would have to read it to Esteban.

She wrote: "Esteban, the pearls you lent me are in the hotel safe with your name on them. *Yo te amo,*" she wrote above her signature.

There were mixed feelings about the *"yo te amo,"* as she folded it. *At least it's something he will understand. And he'll know I didn't change my mind or get cold feet as he evidently did.* She felt a twinge that made the adrenaline pump, his face more real in that second than the memo in front of her.

She prayed he was all right, wherever he was, and brushed her hair again before she left. She picked up the note, the pearls with his name on them, and then her purse with the note in it.

There was nothing else she could do. She looked around the room, giving it a sad half smile. She'd checked the closet, the bathroom, done everything properly, she ridiculed herself, done it all properly. Her Aunt Sophie wouldn't have a thing to remind her of.

And she'd say, "Hold your head up and conduct yourself with dignity," too.

Laura almost laughed. *Well, Aunt Sophie, I can honestly say I'm not the one who got cold feet. My intentions were honorable, Aunt Sophie.*

Stopping at the desk, she gave the jeweler's box with Esteban's name on it to the clerk and pointed out the name, Esteban Aguilar to him. While he put them in the safe, she stole a look at the message boxes. There was nothing in the one for room four-oh-seven.

At least she hadn't had to ask again, she thought. Aloud, she asked, "Is the band leader or any of the band here practicing? I want to leave a note for someone."

"I believe . . ." The clerk was uncertain. "Sometimes they are there. I think I hear them earlier."

"Thank you. I'll just look in and see."

As she approached the large, formal dining room, she heard the din of several instruments being tuned and made her way toward the bandstand.

An older man came to her and asked in English if he could "help the pretty *senorita.*"

Laura returned his smile, thinking he must be the leader. She held up the envelope with Esteban's name on it. "I want to leave this. Will you take it and give it to him when he returns?"

He took the envelope and nodded, "*Si*, I give it to him for you."

"Thank you." She went to the coffee shop to have honeyed rolls and coffee, having taken care of everything else she needed to do.

I'm getting good at piddling around. By the time I get my luggage

Stranger in Paradise

down to the shuttle and make it to the airport, I'll be comfortably early.

Going back through the lobby, she saw people were already gathering to get on the next shuttle boat. She stopped only briefly to pay her bill and have someone go up to get her luggage.

The man had returned with her luggage and she saw the tram waiting to take the luggage to the shuttle boat. The clerk finished her itemized bill and handed it to her. Her month at the Palacio de Isla Verde came to a little over twenty-six hundred dollars.

"Are you sure? Is this correct for the whole month?" Laura asked in surprise. The young clerk didn't look as if he understood her concern, merely pointed to the monitor then to the bill and nodded. She could look at it later.

"I want my luggage on that next shuttle boat." She hurriedly put her check amount down and the clerk just as hurriedly put her check into a bank deposit bag that must be headed for the shuttle too, since an employee seemed to be waiting for it. She saw her luggage go through the door and quickly followed it.

She rode down to the shuttle in one of the golf carts which paralleled the tram with the luggage on it and was soon standing at the rail of the gaily decorated little shuttle boat. She tried not to think of her trips with Esteban to the festival on it.

Standing at the rail, her luggage in the roped-off area designated for it, Laura looked back as they moved out into open water.

The beauty of the hotel, the vivid colors of sea, sand, and palms etched themselves on her mind.

"Isla Verde," she breathed in an agonized whisper, her heart heavy. "Esteban . . ." Isla Verde faded in a blur of tears.

Entering the airport in the wake of the young man with his ISLA VERDE sign, Laura's spirits lifted.

I'm here in plenty of time to call Rose and Daisy. I feel like I'm in charge of my life again. She spotted several phones near where she would board the plane and didn't give herself time to think of anything except calling Daisy and Rose and getting safely home.

It was Rose who answered. Her funny little screech of happy surprise made Laura laugh. "I know I wasn't supposed to leave until tomorrow about this time, but I got here on Sunday, so I might as well leave on Sunday too. I'm at the airport in Puerto Rico. I'm on my way home, or will be in a few minutes."

"That's wonderful. Talk louder and I'll put you on the speaker so Daisy can hear too."

"Hi, Daisy! I'll be seeing you in a little while now."

Daisy said something, but was evidently too far away from the telephone for her words to be heard by Laura.

"What? What is it Daisy asked?"

"She wants to know what flight you will be on and what time it will be in, so we can meet you, or so we can worry what flight it is in case it meets a mountain or something." She teased Daisy, the grin in her voice audible.

Laura gave them the flight number. "But that's only for worrying purposes. Don't even think about meeting me. I've got a long layover in Miami and won't get in till nearly midnight, so I'll just take a cab. But thanks for the offer. And I'll probably sleep late in the morning too. I'm so spoiled about sleeping late, I'm going to use getting in around midnight as an excuse to do it once more."

They laughed with her, and she felt good as she hung up the phone.

"I'm glad she's coming home," Rose said with a smile.

"Me, too. That Greek girl is trying to take advantage of her being gone, I think."

"What do you mean?"

"Well, she was with Mack the last two times he came by here with some excuse to check on whether we'd heard from Laura."

"Oh, that. She was just hitchhiking," Rose laughed. "You notice Mack explained he was giving her a lift on some errands she had to do for the restaurant."

"Well—he didn't have to look like he was enjoying it so much."

Rose laughed at her and shrugged.

It didn't take long to get from Puerto Rico to Miami, and not a whole lot longer to get from Miami to Greenfield, including the commuter plane the airline used to get from hubs to the small towns it serviced.

Nearing Greenfield, Laura looked out into the darkness. *The long layover was the only nuisance, and I guess I needed the time. Isla Verde already seems so far away, I could almost have dreamed it. Maybe, surely, when Esteban comes back, he will call me, or write to me.* She pictured him as she had first seen him at the hotel.

She frowned at her own foolishness. He couldn't write to her, and if he were going to call, he would have done it before now. *I would have known his voice and would at least have known he was still alive and thinking about me. There is no point in telling myself I will get over this in time. I know I won't. I love him and he loved me. I know he loved me, too.*

A tear threatened to spill from the corner of her eye. She dabbed at it with a piece of Kleenex. *Love is one thing, commitment is something else.*

The pilot's voice brought her back to the present. She was home.

When her plane landed, she was halfway down the portable stair when she heard someone call her name.

"Laura!"

"Mack! And Rose and Daisy!"

She hurried to them and was caught up in a three-way hug.

She felt the tears rolling down her cheeks. "How good it feels to be with people who love you." She smiled through her tears.

Mack was dabbing at her tears with his handkerchief as he laughed at her.

"If I'd known you were going to be this glad to see us, we'd have sent you off somewhere before this!"

She laughed, hugging Rose and Daisy again. "Well, it's been a whole month, after all. You mean you didn't miss me?" She gave Rose and Daisy a look of mock indignation.

"Of course, we missed you," Daisy vowed. "Even smart aleck here," she pointed to Mack. "He asked about you, if we'd heard from you, regular as clockwork, every three days, then called on the phone in between visits."

"Thank you, noble friend," Mack scolded Daisy. "You can't have any secrets in this town. Everybody knows everything about everybody else."

Rose took them by the ears. "Now Mack, and Daisy, you two try and behave yourselves or Laura might just get on the plane and go back!"

Laura laughed, her heart warm, as she realized how dear all of them were to her. "Since we're not going to get enough sleep anyway, let's see if my luggage got here all right and go to my house to visit. I'll microwave us something to go with hot chocolate. That won't take very long. Then we can all try and get some sleep, how about it?"

"Sounds good to me. Let's see if we can find that luggage," Mack nodded.

"I think I see the largest one." He pointed when they got inside. "That was a back breaker, if I remember right," he complained with a twisted grin. "You girls must have bought out half the shops in town."

Daisy gave him an indignant push. "You can't go anywhere

without shopping. It's a good thing you're a man. You'd make a lousy woman, Mack." Daisy shot him a disgusted glare.

"Well, I never really considered giving it a try." Mack bent his knees slightly and gave her a prissy little wave.

"Don't pay any attention to them," Rose advised. "If they don't straighten up by the time the hot chocolate gets warm, we'll stand them in a corner."

All of Laura's luggage had made it to Greenfield, and they managed to get everything, and Laura, safely home.

"Just dump it down anyplace when you think it's safe to let go of it, and I'll tend to it tomorrow, or the next day, or the next day . . ." Laura giggled as she headed for the kitchen.

She looked around at the familiar room, everything in its place, just as she had left it. It felt so good to be home. She had the feeling somehow that there was a healing process taking place, until her memory mocked her with Esteban's smile.

"Can we help you with something, Laura?" Rose called. "Mack's taking the luggage upstairs."

"Oh, that's good of him. Come on in here and keep me company, since this is where I do all my formal entertaining."

Mack came in as they seated themselves. "I've got everything upstairs but that monster, and it's not really all that bad. A cup of that hot chocolate that smells so good will give me muscles like Popeye."

"No, just leave it. I'll take the things out of it when I get around to it."

"Tell us about Isla Verde. Is it really as gorgeous as you said on the phone?"

Her mouth full, Laura nodded. "Yes, it is. There is no picture or brochure or postcard that could ever be as pretty. The colors are so vivid, like jewels in the sun."

"And you enjoyed your trip." Daisy smiled.

"I certainly did." Laura didn't lift her eyes from her hot chocolate.

Daisy yawned, covering her mouth with her hand as she set down her cup.

"I guess I'd better get these two back home before the little homely one passes out on me," Mack squinted at Daisy.

That woke Daisy up enough to take a swing at him with her purse, to his delight.

Laura laughed. "I know it's thirteen o'clock for working people. Just leave everything sitting there right where it is. I'm home. Everything else can be dealt with tomorrow."

"To tomorrow." Mack toasted with his chocolate, then followed Daisy and Rose out the door.

Laura leaned against the closed door, fighting tears she was too tired to hold back.

Tomorrow. Another day without Esteban.

Chapter Fifteen

Esteban's face was contorted with physical effort as he swung the razor-sharp machete, clearing a path through the jungle's thick underbrush and vines. Sweat ran down his face and made his eyes smart.

Beside him, Arturo worked just as hard and steadily. Desperation and not a little fear drove them relentlessly on.

"Esteban! Stand still," Arturo suddenly commanded in a stage whisper.

Esteban froze in his tracks, arm still upraised.

The whoosh of air past his cheek told him the force of Arturo's machete strike. He held his breath. Less than a second later he heard the disturbance in the overhead branches as a huge body fell to earth.

He looked down at the thirty-foot anaconda a few feet away from him. The snake's severed head looked up at him, its tongue still lashing.

"Thank you." Esteban grinned, his arm relaxing. "I'd hardly have been a snack for that one."

"You're welcome. I wanted there to be some advantage to being stuck with 'the old one.'" Arturo smiled.

"No problem, my brother. The only advantage Miguel has in being sent with the district guide is being sure of his direction. I would have chosen you if I'd had a choice."

"That they know more about where they're going than we do is a comfort to me, but I trust this compass." Arturo wiped his face and nodded. "We are going right."

"You are sure then, that the informant told us the truth? That he is there?"

"As I said, the foolish devil knows he is dead if he did not. I only hope we are in time. That our father is still alive. If there is any sense in their heads at all, they know their chance of money and escape would die with him." Arturo began hacking even harder at the growth in his path.

Esteban glanced at the anaconda's head and swung his machete with a vengeance, grateful to have his older brother by his side.

Laura woke at ten after eight the next morning and stretched luxuriously. It felt good to be at home again.

I must have relaxed to my bones, being home in my own bed. I don't think I even turned over.

The small case with her makeup in it was sitting in the bathroom, and she looked for her toothbrush. The now familiar ache returned to her chest as she put things where they belonged, and firmly thought of what she had to do instead of Esteban. At least, she tried to.

Laura decided to get dressed and go down to the store; take her time getting everything put up.

First things first. There were lots of things to do that were better than feeling sorry for herself, as Aunt Sophie would say.

Laura smiled, remembering last night. She had forgotten to give Daisy and Rose their souvenirs. She would take theirs to the store and give Mack's to him the next time she saw him.

If I still have the nerve. She grinned at her reflection.

Arriving at the bookstore, there were several people in the store shopping and she went to see if Rose had something in particular she wanted her to do.

Rose shook her head. "When it's slow, I take one shelf at a

time and dust and put all the books back where they belong while I'm at it."

"Okay, I'll start dusting. And Rose?"

"Yes?"

"I brought you and Daisy a couple of small souvenirs and forgot to give them to you last night, it was so late. I put them in the office on the desk, so you can look at them when you have time. The rose is for you and the blue is for Daisy."

"Thank you, but you've been gone so long, all any of us was interested in was getting you back safe and sound."

Rose started toward the office, and Laura beckoned to Daisy as her customer left. "Come back to the office for a minute. When I brought you and Rose a souvenir, I got something for Mack, too."

When they entered, Rose had already opened her decorative shopping bag.

"How pretty! And it smells so good!" Rose held her potpourri up for Daisy to admire as she opened hers.

"Oh, mine too. Here, sniff," Daisy invited.

Pleased that they liked their gifts, Laura picked up another sack. "This is what I got for Mack."

She drew out a tie that was as colorful as the logo on the sack. "Do you think we can get him to wear it?"

Daisy laughed. "I don't know, but I can see the resemblance to all those lawyer jokes!"

"I don't know about that. He looks like quite a nice alligator to me." Rose studied the brightly painted reptile critically. "It's just the right thing for those lawyer-dull, super-conservative suits Mack wears." Her eyes twinkled, meeting Daisy's.

"You're so right. Every one of them shouts 'Attorney at Law' at you. This should brighten them up."

"Anyone here?" A voice demanded querulously from the front. "Does anyone work in this establishment?"

"Mack!" Daisy rolled her eyes. "Speak of the devil."

"We're back here, Mack." Laura winked at Daisy. "Come on in."

Rose and Daisy showed him the potpourri and the simmering pots Laura had brought them, and he admired the scents as Laura held the tie behind her.

"I didn't do any wrapping or anything, but, I bought you a small thing too, Mack. If, that is, you're up to the challenge," she added mysteriously.

"Challenge?" Mack regarded Daisy's grin suspiciously. "Just how dangerous is it?"

Laura held up the tie for his inspection. "It's great!" He chuckled, admiring the tie as he took it from her. "Judge Holcomb would have an attack if I wore it to court—there's a suspiciously close resemblance here." He narrowed his eyes, studying it. "But on my own time, it's a day brightener. Thank you, I'll enjoy it."

Laura was pleased with his response. Rose smiled; and Daisy was struck dumb with surprise. They watched him take off the tie he was wearing and replace it with the alligator's toothy grin.

Hearing a customer come in, Rose left and Daisy followed her.

"I'm glad you like the tie. I got a laugh out of it, and then I got cold feet about giving it to you." Laura giggled. "You sure surprised Daisy."

"I enjoy surprising Daisy. She's my sparring partner." Mack grinned.

"The 'gator looks like he's pleased as punch about something, doesn't he?"

"Probably just ate his opposition. I know the feeling. You do feel like smiling." Mack admired the alligator again, trying to see himself in the window glass.

"It was so late last night; I didn't think to give you your

souvenirs. I don't even remember hitting my pillow. I was out like a light."

"I doubt any of us had to be rocked to sleep. One reason I stopped by is that I have a free meal for two coming up from the Kolivases' restaurant. I did him a small favor and wouldn't charge him. But he insisted on some sort of payment, so we settled on a meal. We can go and take advantage of it any time this week, assuming you would like to go. And I would have an occasion to wear my tie," he added as an incentive.

"What about Friday night? That would give me a while to get all my things put up, some cleaning done, and just get caught up in general."

He didn't answer immediately and she asked, "Is Friday all right?"

"It's all right, but it's so far away. Could we work in a lunch between now and then?"

"Sure. I was just thinking about everything that needs to be done here."

As she answered, Laura glanced at the desk Sophie had shared with her. She thought she'd move it, change things around a little, and put the phone extension on or near it. It also occurred to her that maybe Esteban would call her.

Mack cleared his throat, bringing her back from a memory so bright with sunshine she could almost feel the sand beneath her feet.

"I just need to get a little more organized, I guess. About lunch, give me a little notice in case Rose or Daisy has something for me to do."

"I will. And I'll probably be talking to you soon anyway. I've got a case that has some legwork attached, so I'll drop by."

"Fine, I'll be here."

Mack went out whistling, his discarded tie sticking out of his pocket.

Daisy and Rose looked after him. "Whoever would have thought he'd fall for that tie?" Rose shook her head.

"Maybe the fact that Laura bought it for him had something to do with it," Daisy commented dryly as Laura joined them and raised an eyebrow.

Daisy winked at Rose and looked up innocently,

"I said, 'there goes a really neat guy.' But if you tell him I said that, I'll swear you lied." Daisy wrinkled her nose.

Chapter Sixteen

At home, Laura took her time unpacking. *There are so many memories in here. I'll have to face them some time.*

Every item she took out held some memory of Esteban. She picked up the thongs he had bought her for walking on the beach.

I'll put them in the back of the closet. I don't know when I'll ever use them again. I can almost feel the sand and the water splashing over my feet—and Esteban's hand holding mine.

Laura didn't fight the tears that began to fall. There was no one there to see them.

She picked up the yellow sweat suit and held the soft fleece side against her cheek. Her throat closed on a sob, as she remembered their boat trip to San Juan. She didn't even have to close her eyes to recall that king-sized bed on the boat and Esteban's arms around her. Surely, surely, he would call her. Where could he be? What could have taken him so quickly away from her?

She realized she had stopped unpacking. She sat with her arms on her knees, holding the sweat suit's softness and memories too precious to ignore. She thought of the big, unappreciated house where they had stayed, the warmth of the fireplace they had enjoyed together. Where they had loved each other, basking in the fire's warmth. Her heart lifted. Esteban would call her. He would.

Both pieces of the soft yellow fabric on her arms and held

against her heart, she let the tears flow. *He loves me, I know he loves me.*

She buried her face in the bright softness and sobbed her heart out, the first chance she'd had to do so since coming home. Back to reality? Reality was how her heart ached for him, just hoping he was all right.

She patted her eyes with one of the soft yellow sleeves, determined to face reality no matter the hurt.

But Esteban, you knew when I had to leave. She argued with the beloved ghost of him. *You were there when I told the clerk I was going to stay another two weeks; how could you not know?*

Not forgetting, but numbed by logic, she managed to get everything unpacked and see to the things that had to be done around the house. There was only the small case left to put up, and then the rest of her new clothes. When would she ever need to dress for dinner in Greenfield?

She still wasn't through with the last of the unpacking Wednesday when Mack stopped by the store to see if she could go to lunch with him. The nightly memories of Esteban and Isla Verde were taking their toll on Laura, and she hadn't been sleeping or eating very well.

Mack took her to a steak house close to the bookstore.

"Since it's nearly one o'clock, we won't have to stand in line. How come you haven't already been to lunch?" He gave her a stern look.

"I don't know." Laura shrugged. "Just hadn't thought about it."

He smiled, "Did you ever get all that stuff unpacked? It must take an awful lot of clothes for a month. Sounds like a job to me, just packing and unpacking."

"Yes, a lot of clothes . . ."

The scene in the costume store came back to her, Esteban choosing the ballerina costume with the long skirt. She sighed.

Stranger in Paradise

"I've made a big dent, but there's a little left."

Noting her sad expression, Mack asked tentatively, "Some things left. Some things you got in Isla Verde? Or special things for the trip?"

"Not all that much. I'm working on it. I bought some things I might not ever need again . . ." Her smile was a ghost of pleasures past. "And I got some thong sandals for wave hopping, as if I'd ever need them here." Her expression looked like she had no hope of ever seeing another beautiful, sparkling, foam-breaking wave.

"That sounds good to me. Maybe it's something I can fix. I've always thought it would be nice to go to Hawaii for a honeymoon, and you'll have had some experience wave-hopping." He grinned.

"Mack, what are you talking about? I'm not getting married."

"Perhaps not right away. But when I've had time to demonstrate all my good qualities and lovable traits—I plan on marrying you, Laura."

Laura stared, open-mouthed.

"Mack," she finally managed. "I never know when to take you seriously. I've just told you I have no plans whatsoever to get married. Period."

He nodded, "I heard you. But like taste buds," he said, grinning, "plans can change. The rest of your life is too long to be alone. It's not even practical. I've seen too many bad examples in the scope of my work of people who were alone either by choice or losing a loved one. It's no fun being alone, Laura."

"I know there are some situations like that. But I know of just as many people who are happy as clams the way they are and wouldn't care to take on any more problems, thank you."

Laura realized she had raised her voice and lowered it, glancing quickly around them.

"About those examples? Right here at home, there's Aunt

141

Sophie as an example. She led a happy, comfortable, and interesting life. She had the bookstore and she raised me, and Rose and Daisy have been with us so long they're family by affection if not by blood. No," she said, shaking her head, "I will not marry unless I'm in love."

She looked up, meeting his eyes. "And I do not love you, Mack. No, that's not quite right. I do, I guess. Anyway, I'm very fond of you, and I admire you. Any woman in the world would be honored that you would even consider proposing to her. But I'm not in love with you. Besides that, right now, I'm doing well just to keep managing, with Rose and Daisy's help, trying to do things the way Aunt Sophie taught me."

"That reminds me." Mack did not address the differences in loving and being in love. "I've got everything changed over into your name now. You remember the documents I had you sign. The house, the bookstore, and Sophie's accounts and assets. I need to explain to you about the retirement account Sophie had. You were the beneficiary, so I will explain what your options are, and you can decide how you want the money disbursed or reinvested, whatever you want to do."

Laura was glad to have the subject changed. "I had forgotten about the account. She told me about it quite a while ago. If I remember right, she said I probably wouldn't need any income from it, with the bookstore being so profitable, but it was there if I did need it or if I wanted to use it for something."

Her eyes were on a faraway scene. She remembered the house beneath the crest of the mountain, and wondered about the house she and Esteban would have had for their own on Isla Verde. She hung her head, feeling forlorn. Mack hadn't spoken.

"I'll look into it whenever you have time to explain it to me, Mack. I'm really grateful for your help. I don't know what I'd do without you and Rose and Daisy. It scares me to think about trying to manage without you."

Her heart ached. *I didn't think I would be without Esteban. That I'd just have to go on as if we'd never met, everything all cut and dried and planned and dull . . . back to square one.* She managed to fight back the tears trying to escape.

Mack reached for her hand, holding it in both of his. "It's all right. You're going to be all right. We're here for you. We love you, even if one of us is annoying enough to be in love with you too." He smiled affectionately as she looked up at him.

"I'm all right. I'm not going to make a spectacle of myself." The old Laura surfaced. "Some lunch date I am! Do you think you might ever ask me again?"

Mack considered gravely for a moment. He made a steeple with his fingers, wearing his Judge McKinley expression. "Yessssss, I think I will," he decided. "And don't forget our dinner date Friday night. You'd surely not disappoint that alligator?"

"Heaven forbid!"

Mack walked her back to the door of the bookshop and waved when he looked back at her, as if to reassure himself that she was all right.

I wish I was in love with Mack. He's everything anyone could ask for.

"Except Esteban," her heart whispered.

That night Laura finished putting away the suitcases she had used with the feeling she would probably never use them again. She remembered the sight of them on the little shuttle boat, in the roped-off area. She directed her feet to move downstairs to make sure the doors were locked.

I must have eaten enough calories to last a week at lunch and I don't feel like fixing anything anyway.

She went back upstairs and pulled the colorful shawl from a hanger, remembering when Esteban had bought it at the festival.

To think I worried about whom he might have bought it for. She smiled to herself as she wrapped it around her and sat down in a wicker chair facing the window.

Laura could still feel Esteban's warm arms around her. She drew the shawl closer, her mind following her heart back to Isla Verde.

The window showed only the reflection of a street light, but Laura's memories of the vivid colors on Isla Verde were what she saw through her tears.

Chapter Seventeen

Friday afternoon Mack called Laura at the bookstore to remind her of their dinner date.

"I hadn't forgotten, I'm looking forward to it."

Daisy raised her head above a bookshelf as Laura replaced the phone.

"Must have been good news?" She saw the warmer color in Laura's face and noted the light in her eyes.

"Yes." Laura nodded as Rose joined them. "That was Mack, reminding me about dinner tonight. He calls it a 'negotiated meal.' He did something for Kolivas, the man who owns the restaurant, and he wouldn't bill him for it, so Kolivas gave him a meal for two."

"Mack is good-hearted," Rose said, returning to her work.

"Mack is good-hearted, yes." Daisy came close to snapping. "So is Kolivas, no doubt. But I've got the feeling he'd like to give Mack his daughter, too."

"Mack's about the best catch in town," Rose agreed. "But we know where his heart is, don't we?" Her smile was satisfied.

That night, Laura put on her makeup with special care, thinking she looked a little pale. *Might as well get used to it. I couldn't keep that Isla Verde tan forever.*

The doorbell rang.

"There's Mack," she murmured to herself. "Right on time."

Mack stood there grinning as she opened the door. "I'm

impressed. I was hoping you would wear something to match my alligator." He looked down at his chest with the big-toothed grin on it.

"You and the alligator look nice too." Laura looked him over. She admired his dark green slacks and tweed sports coat. "The shades of green and that alligator smile are the brightest spots in our ensembles." Laura touched the toothy smile lightly as Mack closed the door behind her. "I bought it and the potpourri for Rose and Daisy in the Miami airport. It wasn't until I got back on the plane that I got afraid to give it to you!"

"Worried for nothing. It's priceless," Mack vowed. "I'll be careful not to drop anything on him but a few baklava crumbs."

"And precious few of those, as well as you like it," Laura teased him. *And maybe you like the pretty cook too?*

"Guilty as charged," Mack admitted. "The restaurant's owner's daughter, Kara, makes it, and she's good at it."

When they entered, the Greek restaurant was alive with a good amount of business and other diners coming in. Mouth-watering aromas met them as they were beckoned to a table. Laura stopped, pleased.

"A violinist! Mack, they have a violinist tonight, isn't that nice?"

"Um-hum, nice, but not as nice as the baklava." He waved to Kara, who was standing in the kitchen door looking at him as if Elvis the King had arrived.

Laura tried not to stare, and glanced away. Kolivas was a few feet off and smiled like the godfather at Mack. Laura stifled a giggle.

After their meal, the baklava was served by Kara herself, who accompanied the waiter with their coffee.

As Mack had told her, it was Kara who baked the baklava. She was also, he said, Antonio Kolivas's eldest daughter, and the apple of his eye. In addition to that, Laura noted Kara was

Stranger in Paradise

perhaps twenty or twenty-one, had a wealth of long, dark hair, and was a very beautiful girl. It was also obvious how pleased she was that Mack was so fond of the baklava.

As Kara served them, Laura observed things Mack did not. That Kara was fond of Mack was evident without embarrassment. Kolivas, Kara's father, smiled on Mack like a loved member of the family. Laura doubted all that was due to Mack's accomplishments and talents as an attorney, not that those weren't considerable.

Maybe Kara is really in love with Mack, Laura thought. *And he doesn't even notice the way she looks at him. Men can be so unconscious.* She smiled at Kara.

They were going to a movie after dinner. Mack stood by the car, brushing crumbs off the alligator's smile.

"Absolutely the best baklava anywhere," he declared as he shut Laura's door and got into the car.

"Right. And the way to a man's heart is through his stomach, as Aunt Sophie told me." Laura lifted her eyebrows, giving him a questioning glance.

"What's that got to do with anything? Unless you're going to get the recipe and fix baklava for me?"

"No!" Laura's expression was one of surprised shock. "I'd never be able to top what we just had. But Mack, Kara is also a beautiful girl. And I've noticed the way she looks at you with those soulful, dark eyes of hers."

"Child, Laura. Antonio's child. His eldest daughter, as I said."

"She's a grown woman," Laura insisted. "And I don't blame her. You must be giving all the single ladies a fit, being so fleet footed and uncatchable." Laura grimaced.

"Uncatchable? I haven't noticed you entering the race." Mack nosed the car out into traffic.

"Well, I would if I were in the market." Laura chuckled.

They both let the subject drop. The movie was a well-done

comedy, which left them light hearted, full of good food, and taking pleasure in each other's company.

"I've really enjoyed the evening, Mack," Laura told him at her front door. She got up on tiptoes and kissed him on the cheek.

He gave her a brief hug. "I'm glad. So did I."

She closed the door and leaned against it, the happy comfort of the evening clinging. She realized she hadn't felt depressed and alone once since Mack had picked her up.

But as she climbed the familiar stairs, the ghosts of Isla Verde were not far behind.

She dressed for bed, then, in the dark, walked over to the window to look out at the night sky.

Esteban, where are you? What are you doing? Are you back in Isla Verde now? Are you there, looking out at the night as I am, thinking of me? Her heart lurched at the thought, the image of him never far away.

She drew the shawl closer around her. She had got into the habit of wearing it as she looked out the window. She sat in the old-fashioned rocking chair, unable to sleep, longing for Esteban. She gazed out into the night. *As if I could see all the way to Isla Verde,* she scoffed at herself.

Finally tired and sleepy enough to rest, she laid the shawl on the pillow beside her, wondering if she would dream of Esteban. "I'll be back . . ." haunted her.

Laura drifted off to sleep and the dreams came. She was with Esteban, driving, swimming, laughing, enjoying his embraces, his kisses, touching him, feeling his arms around her. *"Te amo,"* he whispered in her ear.

The running of the business and the tasks Laura set for herself turned the days into weeks as the ghost-filled nights took their toll on her. Rose and Daisy exchanged worried looks behind her back. Fashion model thin, Laura certainly didn't need to lose any weight.

"She's the soul of patience, so I don't think running the store is bothering her. And I don't think she's sick . . ." Rose stood talking to Daisy while Laura was out.

Daisy nodded. "She's just so thoughtful and serious. So quiet."

"Too quiet."

They were not alone in their observations. Mack stopped by one afternoon while Laura was out to talk to Rose and Daisy.

"Laura isn't here," Rose began.

"You don't have to tell me. I can guess. She's gone after things she doesn't have to have that don't have to be picked up, that can be delivered. She's trying to do everything there is to do, for some reason."

Rose and Daisy looked glum.

"She's lost weight, too," he pointed out. "Is it just me, because I want her to show some interest in me, or is her mind somewhere else a good bit of the time?"

Daisy shrugged. "It's about time somebody took notice," she said. "Might know it would be you who'd take the bull by the horns. You're right. It's passed noticeable, and got to scary."

"I thought at first it was just that she missed Sophie so much. But it's more than that." Rose sighed.

"Something must have happened on that island." Daisy stated it firmly. "She stayed for a month. And you know when she went, she was only going to stay for the two weeks we talked about. Then she called and said she was going to stay the whole month. If you ask me, the trouble, whatever it is, started on that island."

"I don't know how four weeks could affect someone so much. But it's more than missing Sophie, and we both know there are no problems here at the store." Rose looked at Daisy for confirmation. Daisy solemnly nodded.

"You mark my words." Daisy was emphatic. "It's something to do with that island."

Mack hadn't commented. "Didn't you tell me she was going to some kind of festival in Puerto Rico when I came by to ask about her one time? Before she decided to stay the other two weeks?" Mack folded his arms across his chest, tapping his chin with his forefinger.

"Yes, that's what she told us on the phone."

Rose thought back to their conversation. "She had been to that festival in Puerto Rico, and she was going back. It evidently went on for several days. When I asked if it was safe, she said she was going with an employee who worked at the hotel and that he would come back with her, so it would be safe."

"He?"

"We both asked about him." Daisy explained, anticipating his next question. "Since she met him there and they went and returned together, she felt she was safe with him. I remember saying it was fine for him to be watching out for her, but . . ." Daisy chuckled. "But who, I asked her, was going to be watching him?" Daisy shook her head. "She laughed about that. I think from what I can remember she said, he didn't speak too much English. But she sounded like he was completely safe and trustworthy."

"An employee of the hotel." Mack thought it over. "That's good. I wouldn't have approved of her going alone. If I'd got a chance to approve." He smiled self-consciously and a bit sadly.

"Anyway," Rose said, "since she had an escort from the hotel to go and come back with her, and he worked there in the hotel where he had people to answer to, we didn't worry about it. We were glad she was having a good time."

"Then it seems, as Daisy says, we've narrowed the source of the problem down to Isla Verde. Or possibly Puerto Rico. That festival in San Juan." Mack said it softly, more to himself than to them.

They stood silent a moment, then Daisy lifted her head and smiled toward the door as she waved. "We have company!"

"Fine," Laura came in smiling, her arms full of supplies. "Mack, I'll put us on some coffee if you'll stay a little and join us?"

"Sure, I'm not hard to get. You only have to ask me. And I've got something I want to talk to you about. All of you." He grinned at Daisy. "Or will that take all the fun out of eavesdropping?"

Daisy wrinkled her nose at Mack. "I'll go make the coffee. You can stay and chat a little, not that he deserves it," she said, taking a parting shot at Mack.

"I'm glad she's gone." Mack stepped closer, lowering his voice. "I came to invite Daisy and the rest of you to dinner at Antonio's Wednesday night."

"How did you know it was her birthday?" Rose gasped in surprise.

"I ran across it in some of Sophie's papers and made a note of it on my calendar. We'll just tell her it's one of my 'negotiated meals,' then spring the cake and presents on her after dinner. Okay?"

Rose stuck out her hand to shake on it, and Laura placed her hand over it, three happy conspirators.

"Coffee's ready," Daisy called from the tiny space they called their break-room. She poured their coffee and sat down where both she and Rose could watch the door.

Mack told them about his negotiated meal, watching Daisy out of the corner of his eye.

"Why, that's wonderful!" Daisy's eyes twinkled as she tempered her enthusiasm with, "Sort of reminds you of the days when the village doctors got paid in piglets and chicken dinners."

Pretending to choke on his coffee, Mack exclaimed, "I had no idea you went that far back!"

"I'm not telling about that." Daisy said primly, pausing to sip her coffee. "But the piglets and chicken dinners beat by a long shot not getting paid at all."

Wrinkling his brow as if trying to figure it out, Mack grumbled, "I think there's a compliment in there somewhere."

"Yeah." Daisy laughed at him. "You done good, counselor."

"Before my head swells from all this appreciation, there's something else I want to tell you about."

Laura tilted her head. "You're getting good at this negotiating thing. Is this something else you've negotiated for?"

"No, you're flattering me now. This is something else. I've heard about a piece of property I can get for a good price, if I decide I want it. Maybe for a summer cottage. A cabin, to get away from the city. I haven't actually seen it yet."

This time he spoke directly to Laura. "It just sounded good to me, from the little I've heard about it. And the price is so low, I'm afraid I may have let myself get excited about it too soon. But it sounds worth looking into the deal, I think."

"It certainly can't do any harm to look at it." Laura encouraged him, since he seemed so interested in it.

"It's on several acres and the cabin is old, but I was told it's been well kept, and it's well insulated. It has three bedrooms, butane gas heat, a fireplace, and of course, it's wired for electricity."

Laura, Daisy and Rose's eyes took on a far-away look, as they pictured a cabin in a woodsy setting while Mack continued describing it.

"It's got a well with good water, and has a septic tank far enough away from the lake that it's no threat to the environment. I specifically asked about that."

"Oh, Mack, it's on a lake?" Laura's eyes lit up.

"Yes, a big lake that runs into the river. And the scenery out there is bound to be beautiful in the fall."

Laura remembered how her aunt used to love the bright autumn leaves.

"There's supposed to be a wide porch where you can sit and look out over the lake."

He had the whole attention of Rose, Daisy, and Laura too, and added as if to be fair, "Of course, the fellow who told me all this is the fellow who's trying to sell it to me. But my imagination kept making me forget that."

"I don't blame you. I'd want to see it too," Laura said. "When are you going to see it? That is, if you decide to go and see it?"

"Yes, when?" Daisy raised her eyebrows.

"I don't know yet, but by the time we go to dinner Wednesday, I'll have had a chance to talk to the owner and I'll know then when I can see it. It may not be such a wonderful bargain," he warned. "Just wishful thinking on my part. The way he made it sound, I could see me teaching my son how to fish out there on the lake." His eyes met Laura's."

"Let's not get ahead of ourselves," she warned, her voice more serious than her smile.

"Right. We can just look on it as a refuge from the rat race in the city."

"Even if it needs a few things fixed and a little work here and there, it would be fun to fix it up. And it's a cabin for fun, after all, not the Ritz Carleton." Laura made a face. "There's no phone out there, is there?"

"No. I asked about that too. The owner never suspected I considered that one of the better selling points—not to have the wired-in aggravation."

"Want some more coffee?" Daisy gestured.

"No." Mack rose. "I've got to get back to my personal rat race and telephone so I can afford a place to get away from them." He grinned at Daisy, who shook her head as if he were a hopeless case when it came to grammar.

"Wednesday, I'll come by and get you and Rose first, since you're closer to me, then we'll stop by for Laura. Seven-thirty all right for everybody?"

Laura and Rose nodded. Daisy jerked him a thumbs up sign.

Chapter Eighteen

Laura waved goodbye to Rose and Daisy, fighting feelings of guilt.

You should be ashamed, she scolded herself. *Leaving the bookstore this early to pick up bread and instant coffee was a flimsy excuse.*

She eased up on the gas as she neared home. *It's a wonder I didn't get a ticket. But I'm not sure of the time difference between here and Isla Verde. I don't know why I didn't think of checking about the pearls before. I can at least find out if Esteban has come back to Isla Verde. I will at least know if he's all right.*

Laura's heart beat so fast she knew she was hoping for a miracle. She tried to silence the foolish hope that ran like a bright silver thread through her mind as she ran up the stairs at home. She had looked for the area code in the office before she left. "It may be listed under Puerto Rico or San Juan," she told the long distance operator. "It's an island not very far from San Juan. Yes, yes. Palacio or Hotel Isla Verde, that's it." She wrote the number on the memo pad and stared at it after breaking the connection.

This was it, this was real. She would know, if he had come for the pearls, that Esteban was back, that he was all right. Her heart cringed at all the reverse possibilities, the familiar ache taking the place of the excited beat hope had caused.

I've got to do it. Something could have happened to him, or goodness knows what other reason there could be for his not coming back when he knew I was leaving. I won't embarrass myself by asking for him. I will know when I check on the pearls if he came back. She took a long, deep breath.

And if he is back, *the fact he hasn't tried to call or contact me will make it clear I was right. He doesn't want to hear from me. Or talk to me. Or be with me.* Tears blurred the number. *At least I will know.*

She hurriedly dashed away the tears, wiping her face. She reached for the phone and began dialing.

There were three rings before someone picked up the phone. Laura held her breath.

"Palacio Isla Verde," a young male voice said.

"I'm sorry to bother you," Laura began politely. "But I left something, a jeweler's box, in your safe. It's a long box, velvet, and it had Esteban Aguilar's name on it. I want to know if it has been called for. Would you please check and see?"

"*Si.* A moment, *por favor* . . ."

Laura caught her lower lip between her teeth, trying to decide if the young voice was that of the boy she had asked so many times if there were any messages for her.

"There is no jeweler's box there, *Senorita.*"

"Then I guess he must have called for it. It was addressed to Esteban Aguilar," she reminded him.

"Oh, *si.*" There was a smile in the clerk's voice now. "He most probable get it when he come back."

"When he came back. When was that?" Laura's face paled as she gripped the phone. "Thank you," she said softly as she hung up.

She stared at the phone as if it had died. *He came back two days after I left, and he hasn't tried to call. He could have got the number the way I got the hotel's, or from their records. But he didn't. He's not called, or written or—*

Tears already streaking down her face, she threw herself

across the bed and sobbed into the shawl lying across her pillow.

The next morning she called Rose. "I must have eaten something that didn't agree with me or have one of those twenty-four hour viruses." She blew her nose. "Excuse me."

"Oh, how miserable. How about one of us coming over and fixing you some soup at lunch time? One of us can manage all right."

"No. No, but thanks. Right now I don't want to think about food, and when I do, there's plenty here to fix. I'll just rest and see you tomorrow night."

"Yes, you take care. Daisy and I are looking forward to Wednesday night. You call us now if you need anything."

"I will. Thank you, Rose."

Laura lay back on her pillow. What an accomplished liar she was getting to be, she thought bitterly.

When she woke later she went into the bathroom and looked in the mirror at her red and swollen eyes. When she went to sleep she had slept hard, emotionally exhausted. She glanced at the clock.

It's after one o'clock. How awful I look!

She bathed her eyes in cold water, carefully avoiding looking at herself, picturing Esteban as he had appeared in his tux.

"I love you—I'll be back." The words ran through her mind like a remembered melody in Esteban's voice, as the whispered *"te amo"* did. She quickly covered her face again with the cold washcloth.

I've got to go down and find myself something to eat. Aunt Sophie would probably kick me all the way downstairs if she were here. What a sorry sight I am. Well, I'm not going to spoil Daisy's birthday dinner. She threw the cloth into the sink.

The nearly empty cabinets reminded her of the full ones in the mansion on Isla Verde. Such a waste that was. She stopped, a can of soup in her hand, picturing Esteban as he approved the pork chops she had cooked for him.

Her face softened in a smile. At least she knew he was all right. He made it back safely from whatever emergency it was that had called him away. But if he had wanted to hear her voice half as much as she had longed to hear his, he would have called. Somehow, from somewhere, he would have called. Or if he didn't want to talk to her, he could have written to her, even if he had to get someone to interpret what he wrote. *He could have got in touch with me somehow by now, if he wanted to.*

Upstairs again, she washed her face in warm water, noting with relief that the swelling was almost gone. She put on a generous layer of face cream. She had to get back downstairs before her soup boiled away. On an impulse, she held her face above the rising steam, letting the cream soak in. *I'm going to hang on to what I learned when I got the works at Pierre's and at least look like I'm still alive.*

Setting her bowl on the table, she faced the soup as if it were an enemy to be vanquished instead of an ally in her quest for survival. In the silence, a small voice at the back of her mind repeated stubbornly, "I love you—I'll be back."

She refused to listen. She closed her eyes and swallowed a generous spoonful of hot soup, as if her heart hadn't heard the persistent little ghost.

Chapter Nineteen

The next day, Isla Verde firmly banished from her mind, the new and determinedly cheerful Laura went to work at the bookstore.

"Hi, we weren't expecting to see you until tonight," Rose exclaimed, critically examining her face. "Are you sure you're all right?"

Daisy gave Laura's arm a pat as she went by with books in her arms, an affectionate smile taking the place of any comment.

"That's part of a new shipment Daisy had," Rose bobbed her head in Daisy's direction.

"Oh, that's great," Laura's eyes lit up. "Let's take first choice to read. This is the best thing about running a bookstore; I don't know how the rest of the world manages." The laugh was only a little forced.

"Daisy already has hers picked out," Rose told her as she followed her to the storeroom at the end of the day.

Laura picked out a gothic romance and two mysteries while Rose balanced the cash drawer to close, and the phone in the office rang.

"That was Mack," Laura called, "just reminding us about tonight."

"As if we would forget." Rose shook her head.

Daisy came into the storeroom to get the books she wanted to read. "Rose and I had lunch one Sunday at the Kolivases' restaurant," she told Laura. "But neither one of us has been there for dinner."

"Mack has taken me there twice. He had done something for Mr. Kolivas then, too. And the second time, they had a violinist. I think that was on a Friday night, though. But it's a pretty place, with the candles and the way they have it decorated. And since you've been there, you know how good the food is."

Rose joined them as Daisy nodded. "It was good of Mack to include us in his negotiated dinner."

"Oh, that reminds me. You remember the cabin he told us about?"

"Yes. Has he made arrangements to see it? Daisy, your mouth's open," Rose added.

Annoyed, Daisy immediately closed her mouth, waiting to hear Laura's answer.

"He wanted me to talk to you about that. He wants to leave on a Friday morning, then we can come back Monday afternoon, have a whole weekend to look it over, if it's all right with you to close the store. Monday's slow, but what do you think about leaving Friday?"

"What Friday is this we're talking about?" Daisy lived up to her practical reputation.

"A week from this Friday. The owner is going up there this weekend to check on it and is going to have a key made for Mack to use, then we can go the following Friday, if you think it's all right."

"We could put a sign on the door saying we'll be closed Friday and Monday," Rose suggested.

"Yes, that's a good idea. Then people would know a week in advance, and that would give our customers plenty of notice." Daisy nodded. "But it's your store, remember?"

"I remember, and I want to go. But I would go along with whatever you two want to do."

"Then it's decided," Rose said. "Even if I wasn't really looking forward to it, I wouldn't want to disappoint Mack. He seems sold on that cabin already."

"It's a good thing the owner is going up there too, to make sure everything's okay before we go. It wouldn't be good to have any surprises after we're already there, like no water or no lights."

"I'm glad I've got you two guardian angels," Laura said as they left. "I hadn't even thought about that."

The birthday dinner was a huge success. Mack enjoyed explaining the dishes to Rose and Daisy and introduced them to Antonio and his daughter Kara.

"And we never put any calories in anything on anyone's birthday," Kara assured Daisy, smiling a dazzling smile at Mack.

Daisy raised her eyebrows as she smiled at Mack, too, taking note of his happy expression as he gazed at Kara.

The entire Kolivas family, the ones from the kitchen in their aprons, came to the table to sing happy birthday to Daisy. She dashed away a furtive tear as Mack kissed her on the cheek. After their meal there was birthday cake to go with their coffee, and Mack signaled the youngest Kolivas son to bring in the presents hidden in the trunk of his car.

Daisy cried, "I've never been so happy or so surprised, Mack! Now with all this happiness," she said, making a sober face, "I've no doubt got to say something good about you—" She wrinkled up her face and donned a far-away expression, as if trying in vain to think of something good about Mack until they caught on and laughed with her.

"Never mind." Mack patted her hand. "I wouldn't want you to strip a mental gear or anything dangerous."

"Thank you, Mack," Daisy said, squeezing his hand. "This has been wonderful. The high point of my year, is what it is."

Laura's hand found Mack's other hand under the table.

"Wonderful's the word." She smiled fondly at him.

Mack thought wonderingly he'd made a lot of points with Laura and the whole Kolivas family, and was very glad to have made Daisy and Rose happy too.

"Have you found out any more about the cabin?" Rose asked.

"Some. I know it's got the three bedrooms I told you about, and the owner reminded me when he gave me the key that it will sleep a lot of people for a weekend or a hunting trip. But I told him no, we only want the three bedrooms to be comfortable for now, so we can have a look around the place."

"All of us are looking forward to the long weekend," Laura said. "I'm glad you arranged it the way you did."

"It wasn't too much of a problem for the bookstore, being closed Friday and Monday?"

"No. We're posting a sign to notify people about it, so they will have plenty of notice and won't have to go without something to read over the weekend," Daisy told him.

"Good. I'm glad the agent doesn't know how close I'd come to buying the place sight unseen if he gave me a take-it-or-leave-it option." He looked at his three happy companions. "I'd blow all my points I've made getting these 'negotiated' meals, wouldn't I?"

"Let me think about that over more coffee," Daisy drew her brows together as if such weighty thoughts were painful.

"All right. But birthday cake or not, I'm not having more coffee without some of Kara's baklava." Mack held up his cup and Kara, who was watching him, came immediately.

Daisy watched as Kara served Mack first, signaling the waiter to bring more coffee. She was the soul of efficient service, clearing away his plate to make way for the baklava.

As Daisy watched Kara, Rose watched Daisy. *If Daisy hadn't noticed it, I might not have either, but Kara is taking care of our host like an old mother cat with only one kitten.*

Mack took Rose and Daisy home, then, wishing Daisy a happy birthday again, left to take Laura home.

"I hope he gets his kiss goodnight," Rose said dreamily.

"I hope so, too, Rose. But I'll tell you right now, it would make me plenty nervous for that Kolivas girl to be looking at my fella like she does at Mack."

Chapter Twenty

Esteban flew into the little airport on Isla Verde with Arturo and entered the Palacio yards ahead of Arturo, looking as handsome and happy as Laura's memories of him. Arturo waited as he went to the desk to announce his return, and a young clerk went to welcome Arturo.

Esteban reached for the phone at the desk and dialed, hanging up when there was no answer. He beckoned to the young clerk, who came to help him.

Arturo's attention was on the young clerk. He gestured to the two small cases, and the clerk took them. With a brief look after him, Arturo went to join his brother. He stopped several feet away when Esteban turned around. The look on Esteban's face was more anguished than it had been in the Colombian jungle.

In his hand, Esteban held a jeweler's box.

Laura went to church on Sunday and then stopped by a steak house for a carryout order.

I'll not bother cooking tonight. I'll just read, even if Mack calls and wants to go somewhere. We're getting to be regular customers at the Kolivases' restaurant.

She smiled to herself, remembering Mack eating Kara's baklava the night of Daisy's party. *You'd think she bakes it just for him, and he doesn't even recognize the crush she has on him. Men!*

She had parked two blocks away from the church and the nearby steak house. She passed a news stand on the way back to her car and stopped to get a magazine. Waiting to pay for it, she glanced down at the papers. There was one from Puerto Rico among the out-of-state and foreign ones.

She hadn't realized they had so many papers to choose from. She picked up the one from San Juan. *I'll take it and see how many Spanish words I can recognize. Heck, it beats the crossword puzzle.*

She tossed the magazine and newspaper on a chair when she got home and went upstairs to change into comfortable clothes.

She straightened her shoulders. *That woman in the bathroom mirror looks healthier and happier than the basket case who placed a call to Isla Verde a few days ago. And I'm looking forward next week to seeing the cabin Mack wants to buy. I think I'll wear my sweats.*

Defiantly, she stuck out her chin at the mirror.

Pulling up the pants and slipping on her loafers, she felt nothing but comfort. But pulling on the shirt, the softness closed around her arms and made her heart ache.

"I love you—I'll be back." The refrain returned to flood her eyes with sudden tears. She dashed them away and went downstairs out into her yard.

After checking on some of the shrubbery, she returned to the glassed-in porch, where the sun felt just right on her yellow sweat suit. She tossed the magazine on a table beside her and unfolded the paper from Puerto Rico.

"San Juan," she murmured to herself. "That name may be all I'll understand of it."

She unfolded the paper and recognized none of the words in the headlines. Then her eyes fell on a picture about halfway down the page.

Esteban! It is Esteban! The wild thought brought her bolt upright in her chair. Her hands wrinkled the outer edges of the paper.

But . . . , but, it couldn't be. Could it? Quickly her eyes scanned the articles around the picture, but she could understand none of the words. She realized they might have nothing to do with the picture anyway.

This article hasn't any words I can understand, and it seems to be about some company called A.M.E.A.

She dismissed the article, her fingers touching the picture, the face that was so like Esteban's.

The newsprint was not all that good, but the caption was plain enough. She read the names. One stood out, unmistakable. Esteban Aguilar. *It Is! It is Esteban!*

Laura studied the picture. Esteban was with two other men and a woman. He had a surprised expression on his face, as if the photographer had called to him just before taking the picture. The woman beside him was young, dark like him, and very beautiful. He was holding her hand, the other arm thrown out in front of her in a protective gesture.

The same gesture he used when the man nearly stumbled into us at the festival. Yes, this is my Esteban. Tears blurred her vision.

"So, that's why you were so long getting back," she whispered to the picture. "How lovely she is. A nice girl from a good family, most likely a very wealthy family, the way she's dressed. Those men are probably relatives. Yes, she must be wealthy. It may be she was wondering why he stayed a month at Isla Verde. It says something about Paris under the picture. Maybe that's where she lives. Where he went in such a hurry."

Anger and bitterness hit her hard, and her hands crushed the paper.

I wish I could think of something hateful to make me feel better, but she more than likely doesn't know anything about us and our Isla Verde affair. Oh, Esteban! How could you? To do this to me. Or to her.

She smoothed out the paper. Looking again at the caption

under the picture, she found the girl's name. "This must be it. She's the only woman in the picture. Amparo Collingwood. It sounds English," she murmured wonderingly. "And these others are Esteban's family I guess, not hers. Their names are Aguilar, like his. Maybe he had to hurry to his own wedding, with his relatives there . . ." She dashed away more tears, useless tears that wouldn't change anything.

Going to the kitchen, Laura wadded the paper up, as if crushing it might give her release from her anguish, and threw it into the trashcan. She gripped the magazine in her hand as she climbed the stairs.

This might be one of those arranged alliances wealthy people enter to keep from being snagged by some social climbing peasant. She stomped on the stair that squeaked. *But maybe he couldn't help it. Maybe he didn't have any choice, and felt he had to abide by his parents' wishes.*

She stomped on the innocent stairs some more. *Bull feathers! He could have told me, somehow. He could have found someone to interpret, or some way, he could have told me. I was worrying, only wanting to know if he was all right. Just to know if he was still alive! And this is the big emergency—no, the small and beautiful emergency—this Amparo! Well, I won't think about him again. I won't! I won't! There is nothing more I can do. He did not try to contact me, didn't even tell me what the so-called emergency was. Well, small wonder about that!*

No excuse or logic she could think of, or even justified anger, seemed to affect the pain still in her heart. The newspaper picture haunted her. *And that protective gesture tells me more than any words could as to where his heart is. He cares for her. His very body language says so, and God knows, I'm familiar with his body language! He prefers Amparo. He is where he belongs.*

She marched into the bathroom and washed away the tears

and put on fresh makeup. *I'm all right. I'll put it behind me. I'm going to make it, Aunt Sophie!*

Monday morning a nearly normal Laura went to work at the bookstore. Daisy and Rose noticed the improvement and silently gave thanks. She wore the makeup she'd bought, fluffed her hair that fell into place so neatly now, and concentrated on her work.

Thursday afternoon Rose was in the office checking an inventory list, and Daisy was busy dusting shelves. Laura went to the cash register to wait on a woman who was holding two books she wanted to buy.

Laura smiled and took the two books to scan the bar codes and the woman said, "You can just put them in here."

She picked up a large shopping bag and set it on the counter.

Laura's eyes widened in horror at the splash of vivid colors on the bag. The palm trees and bright colors on it. Laura burst into tears, then, putting her hands over her face, she ran into the office and shut the door.

Daisy, being the closest, hurried to the astonished customer, and Rose went to Laura.

In the office, Laura leaned against the wall beside the door, uncontrolled tears running down her cheeks. Rose came over and handed her a box of Kleenex, at a loss what to say to comfort her.

Daisy finished helping the customer and joined them in the office, glancing from Laura to Rose. No one spoke.

Laura wiped her cheeks and sat down in a chair at the table. "I feel like a complete idiot, carrying on like this." She blew her nose. "It's just that when she—that customer—put that big shopping bag up there on the counter, it, it reminded me of something. I'm all right now," she assured them as they joined her at the table.

Rose and Daisy looked so worried, Laura tried to comfort them. "It's all right. Don't look so distressed. I'm all right. Really, I am. It's just a thing I didn't want to be reminded of, that's all."

Rose glanced uneasily at Daisy.

"There's no point in going into it, since it's over now. But, when I was on Isla Verde, I met someone. Someone special, or at least special to me. That's why I decided to stay two more weeks."

Still no one spoke or even looked at the closed door. Rose and Daisy's main concern was Laura.

"Anyway, I really cared for this person, and even though he couldn't speak English, I thought he cared for me too." The tears had stopped, and Laura was wiping her face with more Kleenex, not meeting their eyes.

"He couldn't speak English?" Daisy exclaimed in surprise. "Then how—I mean, did you ask someone to interpret for you?"

"No." Laura shook her head, thinking back. "It really wasn't all that hard, Daisy. We both knew a few words, I of Spanish and he of English. But only a few, so we used a sort of simple sign language."

"Like charades." Rose nodded, guessing.

"Sort of like that, yes. There were certain signs we had, like when he was going somewhere but coming back, he would point outside, then down at the floor in front of me."

"Going out?"

Daisy and Rose exchanged a look.

"Yes. I don't know where he lived, but he played in the band, and I thought he must live somewhere in the hotel."

"What did he play?" Daisy put in curiously.

"Something typical of Isla Verde." Laura managed a small smile. "Maracas. At least that's what he was playing the first time I saw him. I was having dinner in the hotel dining room, and he didn't see me. Then later when I met him on the shuttle boat, he was wearing the band uniform for a costume. It was one of those bright colored things with the big sleeves." She tried to make them understand, her hands outlining ruffled sleeves, and Daisy's expression assured her that her imagination was doing a great job.

"So, when I saw him on the shuttle wearing that uniform, I knew who he was and that he worked at the hotel. And I felt safer having someone with me."

Rose and Daisy both nodded solemnly. Not asking questions.

"To make a long story short, about three days before I was to come home, he got some sort of urgent message and signed to me he would be back. And he . . . he just . . . he never came back." Laura's reddened eyes studied the table's surface.

"Maybe he had some sort of trouble," Rose began.

"No. He had loaned me some pearls to wear when we had dinner together." She looked up. "To go with the earrings Sophie gave me."

Rose gave a small nod, remembering the earrings. Daisy didn't comment.

"When I left I had them—the pearls—put in the hotel safe for him, with his name on them. I called after I got home to make sure he got them, and he had picked them up. He came back to Isla Verde, but not to me. He didn't even try to contact me to say goodbye."

Rose unconsciously clasped her hands over her heart, and Daisy, for once, didn't know what to say.

"That shopping bag, the one the woman set on the counter just now," Rose guessed out loud.

Rose and Daisy both nodded, agreeing about the shopping bag. There was no sound from the store.

"We went on two outings while I was there. He took me out on a friend's boat, and the other time we went to an estate on the island. He evidently takes care of the boat and the estate as well as working at the hotel. And both times, we took our bathing suits and things in a shopping bag with the hotel's logo on it." Laura's eyes were seeing their trip preparations, remembering Esteban putting things in the bag, pointing to things in the closet. "I called it our Isla Verde luggage. It was the same size bag as the one the woman set on the counter and had the same bright colors."

"So, he just went off and left you." Daisy's face was turning an ugly shade of brick red, and she had found her tongue.

"Well . . ." Laura defended Esteban. "There really wasn't much else he could do, I guess. Neither one of us spoke the other's language enough to explain, and it had come to a time to get serious about a commitment. We were in love, and that's the natural next step, to make a commitment. Maybe he just thought not coming back was the kindest way out."

"What about this urgent message? Was it really an urgent message, or . . ." Rose's question trailed off.

"Yes, I'm certain of that. It was something urgent enough to frighten him." Laura sighed. "Maybe when he had whatever it was taken care of, he thought it would be better to simply stay away until after I left. He did know when I would be leaving."

Without another word, Daisy and Rose went to her and put their arms around her.

"I'm all right," Laura insisted. "I'll go wash my face. You must think I'm awfully foolish," she said sheepishly.

"No, just a human being like the rest of us," Rose told her kindly.

"The foolishness here is on the part of that-that maracas player." Daisy's hands reached for an invisible throat to strangle.

Rose glanced at the closed office door as she and Daisy returned to the store. "She'll be all right. We'll be here to help her."

Daisy nodded, adding thoughtfully, "And Mack, too."

Chapter Twenty-One

Having confided in Rose and Daisy, Laura felt more comfortable. She thought to herself it was true, as Sophie had told her, that shared burdens were the lightest. And there was the bookstore, something she enjoyed, to keep her busy.

She dusted a shelf as if brushing away her troubles. Some things could be pushed away by work and other things put on hold, if not forgotten. She kept busy, reaching for books to put up.

I guess there are always going to be those little Isla Verde ghosts waiting for a reminder like that customer's shopping bag. And the way we loved each other. The way he looked when he smiled. Well, at least, I'm home now, and Esteban is where he evidently belongs. But in my heart, he will always be my Esteban.

Her two guardian angels watched quietly. "I think sometimes she's going to wear out the shelves, she's dusting so hard," Rose whispered to Daisy as she passed her going into the office.

"She's safe at home now and she's not crying. Count your blessings," was Daisy's practical answer.

About the middle of the week, Laura was sitting in front of the television set having a sandwich for dinner while she watched the news. She left to get something to drink and heard the name AMEA as she returned. The reporter was saying something about a cartel that owned jewel mines and showed a picture of a large emerald from one of the mines. There was nothing else after the picture and, he went on to other topics of national interest.

AMEA—A M E A. It rang a bell in Laura's mind. Then, with a start, she placed it. AMEA was the name of the company or whatever it was in the article by the picture of Esteban and that girl. *Maybe she has some connection with the jewel mines. She did look like a rich girl, or I may just be fantasizing because she was beautiful and I was so envious.* She frowned at her sandwich, remembering the sack lunch she had shared with Esteban in the little park in the village. Memories flooding back again.

The memory of the night she and Esteban sat in front of the fireplace at the estate came back to her, and his voice saying, "*Dinero*—no problem."

Dinero *no problem, indeed!* Her face flushed with anger, Laura's teeth bit into the sandwich. *I suppose if you marry into that kind of money, you won't have problems of any kind!*

She leaned back in her chair, ashamed of her bitterness, no longer hearing the television reporter. No, she could not believe Esteban would leave her for money alone. This must be something in which he had no choice, or . . . or maybe she was still just grasping at straws. *But I know what we felt for each other was real. I loved him and he knew it, and he loved me. No matter what happened, he loved me. But whatever the reason, he did leave me, and he hasn't tried to call me or get in touch with me to explain. It's plain, even if he is somewhere as lonely for me as I am for him, he doesn't want to see me again. Or he can't see me and doesn't want to hurt me anymore, or be hurt himself. No matter our feelings, it's finished.* The hard truth was a stone on her heart.

The office phone rang Thursday afternoon.

"It's Mack," Daisy called to Laura.

She took the call in the office, turning away from the door as Daisy began balancing the day's receipts. Rose put magazines back in the right places in the racks.

"What about having a quick breakfast together in the morn-

Stranger in Paradise

ing and getting an early start for the cabin? I can be there to pick Rose and Daisy up at eight, and then come for you, if that's all right." Laura heard the excitement in his voice. "We can start exploring early."

"Sounds good to me. Let me check with them." She turned to see Daisy and Rose, faces at attention, just outside the door.

"Mack wants to have a quick breakfast together. He'll pick you up, then come for me, and we'll get an early start in the morning, what do you think?"

Rose and Daisy nodded quickly, exchanging an excited grin.

"Sounds good to all hands on deck here," Laura reported. "We're about ready to close. Shall we go home and get ready ASAP?"

"Yes, but it's not as if you have to hunt up something special, you know. Tell Daisy anything the squirrels won't throw acorns at will do." Mack laughed. "Remind them comfortable shoes are the main requirement. Otherwise, just come comfortable to the bone."

"We'll do that." Laura smiled into the phone. "See you in the morning."

She turned to Rose and Daisy. "We're through here anyway, and he says he's picking you two up first at eight o'clock, and he said be sure to wear comfortable shoes." Picking up her purse she added, "He's absolutely yelling about casual and comfortable."

"I'm going to wear a light sweater and a heavier one over it in case I need it and take some of my yard clothes." Rose decided as all of them headed to the door.

"And my two main pairs of slacks are so thin in the knees you can read the paper through them." Daisy chortled. "You can't get much more comfortable than that without getting arrested!"

"Okay—goodnight—scatter!"

Jackie Griffey

I'm going to take my yellow sweat suit, Laura decided on the way home, *and dare any ghosts to spoil my weekend.*

Chapter Twenty-Two

When Mack stopped in front of her house, Laura hurried out immediately, her overnight case in her hand, a shopping bag hugged against her side.

Daisy looked apprehensively at the shopping bag, then at Laura.

"Old habits die hard." Laura laughed at Daisy as Mack took her overnight case and reached for the big bag.

"Well," Mack commented, "all of you look like happy campers."

"I can't think of anything I'd rather be doing." Laura gave him a quick peck on the cheek and settled beside him.

"I should have thought of this sooner. We're off! Anyone with a change of heart will have to jump out the window."

Breakfast and the trip out of town went fast. They almost had the pancake house to themselves, and traffic on the road was light.

"The cabin isn't far off the interstate," Mack told them. "So I'm sure we'll have a good road nearly all the way. I want to get there early so we can explore around the area as well as the cabin. Also, I'm not all that sure where to turn off."

When they came to a large and expensive-looking truck stop, Mack pointed at it. "That's one of our landmarks. This truck stop is only five or six miles from the turn off. The owner says you can come here for supplies or gas, or eat out if you get tired of your own cooking."

"It's a handy thing to have close by," Rose agreed.

"What's the name of the road where we turn? We'll help you watch," Daisy volunteered.

"Lake Road."

"How original." Daisy smirked.

"Don't rain on my parade," Mack ordered. "If I get rich and famous, I'll get it changed to Bluebird Way, or Billion Dollar Boulevard, or Sanctuary or—"

"Or Shangri-la," Laura said, laughing.

"Hey, there it is!" Mack carefully slowed down.

The road he turned onto was gravel, but wide enough for two large cars to pass with plenty of room, and it was in good repair. Mack drove slowly, both because of the dust and in order to watch for the gate to the cabin.

They had topped a small rise and started downhill when Daisy spotted the gate. Mack stopped and got out, taking a key from his pocket.

"I'll change that lock if I do buy the place," he commented when he got back in. He pulled in far enough to clear the gate and closed it without locking it.

He continued down a winding drive, which ended behind the cabin. There was room in the separate structure for four cars, and there was a cleared area to cross to the cabin itself.

"Let's go around to the front," Mack suggested as they got out. "I want to see the front and the view of the lake, and the key I have fits the front door anyway, I think."

They stopped at the corner of the porch, all of them looking down at the lake.

"Mack, he was right about the view. It's beautiful," Laura exclaimed. "Look at the morning sun on the water. This was a good time of day to come."

Rose and Daisy stood admiring the long slope down to the lake. There was a weathered looking wooden pier with two ducks diving near it.

"What an ideal place for a cabin."

"I'm going to see if there's anything in the things we brought to give the ducks," Daisy said. "Fine time to think about it."

"Oh, I think I can come up with something the ducks won't turn down." Mack held the cabin door open for them.

Laura's ghosts chose that moment to return, bringing with them memories of the lagoon on Isla Verde and its swans, and Esteban holding her hand. She pushed them firmly away, glad no one had noticed she had paused.

"Forward," Mack ordered. "Let's see what the inside is like."

He shut the door behind them and they stood looking around them. They were in a large room with a stair in the far corner leading up to a loft of some sort.

"Must be extra sleeping room," Mack said, looking up. The railing went up and all the way across the top so anyone up there could look down into the room below.

On the other side of the back wall was a door leading to a breakfast or eating area with a huge bay window flanked by long windows that went almost to the floor. Laura flinched, closing her eyes briefly, reminded of the windows flanking the double doors of the mansion on Isla Verde.

The kitchen beyond the eating area was large and had a lot of cabinet space, meeting with everyone's approval. Back in the living room they discovered the door next to the stair landing led to a hallway with three bedrooms opening off of it, and one small bathroom. The larger bedroom had its own bathroom, not modern, but in good repair and clean.

"I like it," Mack announced. "We haven't finished exploring, but I've seen enough to know I like it. Shall we take a vote?" he asked, leading them back into the larger room.

Rose and Daisy quickly raised both hands.

"Double ayes," Mack said. "Laura? How say you?" He tried

to look judicial, and Laura smiled.

She raised both hands too. "I think you should grab it before he changes his mind. Even if you don't want to use it, it would be a good investment." Then she added wistfully, "But it would be fun to have it to get away and to fish, and as you said, just rest up from the rat race."

Mack nodded, still looking around. "I'm sold, if nothing happens or falls in on us before we go back. As soon as we get back, I'll call and tell the owner I'll take it," he decided.

He looked up the hall. "I guess we can put Rose and Daisy in the largest room. Laura, you and I can take the two others. Is that all right with everybody?"

"I feel guilty taking the master suite." Daisy spoke before she thought and turned quickly to glare at Mack. "Don't start with me, Mack!" She beat him to the punch, shaking her finger at him.

Laura giggled. "Let's get our things into our rooms and gather some wood for the fireplace. And I've got a few goodies in the bottom of the shopping bag to keep us out of trouble."

They unloaded their things from the car, including three large grocery sacks Mack had in the trunk. There were also some extra blankets and pillows.

Stocking the cabinets, Laura wished briefly for a microwave. She shrugged off the thought, just glad Mack had made sure they would have electricity. She pictured the open fire, smiling till the memory of the fireplace on Isla Verde intruded. She quickly banished that other fireplace from her mind.

We've got everything we need, she told herself firmly.

All of them went out to gather wood, and Mack discovered a cord of wood stacked neatly near the back of the shed where they had parked.

"I'm glad to see that," he told Laura. "But let's bring in all these little branches and bark for kindling, and I'll get one of those grocery sacks to get the fire started."

"What a time to think of matches. Did you bring some? And maybe a useful thing like a can opener?" Laura asked as they reentered the kitchen.

"I was a Boy Scout." Mack pretended to be deeply offended. "Naturally, I'm prepared."

He immediately got hit with a wadded grocery sack and two dishtowels. He grabbed one of the towels and flipped it at Daisy.

"By the way, the agent told me the owner said everything here goes with the cabin. It's not much, and I'm sure we'll all know by morning how badly the mattresses need to be replaced. But it will be nice to have things I can just leave here and not have to do everything at once."

"You're right. That's good." Laura nodded approval, looking around. "I really like the place, Mack. It's a lot bigger than I thought it would be. It's more of a house than a cabin. The big living room and the eating area with all those windows have some pretty decorating possibilities, too."

"I think that part was the only remodeling done on it since it was built to live in. It's probably the mattresses and bedding I'll replace first."

The day went quickly as they explored and generally took inventory, in between getting acquainted with the wildlife in the area.

"Let's go down to the water before we have to decide what will agree with all those pancakes we had at breakfast and the other things we stuffed in on top of them and called lunch."

"All right." Mack was already walking. "I think the pier is in good repair. A little weathered, but in good shape."

He took Laura's hand as they started down the steeper part of the slope, unaware her mind had been borne by invisible ghosts back to the marina at Isla Verde as she gazed at the water.

"The lake is a deep one and there are probably plenty of fish in it." Mack obviously had great hopes for the fishing, his eyes on the water. "The county agent told the man who owns this place that the county stocked the lake about a year ago, and the water is cold just as trout like it."

Laura nodded, looking out across the water. "I heard somewhere that trout like cold water," she mused, pulling her memory reluctantly away from the sunlit waters off San Juan. "It's getting chilly out here on the bank, too." Laura glanced at the lengthening shadows. "By the time you get the fire going and we get something fixed to eat, it will be cold out here."

"But it will be a cool place in the summer. We'll come up here and bring our fishing gear to enjoy it."

Laura noted he made reference to the future every time a chance presented itself. She made no comment.

Dinner was canned spaghetti doctored up with fresh hamburger and onions, served with toasted French bread with garlic. Dessert was a cake Laura had bought at the bakery. Mack made instant cappuccino to go with it.

"This is delicious," Laura pronounced.

"I don't think we could tell if it wasn't," Mack grinned at Daisy. "After a day outside."

"Is that a crack about my age?"

"No, I'm being honest about my cooking." Mack tried in vain to be noble. "Or should I say my doctoring up of the cuisine?"

"Who cares? It's good. It's gourmet fare." Laura laughed away their quibbling.

Hunger satisfied, the women ran Mack out of the kitchen. "Go find something to play Scrabble on," Daisy ordered him.

"A box or something will do," Laura called after him.

As they were finishing up, he stuck his head into the kitchen. "Ready!"

"He seems awfully proud of himself," Laura whispered to Rose.

Finished with the dishes, Laura, Daisy and Rose came into the living room and were impressed. The fire was going well, and back from it a few feet, Mack had assembled a makeshift table. Laura's double Scrabble game was laid out in the middle of it.

"Great. We may just keep you around," Laura admired the table.

"That's what I'm working on," Mack murmured too softly for anyone but Laura to hear.

Chapter Twenty-Three

They played two games of Scrabble before Daisy stifled a yawn. "I'm getting tired, aren't you, Rose?" She tapped Rose's arm.

"What? Oh. Oh, yes. I guess our gourmet meal is telling on me. I'm getting sleepy. Or maybe it was all this outdoors and fresh air, like Mack said." She stifled a phony yawn of her own as she got up, rubbing her lower back.

"We'll see you in the morning."

Laura and Mack watched as they left.

"I guess now we'll have to think of some way to justify all that arranging for us to have some time alone." Mack grinned at her.

"They were a little obvious, all right. But I'm so glad to be back with good friends and people who are real; I'd forgive them about anything."

"People who are real?" Mack weighed the statement. Hesitating. "I . . . that is . . ." Mack spoke cautiously. "Laura, to anyone who knows you, it's obvious you've had something on your mind ever since you got home . . ."

Laura held out a hand to stop him. "Let's go out and sit on the steps. We can take a blanket and look out at the moonlight on the water."

"Okay. There's an extra blanket in the kitchen. I'll get it."

They opened and closed the door quietly and wrapped the blanket around them as they sat down, their feet on the steps.

"Warm enough?"

"Yes, fine. I—" Laura stopped, gazing out at the moonlight's bright path across the lake.

"You don't have to tell me anything you don't want to, Laura. I'm just glad you're home safely and here with me now. With Rose and Daisy and me. We missed you. If we act like Nosy Parkers sometimes, it's only because we're concerned about you. As for life stories and true confessions, I certainly don't intend to play twenty questions," he stated positively. "And since I don't intend to answer any questions, it's only fair not to ask any, is how I see it."

Laura didn't answer. She pulled the blanket closer.

"Just think of me as an 'as is' vehicle. No warranty." His declaration didn't bring a chuckle, and he tried to find words to express his feelings. "There's no apprenticeship for marriage. It's a classic example of calculated risk." Mack sounded like a lawyer, which he was, summing up his case, which he also was.

"I'm not planning on getting married," Laura stated flatly. "And I doubt you will want to take a chance on asking me again when you hear what I'm going to say."

Mack turned from studying the lake to face her, denial written all over him. "There is nothing—nothing, do you hear?—that would change my mind about wanting to marry you."

"Nothing?" Laura's voice was hard with bitter disbelief. "What would your reaction be if I told you I fell head over good judgment in love when I was in Isla Verde, had a torrid love affair, and been abandoned when it came to commitment time?"

It took a moment for Mack to answer. "I wouldn't believe it!" He was vehement. "No man I know would be that stupid."

"Well . . ." Laura gave him a wry smile. "Stupid or not, that's how it was. I loved him, probably always will. But he left about three days before time for me to leave, and he just—never came back."

"That's strange," Mack mused, temporarily at a loss for words. "Just left. Did he not make any attempt at an excuse? Any explanation at all?"

"He . . ." Laura looked away. "He couldn't." Her eyes again avoided his. She gazed at the moonlight on the lake. She finally spoke carefully. "He didn't speak English."

"Couldn't speak English—" Mack started and then shook with laughter. "You're some joker, Miss Smart. What is this, Candid Camera?" Mack gasped, catching his breath. "You really had my motor running there for a minute." Laura still stared at the lake and he stopped abruptly, eyes on her. "Wait a minute. You're not laughing."

Laura sat completely still.

"Are you telling me the truth?"

"Yes. It's the truth. Whether you believe me or not, I loved him." Laura looked as miserable as she felt.

Mack drew in a slow, deep breath. "All right. I believe you. So that's why you called to say you were going to stay two more weeks? Because you had met him?"

"Yes."

"I can't believe it." Mack shook his head, anger beginning to stir. "He couldn't speak English. What did he do to initiate this torrid affair, indicate with some gesture you should undress?" He turned away abruptly, his face angry. "Why didn't I think of that?" He spat the words sarcastically.

"It's hard to explain, Mack. Sometimes I hardly believe it myself." Laura sighed, resting her head on her arms, which she crossed on her knees.

"Tell me." Mack got a grip on his patience. "There must have been something, some reason he just disappeared. Tell me why he left from this affair which began and ended so quickly. What happened, Laura? I don't understand."

"He worked at the hotel. The first time I saw him was when I was checking into the hotel. He didn't see me and I was glad he didn't. He was so good looking I thought he was a movie star or a celebrity. I realized I was staring and made it to the elevators before I embarrassed myself. I didn't see him again until I got bored enough to dress and go to dinner by myself. And there he was. He was in the hotel's band that was playing dinner music. He saw me then, but our eyes only met for an instant, and I left while they were still playing. Then I saw the poster about the festival in Puerto Rico. You had to ride the little shuttle boat to get there, and I met him on the shuttle boat. Recognized him, and he recognized me as one of the guests. He—we spoke enough to know he didn't speak English and I couldn't speak Spanish, but we devised a sort of sign language by exchanging names and making gestures. He pointed to Isla Verde and Puerto Rico to let me know he would see me back to the hotel." She paused. "To be practical, I was glad to have an escort to the carnival. To have someone who worked at the hotel to bring me home."

Mack watched the moonlight on the water. "Anything happen to warn you he couldn't be trusted, or was it love at first sight, no rough spots at all?"

Laura flushed, anger making the blood rise up to color her neck and cheeks. "I'm not a complete idiot, counselor. He was a nice-looking citizen who was responsible enough to be hired by the hotel, and he asked as politely as he could, under the circumstances, to escort me to the festival and said he would see me home—"

"I know you're not an idiot. I make it a practice never to propose to idiots, complete or otherwise." Mack made a polite little half bow without getting up.

Laura giggled, ashamed of her outburst.

"I'm looking for something that will give us a clue to why he left and didn't come back. Did he know you were in love with him?" Mack asked the last question carefully, eyes on hers.

"Yes. He knew." Laura's gaze was back on the placid water of the lake. "And I know he loved me." Her face was sad in the pale moonlight.

"Did he tell you so?"

"He told me in more than words, and I understand the phrase for 'I love you' in Spanish. *Yo te amo* is about the first thing you learn in high school Spanish."

"Told you in more than words." Mack took note of it before continuing. "So he loved you, and he didn't have any problems you could see. Any abnormal behavior or anything?"

"There was one thing," she said slowly. "I thought it was probably normal." She tilted her head, thinking about what she was saying, "I suppose, like everyone else, I've always thought of Latins as romantic and hot blooded. Anyway, a man approached me while he was gone for a few minutes, on the boat, on the way back."

Mack's eyes were alert. "He left for a few minutes. Then what?"

"As I was standing there, a man came up to me and handed me a drink. I didn't like his looks, as the saying goes, but he was all smiles and handed me the Coke, and I didn't know how to say politely that I didn't want it. And I realized I was thirsty, so I said *'gracias'* and drank some of it. Then the man looked scared to death, and I turned and saw Esteban coming."

"His name was Esteban?"

"Yes. Esteban. Anyway, the man hurried away and I tried to explain to Esteban about the Coke. It tasted hot, like it had chilies in it, and I didn't want it. Esteban tasted it, then he threw it into the water and left, looking around for the little man. I was afraid there would be a fight, but Esteban came back in a few minutes and we soon forgot about it. Is that unusual, or an indication he had mood swings? I never thought so. He was always very nice." Laura frowned.

"What? There's something else, isn't there? What is it?"

"The only other time I saw that stormy look on his face was when I went to tell the clerk I would be staying for another two weeks. The clerk said no, that the room was already reserved. Esteban reached across the desk—it was a chest high one—and grabbed the poor boy by his jacket lapels. But an older clerk came out and took care of it, and everything was all right."

"I don't know," Mack admitted. "On the surface, it looks like there were grounds both times for his anger. The strange man approaching you. That's probably not acceptable behavior there. And then, the room." His eyes met hers. "He wanted you to stay."

"Yes. He did. Mack, he loved me and I loved him. I was going to marry him if he asked me. The only reason we didn't sleep together is he didn't seem to want to. Even with the time together, the embraces and kisses—there isn't any mystery there. He just wasn't ready to make a commitment like marriage. There are a lot more people who think they're in love than are thinking about getting married. I felt like the world had stopped when I realized that . . . faced the fact he wasn't coming back. He probably felt it was kindest just not to see me again."

She moved when he would have touched her shoulder, a comforting gesture from a good hearted friend. She didn't want the charity.

"It may have been meant kindly, but that's not the way I felt about it. As Aunt Sophie would say, my intentions were honorable. All the way, Mack. I wouldn't be telling you this now, except it wasn't any vacation fling. I don't think there can ever be anyone who will replace him in my heart, not ever. Are you going to keep speaking to me, or stop the world and just put me off?" She didn't look up.

"I don't know where the switch is to stop the world, and I'm glad this fellow was fool enough to leave. I told you I wanted to marry you, and I still do, if you'll have me. And about the twenty questions, I had a couple of flings in high school and one serious one in college. But no one measures up to you, Laura. I'll do my best to make you forget this fellow with the poor judgment. We can have a good life together."

"Mack—"

"No, don't answer yet. Think about it while we're enjoying our stay here at the cabin and tell me later on, after we get back. We're a good team, Laura. You, me, Rose, and Daisy, are already like family, and I know Sophie would approve. We have years of memories behind us, things in common, and we can make a lot more happy memories together."

"You're making this sound like one of your mergers." Laura smiled affectionately.

"Yes, I know. It's an occupational hazard, I guess. I talk like a small town lawyer because I am one. But I would be proud and happy if you consent to be Mrs. Mack McKinley, and I'll do my best to make you happy."

Chapter Twenty-Four

For the next two weeks, business was good at the bookstore; Daisy and Rose's jobs kept them occupied. Life went on, and so did Mack and Laura's friendship. A couple of days later when Laura left the bookstore, as soon as the door closed behind her, Rose hurried to Daisy. "I couldn't wait for her to leave!"

"Why? What on earth are you so up in the air about?"

"Mack called while you were back there unpacking books."

"He has been known to call before," Daisy pointed out. "Why didn't you run and catch Laura?"

"Because he's going to call when she gets back. But he told me he's inviting us—I mean they're inviting us—to the steak house for dinner with them. This weekend. He said they want to tell us something!"

"Tell us something. You think?" Daisy's eyes grew round. "Do you think they're going to get married?" She glanced at the windows, "But, Laura hasn't said anything."

"No, but I'll bet a cookie he proposed while we were at the cabin."

"You could be right. They probably want to tell us together, that's why she hasn't said anything," Daisy nodded. "You notice they've been seeing each other more often too. She said something about having him at her house for dinner tonight."

"Right on time." Laura opened the door for Mack.

"One of my many, many virtues." Mack kissed her on the

cheek. "That and persistence, like proposing at least once a day. Um, something smells good—besides you."

"It's roast beef, courtesy of my faithful crock pot."

She put her arms around him as he reached for her. "And about virtues, I don't have a lot of virtues. I keep telling you, you can do better."

"I'm happy with my choice." His expression got serious. "And I'm going to keep asking."

"You should call on Kara Kolivas. She lights up when you come in the door. Now there's someone who is in love with you."

"You mean maybe a girlish crush. She'd be bored married to a lawyer and later on a stodgy old judge. She doesn't have the things in common we have, if you want to get technical."

"Mack, you're a snob?"

"No. I'm just practical. Look at the age difference. I'd look like her father in no time."

Laura laughed. "Don't rush into old age, Mack. Marriage is what you make it, and she's not that much younger if you'll just think about it."

"Yeah," Mack was sarcastic. "Think about Papa Kolivas after me with his meat clever."

"Oh, you're impossible. Kolivas likes you and the head of the house is supposed to be older and wiser, look at all the arranged marriages in Europe. Greece is a good example of that too."

"Enough about arrangements. Let's go. No more about Greece and arranged marriages. You're ruining my appetite."

"You mean you're not even going to 'present your case' to Kara then?" Laura persisted.

"Certainly not."

"Mack, really!"

Mack eyed the door. "And let's not have that speech about to love, to be in love, and to like, being three different things." Mack playfully tickled her. "Two out of three's not bad, and I'll have the rest of our lives to work on the other one." He kissed her to end the argument.

"You're a hopeless case. You haven't given much thought about how Daisy and Rose are going to take this trip of ours either."

"They'll be fine. This is not fifty years ago. A trip like this is a great freebie."

"Oh, I know. Have you got everything? The plane tickets, the hotel reservations?"

"Of course. You worry too much."

"I don't think Rose and Daisy will be all that badly disappointed or shocked about our going to Hawaii together. Not really." Laura didn't look like she'd convinced herself. "It was certainly good of the company you represent to give you the free trip to Hawaii for two to go to their convention, though. No one can deny that."

"And they have had several gratis meals from the Kolivas family for things I've done for them. They will be glad for us. I'm sure of it." Mack's grin was back. "I'll whisper to Daisy that I'll be working on wearing down your resistance while we explore among the palms."

Laura shook her head at his persistence.

"Maybe you'll see the light. I'll get you so full of pineapple and coconut and fun, you'll wonder why on earth you couldn't see all my good points before. Then, since we'll know where to stay next time, we can come home and get busy planning the rest of our lives—with Rose and Daisy's approval." Mack grinned looking happy about it already.

"Just one thing. Only one proposal in the whole week. Okay?"

"Oh, okay. Unless, of course, you decide to propose to me."

"I'll chance it. This way we can have all the good stuff without the hassle." That settled, she kissed him lightly, on the cheek.

"Exactly! And Rose and Daisy will think so, too, when we tell them."

"Well, maybe, Mack. I'll have to admit, though, I waited to tell them till now so we won't have to listen to all their reasons why we shouldn't go, since we'll be leaving next Friday. And you're sure you've got everything done?"

"Of course." Mack feigned insult. "That's one of the many advantages in being married to a lawyer, Laura. Things get handled efficiently."

When Mack knocked on the bookstore door the next day to take them to lunch, Rose, Laura, and Daisy were ready to leave.

"Locked up early?" Mack raised an eyebrow at Daisy. He felt vaguely uncomfortable as he looked at her beaming face. Rose also looked like she knew some kind of happy secret. Laura gave a slight shrug.

"Yes, we aren't invited out all that often, in case you haven't noticed, and we want to beat the crowd to the steak house."

Laura's eyes danced, giving Mack a look from behind Daisy's back.

"Well, head 'em up, move 'em out." Mack herded them toward the door.

"It couldn't be curiosity that got you into high gear, could it?" Mack winked at Laura on the way to the car, still teasing Daisy.

"Just drive, counselor," Daisy commanded, getting into the back seat beside Rose.

They chose a table toward the back with no one seated near it, while Mack stood in line to order their steaks. Laura waited for Mack to make their announcement.

Three pairs of eyes turned to him when he joined them.

"I won't keep you in suspense, since I'm hungry and you

more than are about to pop with curiosity. I've got another freebie, girls. But this one is not a mere meal. It's a lot bigger and more exciting."

Rose and Daisy looked at each other, obviously puzzled. "A freebie? A big something?" Rose began.

"Just what are you up to, Mack?" Daisy pinned him down. "Has this freebie got some kind of catch to it?"

"No, no catch. One of the businesses I am on retainer for gifted me with a trip for two to Hawaii, and I'm taking Laura with me." He winced as Laura's foot connected with his shin under the table. "Best hotels and food, double beds and an ocean view . . ." Mack kept reciting the list of goodies as Rose and Daisy simply sat in silence, wide eyes on him.

"I think it's customary to get married before you go on a honeymoon, Mack." Daisy's expression was stern. Rose just seemed stricken and sat quietly. "Aren't you afraid of what people will say?"

"What people?" Laura asked. "We're not telling anyone but you two."

"But things like this get around," Rose said softly.

"No. No, they won't, dear. And this is only a free trip to a convention," Laura explained patiently. "Also, I think you can trust us." She smiled. "There's a double suite complete with dressing room, as well as a view and by the time we get back to our suite at night we'll be hunting rest, not playing hide and seek with each other. This is really a nice thing his customer has given Mack, congratulations are in order."

"Oh. Yes." Rose swallowed, still uncomfortable. "Congratulations, Mack."

"I guess so," Daisy said, looking anything but happy about it.

"Oh." Laura looked up with relief at the server. "Here are our steaks."

"Of course, I'll still be proposing to Laura right on schedule."

Mack looked at Daisy. "I guess I could also point out how convenient it would be for her to say yes while we're there and save us a bundle—"

Daisy cracked up. "You are a bright one, counselor." Daisy laughed so hard there were tears in her eyes as she pictured Mack using this latest excuse to propose to Laura. Rose looked happier too. "When's the happy day?" Daisy demanded.

"It will be Friday. This coming Friday." With a glance at Daisy, Mack anticipated her next question. "We will be leaving early in the morning and the return trip has an arrival date in the dead of night, like Laura's did. So even though there's nothing to be ashamed of, no one will know of our good fortune."

"Except the two of you," Laura finished.

Daisy was the first to find her voice. "That's as it should be. By the way, this steak is done just right."

Mack laughed. "Daisy, if you'd been twenty years younger, Laura wouldn't have had a chance!"

"Sure. I believe that. You ever consider selling used cars?"

"Enough of this character assassination. Our steaks will get cold."

"I've always wanted to go to Hawaii," Mack said, looking like a little boy working on his Christmas wish list.

"So have I," Laura agreed. "We'll bring you back coconuts or a breadfruit plant, or something native to Hawaii," Laura promised.

"We'll leave Friday after our dinner that night and come back the next Sunday after the dinner hour. After we get back, the four of us can start on the cabin."

"I guess it's a good thing sometimes to have a lawyer to arrange things . . ." Daisy mumbled, giving Mack a speculative look.

"That's just what Mack's been telling me. That and all his other good points." Laura laughed.

Chapter Twenty-Five

Life went on like a bubbling, busy wave, cresting over the deeper current of Laura's feelings. Her logical, sane, good sense told her it was time to get on with her life and think of Daisy and Rose and Mack, and make a life for herself somehow. That logic was banished from her bedroom nightly by the ghosts from Isla Verde that transported her to the vivid scenes of its tropical, enchanting splendor. And into Esteban's arms. Arms that were no longer Laura's, but Amparo's, Laura kept reminding herself.

Sometimes she read to occupy her mind, or found something that needed doing in the house, to make her tired enough to sleep soundly.

She knew there would be plenty to keep her busy if she and Mack married. She would have to make a home for them and, and then there was her work at the bookstore. And they'd also have fixing up the cabin to look forward to. The counting of good things always helped at first, but faded as she got sleepy, and the Isla Verde ghosts came creeping back.

She smiled, thinking of Mack and his list of good points. All of which he kept reminding her. *I'll never forget Esteban, no matter how good a life Mack and I might have together. But after telling him that every time he proposed, I'll keep it to myself now. Just me and my own little ghosts.*

Thursday night she got together everything she wanted to take with her to Hawaii.

She suddenly realized she hadn't bought anything new for this trip. And it didn't matter a bit. This was to be a pleasure trip with no responsibilities. She paused, looking at the clothes she was considering. *Mack hasn't seen some of these.* She smiled to herself. Her guilt about the trip finally fading away at the thought of how pleased Mack was at getting the trip from his client. She walked over to a chest as she thought about what to take that would be comfortable—and looked at the yellow sweat suit in the open drawer.

I'll leave you here with the ghosts and get back with you. She addressed it as if it had a personality of its own, unprepared for the kaleidoscope memory of Esteban's face, his smiles, his laughter, his brows drawn together, the little hint of amusement that would suddenly appear. Her heart knew them all.

She closed the drawer softly, as if she didn't want to hurt it. She put together what she thought would be practical and comfortable. Everything was ready for the trip but her.

She sat down in the old rocking chair. She wrapped the shawl around her, tears falling unheeded down her cheeks, and sat looking out into the night.

Where are you, Esteban? Are you finding it as hard to go on without me as I am to be without you? I wonder who sent that message that was so urgent. That message and its urgency had been real; she was certain of that. Whatever it was about, it was a summons Esteban couldn't refuse. It could have been from her, from the beautiful, dark-haired girl whose hand he was holding in that picture Laura saw in the paper. Amparo. Esteban's Amparo.

She sat worrying at the puzzle, knowing she would never find the answer, until she was tired enough to sleep. She never thought once about the coming day as her eyes closed and the soft whispers returned.

"*Te amo.*" The Isla Verde ghosts repeated it in Esteban's voice,

Stranger in Paradise

softly, lovingly, bearing her back to their enchanted island.

Laura could hardly believe it was Friday already. The tile floor of the shower was cold to her feet as she tentatively felt the warm water. Her day had gone so fast. She refused to go home early to change and get ready. The time had passed so fast! She took a deep breath and stretched, as if bracing for this pleasure trip as if it was no pleasure at all. She bit her lip, determined to have a good time so Mack would enjoy the trip too.

She knew herself well enough to know her nerves were caused by the feeling she was making a mistake going on this trip with him, no matter what Mack continually said to allay her doubts and fears. He was still proposing on a regular basis. She closed her eyes and stepped under the shower. She had plenty of time. Her heart warmed, thinking of him. Good, patient, methodical Mack, with all their plans made.

I'm going to do my best to have a good time so Mack will too. I just hope I can manage to keep all my little Isla Verde voices hidden so I won't make him unhappy.

Laura frowned, her eyes closed under the flood of warm water, doubts crowding in again. The shower couldn't drown them. *This is all happening so fast. Rose and Daisy don't think this is a good idea, but they're still hoping I'll change my mind and say yes to Mack. But I've got no intention at all of marrying Mack—or anyone else, for that matter.*

Laura remembered some of the dates she'd had in high school and in the junior college she went to before Sophie got sick. She laughed, picturing those young men now plumper, bald, aging, anniversary after anniversary.

She stood under the water's warmth, conjuring up Esteban's face, the feel of his arms around her. She sighed in the silent, empty house, remembering when Esteban had pulled her into the shower with him, clothes and all. Her smile turned to tears and joined the warm flow of the water until she quickly turned off the faucet and stepped out, rubbing herself vigorously with the towel, scrubbing away the water from her scalp as if she could remove the memories too.

She tossed the towel aside and concentrated on getting her things ready to go.

She chose a tailored suit to wear. One that would make her look like the beloved of a prominent attorney, who would later be a judge. She laid everything out. Everything was planned, down to hose and the purse she would carry. It was all ready. Everything but Laura was ready.

Now, the mask, she told herself sarcastically. *I'll use everything Pierre sold me except the eye shadow, and put on a happy face. I am happy. Mack is a good person, my best friend and fun to be with. On our silver wedding anniversary, if we have one, I'll more than likely look back and wonder why I ever hesitated.*

But she would remember Esteban; she knew that, too.

Laura put both hands on her cheeks as tears threatened. *No, no more tears. Mack and I will soon be on our way to Hawaii. That's better.* Her reflection smiled back at her.

Mack came for her a few minutes early. Daisy and Rose were already in the car. Mack had insisted on taking them and picking them up. All of them were unaware Laura went through the motions like a robot, doing everything, but feeling not much of anything.

The dinner must have gone well, since nothing happened to catch Laura's attention. She felt as if she'd been in some sort of daze and didn't remember much about it. Part of her didn't seem to believe it was happening. She felt pleasantly full and refused dessert. Mack said something about holding out for pineapple and coconut.

She woke again to reality when they took Rose and Daisy home. She hugged each of them and said goodbye. She waved

Stranger in Paradise

to them through the window as Mack pulled away from the curb.

Laura realized Mack was talking as if he were as nervous as she was.

"We'll leave the car at the airport. It won't cost much more than a cab, and we'll have it there when we get back." Mack made more small talk as he drove.

She wondered if he felt as unreal as she did, or the nerves were just because Mack was hoping Hawaii would be the magic setting and she would finally agree to marry him.

It's not going to happen, Laura promised herself.

She nodded absently, watching the scenery go by in a blur. She tried to concentrate on the cabin. On happy things, things they were both looking forward to. Good things and a good life together. Together and as good friends as they had always been. Why couldn't Mack see that Kara Kolivas cared for him? And her father, judging by the way Kolivas always watched Mack, was hoping as much for Mack to court Kara as Daisy and Rose were hoping for her to accept one of those many proposals Mack was vowing to make until she said yes.

Suddenly, Laura pictured Mack standing at the cabin's pier with Kara Kolivas, watching three or four dark-haired children pulling in trout and laughing. Then the scene was gone, and there was Esteban in the little park on Isla Verde, his arms making a cradle as he tried to ask her if she liked children.

Laura bit her lip, her heart aching at the thought of the children she would never have with Esteban. She nodded and made little agreeable sounds as Mack talked. But what Laura heard was, "What are you doing?" Something outraged shouted it from her subconscious. She turned a deaf ear.

"You haven't had much to say," Mack observed as he parked his car at the airport.

Laura didn't answer immediately. Getting their bags from the trunk, he asked, "Not getting cold feet, are you?"

"I don't know," came her honest answer. "It's natural to give serious thought to how other people will look at what you do and make judgments, whether they're right or not. Maybe people will believe this is 'more than business,' this going to Hawaii together."

"No one with good sense will." He grinned. "If they threaten to tar and feather us when we get back, maybe you'll feel sorry for me and make an honest man of me?"

Laura laughed. She was saved from any further comment by the arrival of a small plane. "Is that our commuter plane?" She quickly fell into step beside him.

"Must be." Mack eyed the little plane landing on the runway. "We'll be on a big, comfortable one soon. But you took this one before, didn't you?"

"Yes, it's the same one." Laura smiled. "I'll never forget how glad I was to see you and Daisy and Rose when I got here."

Mack smiled at her, looking happy again. "You just go up, eat a bag of peanuts, then go back down." They laughed together. "That's more like it. Hang onto that smile and your sense of humor and I'll handle the rest."

Laura hurried her steps, keeping up with Mack's long legs.

The little plane was full. People were reading or napping.

Laura wondered briefly where they were all going. Then, tiring of the view of fleecy clouds, and glossy ads in the airline's magazines, Laura laid her head back and closed her eyes while Mack read.

"I love you—I'll be back." The refrain haunted her, vibrant and full of promise as ever. Laura saw Esteban's face, his smile, and his eyes full of love for her.

I'll never forget you, Esteban, her heart promised him as the little plane took her toward a larger plane and another life without him.

Stranger in Paradise

The pilot's voice roused her from sleep. She clutched Mack's hand.

"We're circling the field—"

The next lap of the trip was as uneventful, but Laura and Mack's excitement made it more enjoyable.

"I've always wanted to go to Hawaii," Mack told her as the big plane landed. "We'll look at the brochures and tour and see everything," he promised, holding her hand.

Both of them looked around at everything at the airport like the tourists they were. Mack's excitement was catching. He claimed their luggage as Laura looked around. "The hotel has a van, I'm sure."

"Never mind, we'll get a cab and go on. I hate to wait. How do you vote?"

"I'm with you on that, counselor." Laura took the overnight case and followed him as he walked toward the doors with their suitcases, a happy grin on his face.

"We had a choice of lodging, the convention is so big. The hotel I chose is farther out than the main drag," Mack said as they settled into the taxi. "It has beautiful beaches around it and it's a regular palace, the way the agent described it." He grinned, "But then, I doubt any of them would sound like flea bags in the agent's office, even the flea bags."

"Look, Mack!" Laura pointed out the window. "We may not be on the main drag, but we must be going down it. Did you ever see so many temptations? I wish I had two necks, two heads, and at least four eyes!"

He patted her hand. "We'll see it all, I promise."

As they got farther out, the road paralleled lovely sandy beaches, the waves breaking on the shore and rocks at the edge of the water.

"It's like I thought it would be, only better." Mack's head swiveled, looking at the scenery as she had the shops.

"That's beautiful, too," she said quietly, gesturing at the hotel when it came in sight ahead of them.

"The agent called it 'palacio.' It does look like a palace, doesn't it?"

Laura's heart turned over. "It looks like the palacio on Isla Verde," she breathed.

"The agent said it was the most luxurious lodging here, and it must be." Mack was impressed. "You say it looks like the one on Isla Verde? Must be coincidence. Surely nothing like this could be a chain."

When the cab stopped at the entrance, they were immediately surrounded by uniformed employees who opened the doors and took care of their luggage. Laura scanned the smiles that looked like toothpaste ads, wondering about what Mack had said about a chain.

"I'm impressed. A regular hive of service." The service was as good as it had been on Isla Verde.

"Me too. It's going to be a good week." Mack winked at her.

Laura stood waiting, wondering about the hotel as Mack registered for them. She heard a sharp intake of breath and turned to see an older man in a jacket with the hotel's logo on it. He was the older clerk—or was he the manager—who was at the palacio on Isla Verde. Could he be?

For a second they stared at each other. She started to speak to him, intending to ask if this hotel was owned by the same people or chain as the one on Isla Verde. However, the man recovered himself quickly, and without acknowledging her friendly smile, he hurried away when someone beckoned to him from the office door. He only stopped a moment behind the uniformed desk clerk, who was about to talk to Mack, and then he was gone. He didn't look back.

When he finished registering, Mack turned to Laura. "We're on the eleventh floor with a balcony and a view of the ocean. I didn't realize there was so much identification required. I think I gave them everything but a footprint."

Laura shrugged. "Something to do with security, I suppose. This is a pretty expensive place, so they would certainly have good security. As if I traveled that much." Laura laughed at herself.

"That older clerk who passed by was working at Isla Verde when I was there. I was going to speak to him, but I guess he either didn't recognize me or maybe he thinks I'm a trouble maker."

"Trouble maker?" Mack asked in surprise.

"He's the one who came out and gave me the room I had for two more weeks when I called home to say I was staying longer. A younger clerk had told me the room was not available, that it was already reserved. But the older man came out and let me keep the room I had."

Mack chuckled. "Trouble maker, are you? Great. I wouldn't want to spend my week in Hawaii in dull company."

Their room was all that the agent had promised and a lot like the one Laura had in Isla Verde, though arranged a bit differently.

With mixed feelings, Laura looked around. She had taken her overnight case into the bathroom to make sure nothing had spilled or broken, when she heard a knock on the door.

"Laura," Mack called.

She emerged to see Mack take a large, decorated fruit basket from a man in the hotel's uniform.

"This fruit basket is compliments of the hotel, and these tickets." He held them up. "They're for a tour of one of the parks. He said the tour's just started, but we can go in a van and meet the tour at the park, if you want to go."

"Yes, let's do. It may be one of those that have the lava rocks I've heard about. Anyway, I'm sure it will be interesting."

Mack turned to the boy. "Thank you. We will be down in just a few minutes."

The boy nodded, expressionless, and left. Laura wondered fleetingly, if he understood much English.

"Should we grab slacks and a sweater, or just go as we are?"

"We'll probably be in a tram or something," Mack reasoned. "But maybe slacks just in case?"

"Okay, I'll slip on these lower heels, too, and I'm ready to go."

The boy who had given them the tickets was waiting for them in the lobby and beckoned to them. They followed him out a side door and he held a van door open for them. The toothpaste smile was gone, the ageless brown face bland and expressionless.

Somehow, his face gave Laura a twinge. Or maybe management just told the help to smile at the tourists on the way in? She promptly forgot about it as they settled into the van.

Laura and Mack sat in the middle seats of the van. The driver wore the hotel's uniform, and a man in a t-shirt sat beside him. Behind them sat a large man in a dark suit.

"That one in the back looks like a wrestler in a business suit." Laura spoke to Mack softly, bending to inspect her shoe.

"I noticed." Mack spoke just as softly, not looking back. "Wrestlers have to have vacations too, I guess," he whispered with a grin and a slight shrug.

Laura and Mack enjoyed the scenery on the way to the park and admired the entrance as they went in.

"I wonder where we're going to meet the tour." Laura looked up the winding road. Their van was the only traffic on it.

"I don't know, but we seem to be stopping," Mack observed. He started stretching his long legs. "This must be a scenic overlook or a historic place."

Laura turned back to get her purse before following him. As

she started to walk to where Mack was gazing across the valley, she saw the man in the t-shirt take Mack's arm and with his other hand, quickly press something to his face.

"What—"

As she started to speak, Laura felt her arms suddenly seized from behind. Before she could cry out, something came down over the lower part of her face, covering her nose and mouth. Unable to move, her knees buckled as darkness descended.

As consciousness returned, Laura felt as if she was waking in the night. In the dark, uncomfortable and disoriented, she heard a low moan.

She realized the sound had come from her, but she couldn't get her mouth to work. Her eyes were open, but it was dark. She moved her head and her neck hurt. She moved her head back and forth, wondering what was wrong with it and her neck. Where was she?

Then she remembered getting out of the van in the park and seeing the man in the t-shirt holding something up to Mack's face. She tried to open her mouth to call out to Mack.

What? I can't move my lips!

As Laura struggled, she became aware of light filtering in around a door. She was in some sort of small building. She tried in vain to move her arms and legs and heard a whimpering noise somewhere close by.

She peered into the near dark, able to see better now. She saw Mack. He was sitting in a straight chair, as she must be. His arms and legs were tied, and duct tape was across his mouth.

"Mphs, muphs."

Sounds came from Mack as he tried to get her attention.

The sight of Mack close by brought a rush of relief. Laura strained her eyes to see better. At least he was alive and he was there with her. She peered at him in the near dark. His eyes were open, too. He was looking back at her.

But where were they? She looked around the room. There was no one there but the two of them, sitting there all tied up.

We must be in some kind of shelter in the park. And tied up to make sure we stay put.

Her frightened eyes returned to Mack. *We've been kidnapped!*

Chapter Twenty-Six

Laura tried in vain to open her mouth, to loosen the duct tape. She moved her legs a little. The ropes were tight enough to hold them and her arms and wrists securely without biting into her flesh—if she didn't struggle.

After rubbing raw places on her wrists, she stopped and took a deep breath. So much for that. Whoever had tied them up had sure known how to do it properly. She cringed at the thought. Had they been attacked by professional gangsters? She looked over at Mack.

Mack nodded vigorously, obviously trying to get her attention. So far, so good. She knew he was alert and watching, and they both seemed to be all right, other than being tied so securely. He bobbed his head again and she bobbed hers in answer.

There's not much we can do except be glad we're both alive and conscious. Why would anyone want to kidnap us? This kind of thing doesn't happen to anyone but spies and billionaires. It doesn't make sense.

Her eyes continued to search the near darkness. The place was some kind of little hut, perhaps a maintenance hut on the park grounds. *It smells earthy, too.* Laura's nose twitched.

There was a shovel and some other tools against the wall. She wondered briefly if they were going to kill them both and bury them.

She quickly discarded that idea. This place had all the

earmarks of some kind of utility shed where they wouldn't be found. There was a door on the back wall, so there was another room to the place. The door with the light coming in around it was the outside door.

It's still light outside. What's that?

The noise that made her jump was the sound of running water. Someone was there. She heard water run again briefly, as if someone were washing his hands. Then there were little slapping sounds, like someone patting water on his face to wash or cool off.

Laura raised her head as the outside door opened. The light was blocked as someone came in. It was the man from the van who sat in front with the driver and was wearing the t-shirt.

T-shirt saw that Laura was awake. Bending down, the man gave her a look so sensual and evil, it made her cringe.

A sound made her turn her attention to the door at the back of the shed, where the washing sounds had come from. The man from Isla Verde came through it.

He must have been there in the back room all the time. So, he's a crook of some kind. Maybe they fired him at Isla Verde, is why he's here. He saw the way that other man looked at me, too. His face looks as stormy as Esteban's did when I asked about my room. Laura's eyes took in everything, and she held her breath.

The Isla Verde man nailed the man in the t-shirt with his sharp gaze. He made a growling noise and drew his finger quickly across his throat. Laura watched the threat, frightened of both men. However, the Isla Verde man's threat took the dangerous ideas out of t-shirt's head. He paid no more attention to Laura or Mack.

The Isla Verde man came to stand before Laura. He spoke very politely in English. "I am very sorry, *Senora*. You will not have to be here long, and no harm will come to you. You will be safe."

Stranger in Paradise

Your idea of safe must be a lot different from mine. Laura couldn't speak, but her eyes glared back at him. He simply turned away without saying anything else.

Isla Verde and t-shirt disappeared into the back room again.

Laura wouldn't have known what to say to those two bandits even if she'd been able to talk. She shivered now as much with anger as with fright at how helpless she and Mack were.

And Isla Verde calls me Senora. *I noticed that before. What an addlebrained thing to notice at a time like this. The young clerk on Isla Verde called me* Senorita *when I phoned to ask about the pearls and when I asked him about the room, but this man always, from the time he told me I could keep the room, has called me* Senora . . .

Laura's eyes found Mack. Surely he had heard what was said, she thought. The man said they wouldn't be here long and would be safe.

I wonder if they're trying to figure out where to send a ransom note. She felt hysterical laughter rise in the back of her throat at how foolish the thought of ransom was.

Time passed slowly in their dark prison. Mack nodded from time to time, and Laura nodded back to let him know she was all right, or at least conscious.

As the hours dragged by, Mack varied his nods by tilting his head, and Laura answered, aping the tilts and limited gestures. *That's about as close as we can get to meaningful conversation, I guess.* She tried to move a little to keep from getting stiff.

Laura wondered impatiently how long it would take those two bandits to figure out neither she nor Mack had any money—or even anyone to send a ransom note to.

Or maybe they think they can blackmail the hotel into paying them something. Who knows what people like this might think of to try?

Darkness finally took over outside, too, and t-shirt entered the room to plug a little night light into an outlet in the wall. It didn't make a good light, but forms in the room were as visible as they had been with sunlight coming in the cracks around the door. Laura wondered why they worried about light, since the park must surely be deserted at night.

A movement caught her eye. Mack was trying to move a little as she had been doing, apparently with no more success.

Later, Isla Verde came back and signaled for t-shirt to precede him out the shed's door. Laura held her breath until she heard the motor of a car.

The van must have been out there. She was glad Isla Verde took t-shirt with him.

Laura immediately began trying to loosen the ropes, as did Mack, ignoring scrapes as she worked hard to move her hands and her legs. She even attempted chewing at the tape with a vague idea of yelling for help the next day if she heard people nearby. They hadn't made any headway at all when they heard the van returning.

The shed door opened. T-shirt held it for Isla Verde, who was carrying a tray.

He'd brought food.

Maybe they will untie us. Hope leaped in Laura's heart.

Isla Verde stationed t-shirt beside him and began untying Mack. He retied Mack's hands in front of him and led him back to the other room.

Exercise and the necessary, Laura thought contemptuously as her eyes blazed at t-shirt, warning him not to come any closer to her.

Something like surprised admiration crossed t-shirt's face as he read the contempt in Laura's eyes. He looked away, waiting for Isla Verde to return.

Isla Verde returned with Mack and pointed to the chair. He retied Mack to it, testing the ropes before he signaled t-shirt to bring the tray.

Setting the tray down, t-shirt held up a hamburger for Mack to take bites. Mack ate the burger, but refused the water he was offered. He nodded acceptance and drank from a bottled coke.

Checking Mack's ropes again, their captors turned toward Laura.

Oh, it's my turn, is it?

Isla Verde untied Laura's ropes. Then, taking a firm grip on her arm, he led her to the back room.

There was another night light in the little lavatory and enough light for Laura to see. She was grateful that the place was clean. She relieved herself while she could and took time to stretch her arms and legs before going back out.

She was led back to the chair, seated, and retied. T-shirt brought the tray with another hamburger on it. When he reached for it, Isla Verde held up his hand. He picked up the hamburger himself, and offered to Laura.

That smells so good. Laura swallowed, her mouth watering at the scent. *I'm as hungry as I ever remember being, but I won't give him the satisfaction!* She turned her head away.

Isla Verde tried four times to get Laura to eat, looking more worried each time she refused. Finally he said in a pleading tone of voice, "Please, *Senora*, I have brought this for you and the bottled cola so you would not be afraid to drink. I mean you no harm. Please, eat."

Laura regarded him steadily, not understanding how he could think she would cooperate with them in any way. Again, she turned her head.

With a sigh, Isla Verde stood up. Still holding the tray the sandwich was on, he talked in low tones in Spanish with t-shirt and then someone who stood just outside the door.

Getting a glimpse of a muscular shape, Laura wondered if the other person was the wrestler in the suit.

Isla Verde left in the van, leaving t-shirt on guard. Laura and

Mack went back to nodding occasionally until sleep claimed them.

Laura woke, her neck sore from her head hanging forward as she slept. She tried nodding, but got no answering nod from Mack. T-shirt was sleeping, his dark head leaning back against the wall. Laura struggled with her ropes until she felt one of her wrists bleeding freely, stinging the already sore areas.

She tried moving the chair. It did no good but did wake Mack up. He nodded twice, quickly. She nodded back.

T-shirt woke and rubbed his face, squinting at them as he stood, looking soberly from Mack to Laura as he stretched.

Maybe it's finally dawning on him what he's doing, and what the consequences will be.

She watched him from the corner of her eye. She sure didn't want to attract his attention, Laura thought uneasily. *It must be morning. I see pale light coming in the cracks.*

She heard the sound of a motor, and a few minutes later there was a furtive knock at the door. T-shirt opened it to admit Isla Verde.

He glanced uneasily at Laura and then went to Mack. He released him for a trip to the lavatory, then tied him up again before picking up a covered dish.

As soon as the tape was taken off Mack's mouth, he said quickly, "Laura! Please! Do eat! You've got to keep your strength up. When he brings the food, please eat."

Isla Verde turned to Laura and nodded agreement. He fed Mack scrambled eggs and bacon, slowly and carefully.

Scrambled eggs and bacon. Oh, that smells so good. Laura's lips felt dry as Isla Verde approached her. Mack would have urged her again to eat in order to keep up her strength, but Isla Verde had replaced the tape.

"Please, *Senora,* to eat this good food I have brought for

you." Isla Verde said it humbly, raising the fork toward her dry lips.

Laura shook her head.

"I have brought hot coffee, and it has the one spoon of sugar in it, as you like it," Isla Verde added hopefully.

Surprised, Laura's eyes met his. "You remembered that I like one spoon of sugar?"

"*Si,* and it is hot. You will like it." He smiled kindly.

He lifted the cup carefully to her lips, and Laura sipped a little of the coffee. He had told the truth; it was just the way she always drank it with the honeyed rolls. But after tasting it, she turned away.

"It is not to your liking?" Isla Verde was puzzled.

"Yes. The coffee is fine. But I am here, and so is Mack, against our will. You have kidnapped us, and I will not cooperate with you." Her eyes flashed. "Do you know the consequences of—"

With an audible sigh, Isla Verde put down the cup and replaced the tape on Laura's mouth. He looked sadder and more worried than she was.

I'm almost sorry for the poor wretch, she fumed in her forced silence. *But that's silly. He deserves whatever's coming to him.*

Isla Verde left, and the day finally gave way to another dark night. Isla Verde again brought food. Mack ate; Laura would not.

The next day, on the usual trip to the necessary, Laura almost fell on the way back. Nothing seemed real to her anymore. Not the strange, dark surroundings, or the times when she felt she was floating in a daydream or struggling helplessly in a nightmare.

It's the inactivity, Laura reasoned. *I must appear as unreal as I feel, judging by the way Isla Verde keeps looking at me. Well, good! I hope it scares the juice out of him. Serves him right. I'll bet they did fire him on Isla Verde.*

Mack heard her chuckle to herself. Dismayed, afraid her condition was even worse than he feared, he watched helplessly as her head drooped forward and she slept again.

By the next night, Laura needed help rising from her chair. She fell against Isla Verde when she came out of the lavatory. She heard him shouting something in Spanish to t-shirt, but she didn't know what it was, and she didn't care. Somewhere between waking and sleeping, she felt her back being eased onto a mattress instead of the chair.

Must be the little cot by the lavatory, she thought. It felt better. Much better. Almost like the big bed on the boat. Esteban's friend's boat. A pleasant memory . . .

She floated, smiling to herself. "I love you—I'll be back." She murmured the words softly, realizing the tape was gone from her mouth as the dream claimed her.

Mack could only sit and worry. Laura had not returned from the lavatory. The shouting in Spanish was all Mack could hear from the back room. He didn't understand what it was all about, and they didn't tell him anything.

I've got to do something! Mack tried to move, to make a noise, to move the chair. Nothing worked. He watched helplessly, raging against the tape on his mouth as Isla Verde left.

Laura! Oh, God! Laura!

Light coming in the cracks of the shed woke Mack.

It was morning. He felt like he'd hung from the ceiling all night.

Mack's gaze went to the empty chair across from him. He strained his ears, trying to catch any sound from the next room to reassure him. There was none.

There were no signs of the two guards, either. They were either gone or standing watch outside. Laura must be too weak from not eating to be brought back in to sit in a chair as he was.

Mack clenched his fists. *If anything happens to her—*

He struggled frantically with his ropes in spite of sore wrists, until he heard the purr of a motor outside.

Mack's brow drew together. He tilted his head, listening. That car didn't sound like the van.

The motor stopped and he heard voices outside, approaching the door. He couldn't understand what they were saying. He stared intently as the door opened to admit three men, the morning light behind them. To his strained eyes, they appeared as tall, dark shapes, and they moved with an air of authority.

Inside and closer to him, Mack saw the men were wearing conservative but expensive-looking suits. When they spoke to each other, Mack realized they were speaking Spanish.

Mack's heart contracted at the looks of the expensive suits and the Italian shoes.

These aren't park employees, that's for sure. Mack's sarcasm surfaced in spite of his pain. *We must have stumbled into a drug deal or something. These are not on the same rung of the social ladder as those we've been dealing with, not in those three hundred dollar suits. What is this?*

One of the men leaned down to look into Mack's face in the dim light. Their eyes met briefly. The man rose. He gestured to the other two to watch Mack, and he entered the back room.

"*Laura!*"

Chapter Twenty-Seven

Mack jumped at the sound of that voice, which bounced off the walls in the small space.

The cry that came from the back room was filled with such anguish that Mack was shaken, a chill running down his backbone.

Dear God! Let her be all right! Why did he cry out like that? And he knows her name! He called her name—

"Arturo! Miguel! *Aqui!*"

Instantly, the other two men disappeared into the back room. Mack heard their voices. There was a low conversation in what Mack thought was Spanish. The older one, with a bit of white above his ears, came out and glanced briefly with cold eyes at Mack. He passed on, going outside.

Looks like the chairman of the board for whatever this group is, was the thought that went through Mack's mind as he stared back at the man.

In the other room, Laura opened her eyes a little and looked at the man beside the cot. He had touched her dry lips with his fingers. He wet them with cool water, tracing them as he spoke softly to her.

"Laura, my Laura, *mi corazon*. It is Esteban, I am back. I have found you, *querida*." He kissed the hand he held and pressed it to his cheek.

Laura couldn't see very well in the dimness. She knew only that someone was there, kneeling beside her.

Stranger in Paradise

"I . . . I thought I heard . . . But no, it couldn't be. It's not Esteban's voice." She sighed. "I must be dreaming again."

"No, no, I am here. I am Esteban, I am here, Laura."

"Esteban?" She breathed softly, hopefully. "Esteban?"

Then her eyes closed again. "No," she told him sadly. "You are not Esteban. Esteban left me. He is gone."

"Laura, *querida,* I am here," he insisted. He bent to kiss her dry lips, her cheeks. He buried his face in her hair, nuzzling her neck. "I love you, Laura, and you will be all right. We have a car outside to take you back to the hotel. They said you wouldn't eat. But we will get some food to nourish you and make you strong again."

Laura did not answer or open her eyes again. Concerned, he leaned closer. "I am here. You will be well and strong again. I have been searching for you."

Laura sighed, not opening her eyes. "No. No. You are not my Esteban. My Esteban could not speak English. No. You are not my Esteban."

Brushing her hair back, Esteban kissed her forehead and laid his head beside her on the bed.

"Esteban," a voice called from the door.

Esteban rose and spoke briefly to the other man in Spanish, then turned back to Laura. He bent and picked her up in his arms.

In the outer room, one of the other men cut the ropes off Mack and then held the outside door for Esteban.

Mack stood up, stretching and rubbing the muscles in his arms and legs. One of the men stood watching him as Mack jerked the tape from his mouth.

Mack went out and joined the other two men and Laura in the car, glancing at the leather interior of the limo. As he sat down, he looked at Laura. The man who had stopped to peer into his face when they came in was holding Laura in his arms, cradling her head against his chest.

"I am Esteban Aguilar," he told Mack uncertainly.

"The Esteban Laura met on Isla Verde?"

"Yes." His eyes met Mack's. "She spoke to you of me?"

"Yes. She said you deserted her a few days before she was to come home. You never called or tried to reach her or give her any explanation." Mack gave him a severe look. "She took that pretty hard."

"I told her I would come back, and I did. But when I returned, she was gone. I've been looking for her ever since."

He seemed to feel his guilt so keenly, Mack could almost grant him a little sympathy. But only almost. *No jury would believe that story,* he thought. *And Laura won't either.*

"Laura said she had told you about the bookstore, and that she was from Greenfield. You could have looked on the hotel register. That shouldn't have been so hard to do," Mack accused, remembering Laura's sad face in the moonlight at the cabin when she talked about Esteban.

"Yes, she told me of the bookstore. And of her Aunt Sophie, and about her home in Greenfield."

"Well?" Mack folded his arms.

"Whoever did the registration put only Greenfield, USA as her origin. There was no state or street address or any further information." Esteban paused. "Do you have any idea how many Greenfields there are in the USA?"

"Hmm." Mack began to see the problem. "Quite a few, I guess. And her phone is not listed in her name yet. It's still in Sophie's, and only as the bookstore." His mind turned over the identification problem Esteban had just pointed out to him.

At that point, they pulled up to the back of the hotel and the driver opened the door for them.

Mack got out of the limo and held out his arms. "I'll take her now."

"You will not."

"We came here together." Mack pointed out.

"Get—out—of—my—way."

Esteban pushed his order through his teeth, and it was accompanied by a thunder-and-lightening expression. Mack instinctively moved aside.

Escorted by the other two men, Esteban leading the way, they made their way to a service elevator near the door.

"Our room is on the eleventh floor," Mack looked up at the directory.

"*Your* room is on the eleventh floor," Esteban corrected him firmly.

As they passed the eleventh floor, Esteban still tenderly holding Laura, Mack spoke again, slowly, so he was sure Esteban would understand.

"Laura and I came here together. I was hoping she would accept my proposal of marriage while we're here. I'm an attorney and clients of mine gave me this trip to their company convention. We came here together, as I told you."

"You may have come together, but you will go back to Greenfield by yourself. I have searched all over for Laura and now I've found her. She won't be going back with you."

The elevator stopped at the penthouse and Esteban stepped out with Laura. The other two men stopped, eyeing Mack.

"Let him come," Esteban said without turning.

"Well, thank you," Mack said sarcastically to Esteban's back. He followed him to a bedroom where Esteban carefully laid Laura down on the king-sized bed.

"Stay here with her," he ordered Mack. "And you, watch him," Esteban told the other man who had entered the room with them. With that, he disappeared through the bedroom door.

Chapter Twenty-Eight

Mack sat down in a nearby chair, his attention on Laura.

The man Esteban had told to watch him spoke quietly. "I am Miguel, Esteban's brother. The other man with us is our older brother, Arturo."

"Miguel," Mack acknowledged. "My name is M. L. McKinley. Mack. I am going to marry Laura. We came here together," he stated positively.

Miguel averted his gaze. Mack felt his stony silence more keenly than any comment he might have made.

Esteban returned, followed by a man in a white coat who carried a tray. Esteban sat down on the side of the bed, and raising Laura in his arms, began piling pillows behind her. Mack saw what he was doing and came around to the other side to help. He watched as Esteban slowly fed a rich looking broth to Laura. As he fed her, Esteban talked softly to her.

When she opened her mouth to question or deny him, he put in more of the broth. She had nearly finished the bowl and Mack, watching her, could see her eyes were clear and her color was better.

After the broth, the houseman brought a small bowl of ice cream with a layer of whipped cream on top. Esteban fed her this more slowly, still talking to her.

"Do you remember how rich the chocolate and ice cream is on Isla Verde? I have some here for you."

"Esteban? It really is you, isn't it?" She reached up to touch his face.

"Yes, *querida*. I've been looking for you ever since I came back and found you had gone."

He handed the houseman the empty bowl and held a warm cup of chocolate to her lips. "Drink this and rest, and we will talk more later."

Laura obediently drank the chocolate, and then lay back, exhausted. Esteban reached under the coverlet to remove her shoes.

He rose, looking down at her as she drifted off to sleep. He beckoned to Mack as he went toward the door.

Mack followed him to the kitchen. His hands on his hips, Mack spoke. "I'm sure you must have guessed by now, it will take more than all three of you to get me out of here. I love Laura. We've been friends for over twenty years."

Alone in the kitchen, they stood face-to-face, Mack and Esteban.

Esteban observed the stubborn jut of Mack's chin, and his stance that said he would not be moved. Esteban's features softened as he spoke.

"I would do the same. You are welcome to stay until Laura is recovered and able to tell you herself that she is staying with me."

He turned his attention to making coffee, and set out cups for them before Mack replied. "What makes you so sure she will not want to go home with me?" He sat down, not looking at Esteban.

"I know." Esteban's voice held certainty. There was no trace of doubt in his tone or his face, when Mack looked up.

"As you said, we will wait and see what Laura has to say," Mack conceded. "I'm glad you got to us when you did," he said, changing the subject.

Esteban offered sugar for Mack's coffee, not commenting.

"Laura wouldn't eat. It was a matter of principle with her. She regarded that as cooperating with the enemy. She was so weak, she nearly fell the last time they let her get up." His face was anxious, remembering. "I tried everything I could think of to get loose. The whole thing must have been a case of mistaken identity or something."

Esteban looked out the window and picked up the remote control of a television set across from the table. After watching a weather report, he glanced at his watch. "Let us return and relieve Miguel." They took off to Laura's room.

As Miguel left the room upon their entering, Esteban gestured at the large chairs they had put beside the bed and said to Mack, "These are comfortable enough to sleep in, if you feel like it."

"I'll make it all right." Mack was torn between gratitude for Esteban's consideration and his own naturally suspicious nature.

Soon Mack and Esteban both slept. The next thing they heard was Arturo's voice.

"Fine pair of watchmen you are!" Arturo's voice was low, and he glanced at Laura as he spoke. "Ling has anything you might want for breakfast, and coffee and toast are ready."

Looking sheepish, Mack followed Esteban to the kitchen. Both of them did justice to Ling, the houseboy's, good cooking. Esteban and Arturo talked in Spanish.

Suddenly Esteban raised his hand for silence. He rose and went toward Laura's bedroom, Mack right behind him.

She was sitting up on the side of the bed, looking down at her rumpled clothing.

"What a mess I am. Esteban." She smiled up at him. "I was afraid I might have been dreaming you're here." She stretched her arms and looked around her, beginning to appear puzzled. "This is a different room, isn't it?"

Mack appeared from behind Esteban.

"Mack!"

Laura put her hands over her eyes. "Now I remember. That awful place, and sitting in those chairs." She reached out to Mack and he took her hand. "Are you all right, Mack?"

"Yes, I'm fine. You are too, now. You were weak from not eating." He sat down beside her.

Esteban sat down on the other side of her.

"We are in Miguel's apartment." Esteban gestured toward the door where Laura saw the two men. "These are my brothers, Miguel and Arturo. They have been helping me look for you."

Laura's hand found Esteban's, her eyes were haunted with guilt and worry, glancing at Mack.

"Esteban, I thought you weren't coming back." Her voice grew stronger. "You knew when I had to leave, and I had not heard from you. Then you didn't call or try to contact me after I got home."

She stopped, and meeting Esteban's eyes, said solemnly, "Esteban, Mack and I—we came here together. I will go back with him."

"No, you won't." Esteban shook his head. "You will stay here with me, now that I've found you."

"We came here together, Esteban." She blushed. "We are not lovers, but we are very good friends—"

"I know." Esteban smiled. "He says you have known each other for twenty years."

Mack watched, saying nothing until Laura turned to him.

"Mack," she began. The regret in her voice sank his hopes. "I'm sorry. I'm so sorry." A tear rolled down her cheek, but she held tightly to Esteban's hand.

It took Mack a few seconds to speak. "I guess this means you do want to stay here—with him."

"Yes. I still don't know why Esteban left, or why he didn't contact me. But he is here now, and I love him, Mack. I told you I did, remember? Please, will you try and forgive me?"

"You were honest with me. I was never misled about your feelings." Mack spoke as if they were alone together, as they had talked at the cabin. Taking a deep breath, he pressed the hand he still held. "If this is what you want, I'll arrange to go back alone. But . . ." He hesitated. "Are you sure? Don't you think it might be wise to give it some thought—"

"I'm sure, Mack."

"Then I'll arrange it." Mack faced defeat, but he was still concerned for Laura. He sat down in the wide chair from which he had watched her sleep and turned his attention to Esteban.

"Now that we have that settled—" He eyed Esteban sternly. "I have been Laura's friend, and my father and I have handled their business affairs for nearly twenty years." His attorney eyes bored into Esteban's. "I want to know why you left her."

Chapter Twenty-Nine

Laura moved, getting more comfortable on the side of the bed. This had her full attention. She watched Esteban, remembering that urgent message that had torn them apart.

"It was a family emergency," Esteban explained. "Most of our family business is very confidential." His gaze went to Laura, then to Arturo, who nodded slightly from where he stood in the doorway.

Laura saw the look. "Mack is my oldest and dearest friend. I'd trust him with my life." Laura's voice had an edge of resentment to it, which wasn't lost on either Esteban or Mack.

Mack's lips turned up, but the faint smile was grim. He waited with the air of a judge waiting for a plea.

"Have you ever heard of a mining operation called AMEA?" Esteban asked them both.

Mack hesitated, then nodded. "There was something about it on the news before we left, a brief mention. I don't remember what it was," Mack admitted.

"I saw it on the news, too," Laura said. "But whatever it was about was over before I got into the room, so I missed most of it." Laura nodded, her eyes on Esteban. "What I saw was someone showing a very large emerald that came from one of the mines the company owned."

"El Verde, one of the largest emeralds ever mined, and the most beautiful," Arturo said from the door.

Esteban nodded. "The AMEA stands for Arturo, Miguel, Esteban, and Amparo. My brothers, my sister, and me."

"Your sister! Amparo is your sister?" Laura's eyes widened.

"Yes." Esteban seemed puzzled. "Have you met her, or heard her name somewhere?"

"I saw a picture of you in a Spanish paper, I think it was from Puerto Rico, a San Juan paper. You were holding her hand, but all I could understand about it were the names under the picture." Laura looked down, studying the coverlet. "I thought she might be the reason you left me. The one who sent the message to you."

Esteban moved to pull her into his arms and held her close a minute before continuing.

"You were saying?" Mack prodded unmercifully.

"The message I got, it was from Arturo. My father had disappeared without a trace somewhere between his office and where he was to be picked up in the parking garage. We suspected he had been kidnapped, and this was found to be true before I got to Arturo. A ransom note was received. We had some suspicions that our security forces had gathered for us. We had to move quickly and in concert to find him. And to find where our security had failed."

"Your father?" Laura's hand went to her heart. "Kidnapped! Is he all right, Esteban? You found him?"

"Yes, we got to him before any harm came to him." Esteban smiled. "He was in better condition than you were, *mi corazon*. The two culprits who betrayed us were members of the family of some friends of ours with whom we do business. They—the rest of the family—helped us cut off any means of leaving the area where he was imprisoned, and they also helped us find him. Our father was being held in one of the smaller mines in a remote part of the jungle, but he was unharmed. The family—the kidnappers' people—were as concerned as we. Their son had fallen in with bad companions—a bad lot who planned to hold my father for ransom. They helped us and insisted on punishing the son and the other culprits themselves."

Mack and Laura were both imagining dire consequences, all their attention on Esteban. He saw a little of the horror in their eyes.

"We were not going to stick their heads up on the mine's gateposts," he assured them. "In fact, I'm sure they fared worse at the hands of their relatives, whom they dishonored, than they would have with us. All of our organization is made up of family members or friends of long standing," he explained. "Everything, including the location of the major mines, is confidential."

Laura drew a deep breath. "It sounds so frightening, Esteban. I certainly understand why you left so suddenly. But, why didn't you contact me? The address was on the hotel's register."

"All that was on the hotel register was Greenfield, USA. There are stacks of computer pages of Greenfields in the USA. We had a staff checking all of them. None of them came up with a Carroll's bookstore, a Sophie's bookstore, or a phone number for a Laura Carroll. Then my brothers and I started checking each of the Greenfields, every one of them, to search until we found you."

Laura bowed her head at the pain she had caused him and Mack. "To find me." Her voice was just above a whisper. "Even if I was with someone else?"

Esteban's jaw set. "To the gates of *el diablo,* if I had to." His eyes met Mack's.

"Wait a minute." The counselor in Mack stopped Esteban abruptly. "Where was all that security you mentioned when Laura and I were kidnapped?" He demanded.

Esteban glanced at the door; Arturo and Miguel were gone. "It was our security that helped us find you. They had penetrated our work force and were watching us. You too, Laura."

"Me?"

"Yes. That is why I dared not contact you, to risk putting you in danger. They had pictures of you, of us together. After they were arrested we found the photos. They knew of you through some employees who didn't know any better than to talk to them, and they placed their own accomplices in minor jobs to watch, too. The manager at the Palacio Isla Verde held himself to blame for my not being able to find you and banished himself to Hawaii as Assistant Manager here, though we did not hold him responsible. As soon as he saw you, he sent a message to me and pretended to work with the kidnappers so he could watch over you until we could get to you."

"So that's how he knew I was a prisoner, and he really did come to see that I wasn't hurt?"

Esteban nodded. Mack looked down thoughtfully, remembering how the man had tried to get Laura to eat.

Mack's anger rose. He stared, aghast and unbelieving. "You waited long enough to come to our rescue."

Chapter Thirty

"Let me explain." Esteban glanced at Arturo, who had come to peer into the room again. "All of our offices and hotels, worldwide, had been alerted to look for you, or to tell us if your name came up on any of their computers anywhere. Juan, the man you saw—his name is Juan Delgado. He felt so keenly his guilt at the series of errors that occurred when you left Isla Verde, he imposed a punishment on himself. When you checked out, no one noticed that there was no state listed on the registration, that the registration information was not complete. There was only the city and USA. The check you paid was not at the hotel because the bank deposit went back to San Juan on the same shuttle you did. We simply had to look for you—and the USA is a big place." He smiled. "Juan was born on Isla Verde. He loved his home, but he banished himself to Hawaii and took a demotion for not having watched the new clerks he hired closely enough and not getting your address down properly. He took the blame personally."

"I don't remember," Laura admitted. "I don't know who was at the desk when I first arrived in Isla Verde."

"He blamed himself, and he's been in Hawaii ever since. Then when he saw you come in, booked into the suite with him—" He gestured at Mack. "Juan sent a message, or tried to, as I said. But the message was sent through our private communications, and it took a while to find us. Arturo, Miguel, and I were checking names, phones, bookstores and any other available lead or source, in one of the Greenfields. I got here as quickly as I could when his message finally reached me."

Silence fell as Esteban finished. It was a lot to take in and consider. He sat silently, as if willing Laura to understand, his hand near hers on the bed.

Resting his case, the counselor in Mack sneered inwardly, although no hint of his feeling reached his face.

Laura picked up Esteban's hand and held it to her cheek. "It's over now. Your father is found, and Mack and I are rescued. And in support of Juan Delgado, he did try to get me to eat, Esteban. And he told us no harm would come to us."

"As if anyone would believe that, in the circumstances." Mack defended the resistance he and Laura had put up. No pity for the kidnapper who broke the law and held them prisoner showed in his cold expression.

Laura looked down at herself. "I'd like to have a shower and rejoin the human race."

"Fine," Esteban said, relieved. "I'll have your luggage brought up here while you wash up."

Mack stood, his stubborn chin jutting out again. "Don't you think it would be better to wait until you have the marriage ceremony? There's no shortage of rooms here."

Laura stopped, standing between Esteban and the bathroom door, at a loss for words.

Esteban answered Mack without a glance at her, his face hard as stone. "Do you think a piece of paper makes any difference to me at this point?"

"Then never mind." Mack spat out the words. "I'll go now and have someone come for the luggage." He walked as fast as he talked, heading for the door.

He turned back when he reached the door. Laura had gone and his eyes met Esteban's. "I'll go, but I'll have my eye on you, too. Security. Bah!"

As Mack stalked out, Arturo stuck his head in the bedroom door. "Esteban, Miguel and I will be one floor down. And I admire your choice." He smiled at his brother. "I'd have searched the world, too. Anything else needed?"

"Nothing I can't handle." Esteban grinned.

When Laura reappeared from the bathroom, Esteban went to her and held her close, their search and fear and loneliness at last behind them.

"Your luggage is here." He pointed. "And I talked to Mack on the phone. His airfare is taken care of, although he argued about it. He got a ticket on a plane leaving an hour from now." He added defensively, "That's the one he chose himself."

"He's right. It's best for him to go now. As soon as possible."

Esteban nodded. "I'm sure that's what he thought. And he said he would talk to Rose and Daisy. He said to be sure to tell you he would."

"Good, I appreciate that. He is a good friend, Esteban. A fine person." She turned to face him. "He just isn't you. I thought you were lost to me, that I would never see you again. I tried to explain to him that to love and to be in love are two different things. But I do love him and Rose and Daisy." She smiled. "Just in different ways."

Looking uncomfortable, Esteban finally came up with, "I felt he was—dependable."

Laura laughed. "Dependable. He'd like that. And he is."

She had started drying her hair and continued as she talked. "As soon as I can—I mean we can—" she smiled at him. "I'll have to go back and take care of the house and the bookstore. Mack, and his father before him, have always handled our business for us, for Aunt Sophie. He took over his father's practice. Mack will get things done the way I want them."

"Then that will be taken care of. All I have to do is show you how much I missed you." He kissed her, setting off all kinds of ringing bells and fireworks in her heart. *"Bueno,"* she whispered.

"Bueno?"

"Better than Isla Verde ice cream." She snuggled close to him, comfortable in the big terry robe and his arms. "Please, don't ever leave me again, Esteban."

"If ever I have some crisis to take care of, you will not doubt I am coming back, because you will be my wife, and wives should have faith in their husbands, no?"

"Of course. Whatever you say."

"Right now, what I say is we will be married as soon as it can be arranged. My family is so happy I found you. Arturo called them and he says they may smother you! And Amparo wanted to come with us to join in the search, but she had just found out she is with child, so we would not allow it. Arturo has called her and told her everything."

"I'm looking forward to meeting them." She kissed his cheek. "And now that we're alone, how about that long-awaited explanation?"

"I thought it had all been explained."

Laura shook her head.

"All right. Where shall I start with this long-awaited explanation?"

"At the beginning, of course. Where else?" Laura propped herself up on her elbow to look at him. "From that first night, on the shuttle boat."

"I had seen you in the dining room and I looked on the register, trying to guess which name was yours when no one behind the desk was watching."

Laura smiled, picturing him sneaking peaks at the register with the elderly Juan always coming in and out.

"Then I saw you on the boat. I looked at the people around you to see if you were with anyone."

"And suppose I had been?"

"No idea. Maybe throw him overboard?"

"Be serious!"

"I am." He tried to look innocent. "Then when I asked you to accompany me to the festival, I found you didn't understand me. It is an aggravation that most of our guests from the north have not bothered to learn our language. So I let you think I didn't understand your English and made a game of it." He chuckled.

"You dog! It never occurred to me you weren't telling me the truth!"

"Then coming back to the island, that toad, the one on the boat, gave you that hot drink—"

"Hot drink? Oh, yes. It tasted like it had peppers or something in it."

"It was 'or something.' It had an aphrodisiac in it, and quite a lot, too."

"You mean . . ." Laura was appalled. "You mean it was what we call 'doped up' back home? I thought it was just a combination of too much food and drink that was strange to me. And you knew when you tasted it! No wonder you looked at me so angrily."

Esteban's face froze into a merciless mask. "Not at you. At that toad. It didn't take me long to catch up with him. I threw him off the shuttle boat."

She gasped. "That's what all the commotion was on the other side of the boat was, and you looked like you didn't know a thing about it. But, what happened to him?"

"I don't know. The crew may have thrown him a rope. I didn't care. I was concerned for you. The drink didn't start affecting you until we were almost back to the hotel."

"Is that why, when I turned to you in the elevator, you wouldn't kiss me? Because I was—worse than intoxicated?"

"I wanted to kiss you, *querida*. It hurts to remember how

much I wanted to hold you and kiss you. But I had already let you believe I could not speak English, and it was the drink that wanted a kiss, not you."

"So you were going to see me safely to my room and just go away?"

"I was going to call on you the next day, and introduce myself properly."

"But, you didn't leave—"

"*Por Dios,* Laura, I am only flesh and blood." He closed his eyes as if in pain. "And I could not leave you. I had to stay and make sure you were all right."

"You didn't think it was safe to leave me alone? You must have thought I was awful. A . . . a tramp."

"I thought you were wonderful, never anything else. What happened was awful, but it was good that I had found you. But it happened so fast, not like it should have, because of the drug. I was afraid you would send me away when the drug wore off. So. I pretended to speak no English, so you couldn't tell me to leave, or not to come back."

"You were afraid I'd tell you to go, and I was afraid you would go. I was always afraid when you left that you wouldn't come back."

"I looked for things you might enjoy. I showed you my boat—"

"It's your boat? It doesn't belong to an *amigo?*"

"Yes. The estate I showed you is mine too. Ours. The land was bought at the same time as the land for the hotel. The house was built in hopes I'd settle down." He smiled at her. "The only member of my family who didn't push me to marry was my Aunt Serafina. She told me I would know when I met the one made for me and to ignore the rest of my family. She always took up for me, *Tia* Serafina."

"She sounds like my Aunt Sophie. My parents were killed in

Stranger in Paradise

an accident, and Aunt Sophie raised me. She was my mother's sister. She and Rose and Daisy have been my only family for as long as I can remember. And Mack and his father, too, who handled Aunt Sophie's business affairs."

"That's what you meant when you said he's your oldest and dearest friend?"

"Yes."

Laura suddenly wondered what Daisy and Rose might be thinking right now. She remembered Daisy's face when she had referred to Esteban as "that maracas player."

Esteban noticed the worried look. "What is it? You are worried about them, about Rose and Daisy?"

"They will understand, but it may take a while. You must remember, they wanted me to marry Mack and settle down in Greenfield. They really thought I might accept his proposal in Hawaii. All of us have been friends for a very long time. We're family, the only family I have—or had, until now."

"And now he must explain why he returns to Greenfield alone. This is why he wanted me to tell you he will talk to them."

"Yes. It's going to be a shock for them." She reached for his hand. "But they don't know you yet, Esteban. When they have met you and see us together, they will understand and be happy for us."

Esteban did not answer, picturing Mack's face when he left.

"I did tell them about meeting you," she said. "And how handsome you are. They know I love you and will be happy for both of us. Tell me," she said, changing the subject. "If your family couldn't persuade you to marry, when did you build your house?"

"After the hotel was finished, a friend's construction company wanted to do it, and it pleased my family for me to have a suitable home in the hope I would marry. That was three or four years ago. My poor mother. The last time I visited her and my

237

father, she said I had a home, but used it like a gypsy camp." Esteban thought back, remembering the time he and Laura had spent there.

"By the time we went to the estate, I was trying to find some way to let you know I speak English without making you so upset and angry with me that you wouldn't marry me. I didn't want to take any chances, so I tried telling you I love you in Spanish, and you understood."

"I understood, but I wasn't sure when I heard the words. It's been so long since my school friend who took Spanish told me the words. Then when you said it again, I said it back to you. So you would know that I love you, too."

"I was still trying to find the right way to tell you I understand your language and talk to you of marriage when I got that message from Arturo that my father was missing."

He picked up her hand and kissed the palm. "I had to go, *querida.*"

"I know. It's only that I didn't understand. I didn't know, either, about the incomplete address on the hotel register. After I got home and didn't hear from you, I only wanted to know if you were all right, that you had come back to Isla Verde. I called and asked if you had come to pick up the pearls you let me wear, and you had. So I knew you were all right, but you didn't contact me. That made it pretty plain you didn't want to see me again, Esteban."

"No, no. I came back to find you were gone and had left no address except Greenfield on the register. Then the clerk told me about the pearls and I got them and the note you left with the bandleader. Returning the pearls made me think your were rejecting me, but your note did say *te amo*—"

"I left the pearls because they were your mother's. I knew I should return them to you."

"My mother gave each of us something from her jewelry box

to give our chosen ones. Arturo took an emerald pendant, Miguel, sapphire earrings. I liked the pearls. And Amparo, who is the only one in the universe who could do this, held out her hand for my father's ruby cufflinks," he smiled.

"His only little girl among three sons, and she must have been such a pretty little girl." Laura remembered her picture in the San Juan paper. "I won't ask anything about the mines, since that's so confidential. But the hotels. Are there more of them than the ones in Isla Verde and here in Hawaii?"

Esteban nodded. "The bulk of our money comes from the mines, but, to the rest of the world, we are innkeepers. My parents have a hotel near Paris. My sister Amparo married a citizen of the United Kingdom. He is an only son and wished to stay near his parents, so they have the hotel in London. Arturo and his wife have the hotel in Roma. Miguel is here in Hawaii, and I have the one in Isla Verde."

"I thought your job was playing in the hotel band. That's why I left a message for you—"

"I got it, *querida*, and I brought the pearls with me." He pulled her up to hold her close in an excited hug. "You can wear them while I show you Hawaii."

Looking around a plantation, Laura stopped to admire the view. "You must be the best tour guide in Hawaii, not that I intend to share you with anyone." Laura held his arm as Esteban showed her around.

"I wanted you to see the real beauty here. Have you bought something for Rose and Daisy?"

"Not yet. I was enjoying seeing the plantation so much, I haven't decided what to get. I promised them I'd bring them something native to Hawaii."

"You could get them pearl rings. The cultured pearl business is good here."

"There is a shop in the hotel. I'll take your advice. I know they will like them."

She stopped in the gift shop when they got back, to pick out the rings.

Upstairs, he admired the choices she'd made for Rose and Daisy and asked, "Did you bring that yellow sundress with you?"

"No, but I have a green one a lot like it," she answered, curious why he'd asked.

"We are going to a luau for dinner tonight."

The luau was on the hotel's grounds, the scenery and entertainment as impressive as the huge variety of food.

"This is—is . . . I'm enchanted," Laura exclaimed, the dancer's flaming torches reflected in her wide eyes.

Esteban kissed her hand, watching, too. "That's exactly the reaction Miguel strives for." He laughed.

"Oh, there are Miguel and Arturo over there. Arturo is still here," she said uncertainly.

"They are our guardian angels. They will be here with us until we leave."

Laura turned a surprised look on him. "You mean, in case Mack comes back with a shotgun? That would be completely out of character!"

Esteban laughed. "No, I don't expect anything so uncivilized from Mack. But still they will be with us until we leave."

Laura still puzzled over why she and Esteban would need guardian angels as she welcomed Arturo and complimented Miguel on the luau. They had with them a bronzed and genial giant who was obviously Hawaiian to the bone and wore a black suit.

He was a bishop, and Esteban told Laura he would bless their union here, and then they would be married on Isla Verde.

It was a solemn and beautiful interlude, which brought tears to her eyes and made her feel she had gained two brothers as all of them held hands.

She did not see Miguel's signal, but a man in a bright shirt along with and two musicians came to sing the "Hawaiian Wedding Song" to them. "I will love you longer than forever," were forever etched into her memory, along with, "I love you, I'll be back."

When they had enjoyed their meal, Arturo reached into his coat and handed Esteban the fax he had been waiting for.

"I made reservations for Roma before I am divorced," Arturo smiled at Esteban. "The ones I made for you for San Juan, you may cancel if you want to." He handed Esteban the tickets. "I must go."

With hugs from Arturo and Miguel, Esteban and Laura went back to the hotel.

"Are you going to cancel them?" Laura asked in the elevator. Touching the tickets in Esteban's pocket.

"No. We will leave now."

Chapter Thirty-One

When Esteban said *now,* he meant now. Their things were gathered up by a small army of the hotel employees, and they were in the air within the next hour.

On the plane, Laura talked to Esteban about things she had to do. "I've been thinking about the house in Greenfield, the bookstore, and Aunt Sophie's furniture, too."

"It is your decision. What do you want to do?"

"Daisy and Rose once made Aunt Sophie an offer for the bookstore. But Sophie thought it would be a good income for me. She told me about it, that I could also sell it and invest the money, if I wanted to." She turned to face him, and his arm went around her shoulders.

"I would like to give the shop to them, to Rose and Daisy. What do you think?"

"We don't need it, and you can't run it from Isla Verde." He leaned over to kiss her forehead. "There's no way I could spare you. I think it is a good thought to do that. What about the house?" He asked, smiling. "That house of yours that is big enough for you and me and my son and your daughter?"

Laura smiled, remembering the little park where Esteban had played with the children. "The one on Isla Verde has room, too, and it already has some good memories waiting for us. So, I will also give Rose and Daisy the house."

"This is something else Mack will arrange for you?"

"Yes, he will know how to do it. I won't let them know the

details until we've gone back to Isla Verde, and then Mack can tell them about it."

"What is this secret arrangement?"

"I will have him tell them I want them to live in the house as long as they live, so there will be someone there to watch over it. Then it will revert to my estate. Mack will know how to word it. That way, they won't object to Mack's seeing to the upkeep and expense on it."

"Mack will see through that immediately," Esteban said. "He's what you call in your country, pretty sharp."

Laura wondered at his tone of voice, and if jealousy still lingered. As if there could be any doubt how much she loved him.

"Well, yes, I expected that. But it will look good on paper. He will know how to manage them. And Esteban?"

"Yes?"

"Aunt Sophie's furniture. She has an antique bedroom suite in her room that's been handed down since before the flood, I guess, and some other things she's bought. The antique dealers hounded her for them constantly. I would like, if it's all right with you, to take some of her things with me. Rose and Daisy will have plenty of furniture without the things I have in mind. Would you mind if I put them in our house?"

He smiled, his arm around her tightening. "Our house. Right now, *querida*, I wouldn't care if you wanted us to spend the rest of our lives on the floor!"

Back on Isla Verde in Esteban's penthouse suite, he put down the phone. "We will be married in the village church tomorrow in the chapel."

"Oh! Tomorrow?"

"*Sí.*"

"It's a good thing I'm a Catholic," Laura said, smiling.

"Otherwise, I don't think the priest would approve."

"We will call my father now." He added, "Since I'm going to call my father, we may as well talk to everyone. It will take only a little while to set up a conference call."

Laura simply nodded, mute, at everything that had to be arranged. Feeling suddenly weak, she sat down on the sofa. "In the chapel here," she breathed softly. "I've never even been in it. What will I wear that will look appropriate? Or even presentable?" Doubts and questions left her feeling weak and vulnerable, with nothing but her sure knowledge of Esteban's love to hold to.

The conference call came through, and Esteban's father talked to him briefly before Esteban handed the phone to Laura. *"Mi madre,"* he said affectionately.

Laura swallowed, but managed to talk a few minutes before tears started down her cheeks. She smiled up at Esteban as she listened to *Senora* Aguilar's happy welcome.

Arturo Aguilar, Senior, took the phone briefly to offer any help she might need in housebreaking his youngest son.

Esteban shared the phone too. He spoke with Arturo, laughingly checking to see that he was safely home and the dogs still recognized him.

Next, Amparo spoke to Laura from London.

"She is as sweet as her picture in the paper looked." Laura put her hand over the phone to whisper to Esteban. "She's saying something I don't understand about a dress. I hope I don't embarrass you." Into the phone she said, "Yes, of course, I know it must be beautiful. And I love your brother, and I don't want him any tamer than he is!" She laughed with Amparo before she gave the phone back to Esteban.

That night as Laura slept in Esteban's arms, planes arrived from Paris, Rome, and London bearing Esteban's immediate family.

Stranger in Paradise

Neither Esteban nor Laura knew what was in store as they returned to the penthouse from breakfast.

Arturo met them at the door and stepped aside to make room for all the hugs and good wishes awaiting them. Laura could not believe Esteban's father, mother, and Amparo were there, along with Arturo, Miguel, and other family members.

Esteban's eyes were moist as his father embraced him. Laura didn't try to stop her tears.

"Your *madre* is as *hermosa* as her pearls, Esteban," Laura managed to whisper to Esteban in the chaos of greetings and outpourings of love.

Amparo beckoned to her, and Laura followed her into the bedroom. A small woman in a black dress stood up from her chair, bobbed a small curtsy, and smiled at her. Amparo gestured excitedly at the bed.

"It's—it's a wedding dress! Oh, how beautiful! *Hermosa*," she said, smiling at Amparo. "It's yours. That's what you were trying to tell me on the phone?"

Amparo nodded. "I still am working to speak better," she explained. "Sarita will fit to you the dress, if you like it."

"Oh, of course I like it! It's beautiful, Amparo, as you are beautiful!"

"Come, let us—before the others—"

Amparo quickly latched the door as Laura took off her clothes and held up her arms for Sarita to carefully put the dress over her head.

The dress needed very little alteration; it was only a little bit short. "It will not make the difference, with the train," Amparo said hopefully.

"No, it's just right. I wonder if Esteban will be pleased. He thinks I am going to wear the white dress I showed him once. But surely he will be pleased."

"He will be pleased or—" Amparo quickly drew her finger

across her throat.

Laura laughed. "I must remember not to make anyone in this family angry!" She giggled with Amparo as Sarita removed the dress.

"Shhh," Amparo held her finger to her lips and Laura nodded. She folded the dress carefully and handed it to Sarita. "We dress you in the sacristy in the morning."

"That's wonderful, we'll surprise him!"

The next morning, by the time they got to the chapel, someone—or more probably a whole staff of someones—had worked miracles with flowers and decorated the small and already beautiful Catholic chapel.

Esteban's face was worth the preparations they had made, as he watched Laura come to him on his father's arm in Amparo's designer wedding dress. He glanced at his sister and threw her a kiss as Laura joined him at the altar.

After the ceremony and toasts to offer every good wish in at least two languages, Esteban's father called him aside.

"You will come to us in Paris after you go to Greenfield?"

"We will be there. Thank you, Father, for everything."

"These things, all of this and our adventures, they will be tales to tell *los ninos*, no? For now, thank the Lord, my son, the future is in your hands." He gave Esteban a hearty embrace and signaled to his family.

Laura hugged Amparo, and waved at Sarita, who hovered in the background. "The dress. Amparo, can you wait just a couple of minutes, it won't take me long—"

"I would have to swim back to London!" Amparo made a face in the direction of her father. "You can return it when you get to Paris. Just bring it with you. We will be there so you can meet my husband, and then they take me back to jail—until my child is born!" She grinned and hurried after her father.

Chapter Thirty-Two

"As soon as we find out when we will get to Greenfield, I'll call Rose and Daisy. No, I think I'll call Mack. We need to see him first anyway, to tell him what I want and sign whatever I need to sign. Then he can call them for us."

Esteban only nodded, leaving her to make her own decisions about the Greenfield arrangements.

When the little commuter plane landed at the airport in Greenfield, Laura said, "This is the price you pay for living in a more or less rural area."

Esteban shrugged. "I've traveled by ox-cart to some of our mines." He remembered hacking his way through the Colombian jungle at Arturo's side.

"I guess it will do, considering ox-carts." Laura laughed, excited at being home again.

She stepped off the portable stairs and pointed. "There's Mack!"

Laura ran to him, grasping his hand. "It was good of you to meet us."

Mack smiled slightly at Laura before extending his hand to Esteban to welcome him as he caught up.

"I would have brought Rose and Daisy, but you said you had some things you want to get settled first. I made arrangements for all of us to have dinner tonight at Antonio Kolivas's restaurant, if that's all right with you?" He included Esteban in his quest for approval.

Esteban nodded, glad Mack was offering his acceptance, if not yet friendship.

"I'm glad you did. You will like Kolivas, Esteban."

Laura returned her attention to Mack. "I would like, if you don't have too much to do, to get things squared away this afternoon. About the house and the bookstore. I'm still depending on you, Mack. You know what's involved, and you know Daisy and Rose, and that's essential in this."

"I know. And don't worry about time. I've made arrangements to have all the time we need. I will take you to the house to leave your things, then we can go to the office and finish up whatever you want done. I've anticipated some of it, and you can straighten me out on other things. Our dinner reservations are for eight. I'll pick you up then, unless there is something else you want to do?"

"This couldn't be better," Laura answered gratefully. "Thanks for arranging it. I don't know what I'd do without you, Mack." She pressed his arm and walked beside him to the car.

Mack grinned to himself at Esteban's grim expression. *Darned if I'll be stripped of even friendship!* He looked away to hide the gladness this bright spot in his day had caused.

At Mack's office, Laura laid out her plans about the bookstore and the house.

"You've got this all figured out so you won't have to argue with them, haven't you?" Mack chuckled. His eyes danced as they met Laura's in a close confidence Esteban couldn't share.

"Don't kid me. You love arguing with them! I'll admit it's sneaky of me, but you can arrange it, can't you?"

"No doubt," Mack agreed. "But I see I'm arranging a job for myself, right?"

"Yes, Esteban said you would see that." She smiled at both of them. "But it's the only way they can live there and have the expenses paid for them."

"Did Esteban think of this, or were you smart enough to figure it out all by yourself?"

Esteban smiled at that suggestion. "No, this is all Laura's plan. I can't claim any credit."

As Mack separated the papers he had for her to sign, Laura said tentatively, "There are some things I want out of the house, too, Mack. Some of the furniture and Aunt Sophie's silver, and some of my books . . ."

Mack nodded and pushed his chair back. He opened a drawer and pulled out some gummed labels. "This should do it." He laid a big roll of them on the desk. "Put one of these gummed labels on whatever you want, and write Isla Verde on it. The silver, books, or loose things, put in a box or a sack and stick a label on it. Then, when I can get to it, I'll have them shipped to you."

"Mack," Laura said, beaming, "you're a genius!"

She took the gummed labels from him. "And if I don't get a bill for all this in thirty days, I'll . . . I'll—"

Mack waited with an amused grin, wondering how she thought she could threaten him.

"I'll sic Daisy on you!"

Mack let out a horrified screech. "No! No! Not that!"

He turned to Esteban, still laughing. "You'd have to know Daisy to appreciate what a scare tactic that is."

"They fight all the time, Esteban," Laura explained. "But they are really good friends. They just argue to keep in practice."

As they stood up, Esteban extended his hand to Mack. "I want to thank you for your help, too," he said sincerely.

"That's all right." Mack's good-natured grin was back. "You'll get the bill. Laura knows my weak spots." He chuckled. "Wait until you meet Daisy."

"Goodness! Have mercy, Mack," Laura pleaded. "He's

already dreading meeting them."

"Dreading?" Mack raised his eyebrows.

"This *Senora* Daisee, *una mujer para el Diablo?*" Esteban's eyes searched Mack's face.

"Oh, hell yes, and I don't even know what that means!" Mack put his hand on Esteban's shoulder as they went out, laughing together.

"I'll pick you up at seven-thirty," Mack promised when he left them.

Esteban stood with Laura in front of the house before they went in. Laura looked up and pointed.

"That window up there is where I looked out at night, after I came home, looking back toward Isla Verde. Wondering where you were, and if you were all right."

Inside, she showed him family pictures and the antiques Sophie had collected.

Esteban put down a picture of Sophie he had been looking at. "She has a kindness in her eyes, like my Aunt Sarafina," he said.

"Yes, she was a dear, and I'd like to keep some of the things that were dear to her. I'm going to start putting labels on some of these things. If you see one if them on something you don't want to take, you can tell me."

"Whatever you want is what we will take. I will see to our tickets to Paris. Is there a good travel agent here?"

"There's the one who arranged my trip to Isla Verde."

"He deserves my business." Esteban grinned. "Who?"

"The name is Carefree Travel, on Elm Street." Laura answered as she bent down to stick on a label.

They had time to freshen up and were ready when Mack came for them.

Rose and Daisy were seated in the front seat with Mack in

Stranger in Paradise

his van. He came around and opened the back door for them.

"Pretty dress," he said to Laura as she got in.

"This is one Rose and Daisy and I picked out on our shopping trip," Laura replied, getting comfortable beside Esteban. Rose and Daisy sat still as little girls at their first dance, but with a mixture of curiosity and concern, slowly turned their heads.

"Rose, and Daisy, I'll owe you a hug when we get out at the restaurant." Laura patted Rose's shoulder. "Right now, I want you to meet my husband, Esteban Aguilar. Esteban, Rose and Daisy and Mack are all the family I've got. I guess if you had to give Rose and Daisy a title, it would be honorary aunts—or maybe guardian angels!"

Rose and Daisy laughed, the ice broken. They both now eyed Esteban with open curiosity.

Esteban smiled his toothpaste ad smile, still unaware of its devastating effect, and held both hands over the seat. They took his hands and he pressed them briefly. "I'm glad to meet you, Laura's family. I love your Laura." He looked into their eyes. "And I'll take good care of her," he promised solemnly.

Antonio himself greeted them when they arrived at his restaurant, and talked with Mack as he led them to a table.

The food and service was excellent, as it always was, and Laura noticed Kara watching them. She touched Esteban's hand under the table and gave a tiny nod that only he noticed. Esteban looked at Kara, but didn't understand what Laura was trying to tell him.

Kara's beautiful, dark eyes glanced around the restaurant often enough to keep an eye on everything needing attention. But they always returned to Mack. When they were nearly finished with their meal and Mack put down his fork, Kara immediately disappeared through the kitchen door.

The waitress came to take away their plates, and they saw

Kara approaching. She came bearing coffee and baklava for Mack and had another waitress in tow bearing a wide dessert tray for the rest of them to choose from. Esteban glanced at Laura to let her know he now understood her nod at Kara.

Esteban watched thoughtfully as Mack picked up one of the pieces with obvious appreciation, and smiled happily in Kara's direction.

The beautiful, dark eyes lit up as Kara smiled back at Mack with her heart in them.

"She anticipates your wants, this pretty one." Esteban's eyes went from Kara to Mack with a knowing expression.

Mack swallowed, looking annoyed. "She is Antonio's daughter. He is my friend and a good client. Kara makes the baklava."

Mack chased the pastry down with coffee, trying to make light of Kara's continuing attention.

Esteban and Laura exchanged a smile, which didn't go unnoticed by Rose and Daisy.

Rose smiled her approval at Kara, who didn't see it because her eyes never left Mack. Daisy sipped her coffee, looking speculative as she watched Kara bringing Mack more baklava when he asked for more coffee.

"What are you doing?" Mack asked as Laura raised her hand.

"I want to introduce my husband to your friends," Laura said with as innocent a face as she could manage.

Kara saw Laura's raised hand and after a moment's hesitation, on seeing their waiter was across the room, she came to the table.

"May I bring you something else?"

"No, thank you, everything is fine. But I know you are the one who makes the baklava—"

Kara's face broke into a delighted smile. "I will bring you some."

"No, no. I only wanted to compliment the food, and the

Stranger in Paradise

baklava, and to introduce my husband—"

"Your . . . husband?" Kara's face managed to remain blank as she tried not to glance at Mack.

"Yes. We were married last week. I will not be living here any longer, and I wanted to tell you how much we have enjoyed your good food and introduce my husband to you before we leave."

Laura laid her hand on Esteban's arm briefly. "This is my husband, Esteban Aguilar, Kara Kolivas."

Esteban rose from his chair. "It is always a pleasure to meet a beautiful woman." He raised Kara's hand to his lips. "And one who cooks like this is a gift from the gods."

Laura suddenly wanted to kick him, but restrained herself when she saw Mack's reaction. A tide of red anger was rising up his neck.

Kara flushed, looking pleased. "I—I am pleased to meet you, and I and my family wish you much happiness."

Mack watched all this, silently smoldering. When Kara left without a word, he abruptly got up and stalked toward the restrooms. The red flush had reached his face, and his feet were punishing the floor in what was nearly a hard stomp. He made no apology and didn't look back.

Laura dropped her napkin on the table and followed him, catching up with him on the other side of the restaurant. She grabbed his arm, making him stop.

"What's the matter," she teased him unmercifully. "Can't take the competition? I thought you said Kara is only a child. She's a woman, Mack. A beautiful, desirable, woman. And you're jealous. Admit it! You're used to having all her attention, and you're jealous! Jealous! Jealous! That's what you are."

"Jealous? That's ridiculous. Even if I 'had idees,' as the old folks call it, about Kara, Antonio would be chasing me out of here with his meat cleaver—"

"He would not. He likes you, Mack. He admires and respects you, and you're a good catch for his daughter, who obviously thinks you hung the moon.

Laura looked around. No one had followed them or was close enough to hear their conversation. At least Mack had calmed down and was listening to what she said.

"Mack, get off your back side and start courting Kara, or you may have more competition than you bargained for." He didn't answer. "Do you hear me?"

"I don't know . . ." He spoke slowly, eyes going to the kitchen door. Kara had not returned.

"She is not a child, Mack. You only think of her as one because she's Antonio's daughter."

"Sure." Mack hid behind sarcasm. "The old hag must be pushing twenty-one."

"Cut it out. This is me, Laura. I know you. And I'm not blind as you act like you are. Kara's not that much younger than you, she's beautiful, she's your friend and client Antonio's daughter, and she likes you, Mack. Everyone can see that but you. And . . ." Laura narrowed her eyes, reminding Mack of Daisy. "There's that baklava you like so well."

"I think," Mack said, not looking quite so grim now, "that she did mention about a bake sale of some sort sometime next month. I think maybe she might have been going to invite me to it or something."

"And what did you tell her?" Laura demanded.

"I said I'd see what I had to do around that date. But isn't it a little late to remind her of that? It was right after I got back from Hawaii. She didn't know about us, and besides, I only see her here when I come to dinner, and . . ." He was full of excuses. "I've got to see to all the things you want sent."

"That's perfect!"

"What's perfect?" Mack regarded her suspiciously.

Stranger in Paradise

"Call her. Call Kara and ask her to help you with it."

"You think she would?" The thought came as a complete surprise.

"I'd bet your baklava on it." Laura grinned. "And, of course, you'll talk to each other as you work, and if she doesn't bring up the bake sale, you can, and then—"

"Wait just it a minute, will you?"

"What?"

"You've spoken your piece, as Daisy would say. Now, allow me to plan my life myself, will you?"

"Oh, all right, as long as you get on with it. I've got to get back to the table before Kara decides she'd rather have Esteban!"

"Yeah." Mack grinned. "Protect my baklava rights—hurry!"

It wasn't until Laura and Esteban were back home and getting ready to leave the next morning that they had a chance to talk about Mack and their dinner with him, Rose, and Daisy.

"I was almost as upset as Mack when you kissed Kara's hand and looked into those big, dark eyes of hers." Laura confided to Esteban.

He looked around. Everything was packed except what they would need the next morning. He came and tenderly put his arms around her. "The only eyes I searched the world for are blue." He kissed her cheek, then her ear. "And to see that hand kissed by another's lips, it had the right effect on Mack." He chuckled.

"You were absolutely right. Mack was so upset. I knew he couldn't deny his feelings any longer. So now he's finally on the right track. And Kara loves him. Everyone but him could see that."

"So now we can go to Paris and home to Isla Verde."

"And live happily ever after," Laura said, smiling. "There's just one thing." Her smile faded.

"What?" Esteban's arms tightened around her. "Everything is arranged, and Mack is, as you say, on the right track." He smiled. "You said he can 'plan his own life' from now on? What else needs our help?"

"It's not what, it's who. Please, when we get home to Isla Verde, tell Juan Delgado he can come home now."

ABOUT THE AUTHOR

Jackie Griffey fell in love with books before she started writing and has written novels in the cozy mystery, horror, romance-suspense, and contemporary genres. She and her family live in Arkansas with a big cat whose main talent is finding places to relax in the sun, a tiny Chihuahua with a long list of stuff to bark at, and lots of books. She is currently working on another cozy mystery.

CASTROVILLE PUBLIC LIBRARY